DOG-HEART

DOG-HEART

DIANA McCAULAY

PEEPAL TREE

First published in Great Britain in 2010
Peepal Tree Press Ltd
17 King's Avenue
Leeds LS6 1QS
England

ISBN13: 9781845231231

Supported by
ARTS COUNCIL
ENGLAND

This is a work of fiction. Except for historical figures, all characters are imaginary. To the best of my knowledge, there is nowhere in Kingston called Jacob's Pen or Nevada and no schools called Nightingale All Age, Holborn Preparatory or St. Stephen's. I have taken liberties with geography – a reader who knows the city of Kingston will not find the layout of streets accurate.

This book has been a long time coming. To my husband Fred, my son Jonathan, my friend Celia and my teacher David – I'm grateful for your faith in its uncertain progress.

For my mother

...You still had
this burning
desire
to set sail
even though
(now and always)
and despite
what long ago
the fortune teller
said –
"I see something great
in your hand, something noble" –
you were
rudderless.

Olive Senior, *Gardening in the Tropics*

JACOB'S PEN, KINGSTON
JAMAICA

The three boys stood by the zinc fence in the shadows, waiting. The tallest of the three had one arm and a massive torso. He was about seventeen; facing manhood. He could see over the fence and he gazed out into the night. The second boy was thin with wiry arms, nappy hair and scars on his face. He might have been fourteen or twenty. The third boy was the smallest of the three and had suffered a recent beating – one eye was still swollen half-shut and his mouth was split, but healing. His head was bandaged. He was almost fifteen and had not yet learned the still watchfulness of the other two. He seemed exhausted, shifting from one leg to the other, squatting and getting up, rubbing his wrists as if to restore circulation.

Across the dirt yard, a group of men sat on the verandah of a slab-roofed house. There were lights on in the house, but the men on the verandah sat in near-darkness. The door into the house was open and behind the men, women moved around, putting food on a table. The voices of the men rose and fell. The waiting boys could not hear all they said but they heard the men curse and they heard the word "blood" many times. The men smoked ganja and drank white rum, except for one man who sat apart from the others. He spoke little and did not drink or smoke. His hair was styled like a woman's with plaits and beads, dyed reddish blonde; he looked no older than the boy with one arm who waited in the yard. He wore two sets of earrings in each ear and a heavy gold chain around his neck. He was the don of Jacob's Pen and he would soon make a decision about the three boys.

Two older men stood in the corners of the verandah, their eyes moving from the three boys in the yard to the don and back again. They wore loose shirts over the hand guns stuck in the waistbands of their trousers. It was their job to ensure the safety of Merciless, the young don, and to carry out his wishes. Those wishes could include the summary execution of the three boys that very night or simply an invitation for the boys to join the men for curried goat and reasoning until the early hours of the next morning.

"You know Lasco from time," one of the seated men said. "Dese two, mi no know. Di one wit' di one hand, Boston – him is from Nevada – mi hear say is A.K. chop him hand clean off. Him tek it like a man, so mi hear. Di odda one, Dexter – dey call him Matrix – him a fryer. Bloodclaat Babylon pick him up inna raid last month. Him mek bail by a white man; one lawyer. Is dis new bwoy mi nah check for. Mi hear say him have big man frien'. A pure crosses dat."

"Is not di first wi a deal wit' fryer," another man said. "We know what fi do wit' dem." The light from the room behind him framed his dreadlocks and he took a hit of a large spliff. The smell of marijuana and roasting breadfruit wafted out of the house and the boy who had been beaten fidgeted more urgently. A thin, brown dog walked from behind the house and lay at the front steps of the verandah, looking up at the men.

"Plenty heat dey 'pon us now, all di same. Nah make sense do tings bring Babylon a Jacob's Pen again," said a third man, sitting completely in darkness.

A silence fell and the men looked to the don. "Mi hungry," Merciless said. "It late. Make di bwoy dem eat wit' us. Dem can sleep inna Jambo house down a street. Tomorrow wi deal wit' dem."

The next evening, the boys had to perform a task their lives depended on. They were fryers – young aspirants – to Merciless's Racehorse Gang. They had eaten and slept well for the first night in many and were grateful to the don. They thought little about what they had to do. The boy who had been beaten, Dexter, had been given a gun and shown how to use it. A white

Nissan Sunny had been provided; only the one-armed boy, Boston, could drive. The car should have been automatic – they had told Merciless this – but the Sunny had a gear stick. The don had been uninterested in this problem. "No worry," Lasco had whispered to Boston, "mi will change gear. We practice down a di river firs'."

Dexter was nervous and wanted to talk about escape routes. "Yout' man, you a watch too much TV," Lasco told him. "Is only a white woman. We look for one old one. She nah have no gun."

To gain entry to Merciless's crew, the three boys had to commit a crime. Reports of the crime had to appear in the newspapers, so the don would know his orders had been carried out. Within a week, the boys would either be wanted men or dead. They had not expected to live to adulthood anyway.

PART ONE

DEXTER
Car Park Runnins

Been out here long-long, since around seven, beggin. Mumma, she don't know how it hard. If I go home now, she going beat me, say me wut'less. She don't understand plaza runnins. People don't like see boy inna plaza; girl, now, they don't get chase like us. Not many girl out here all the same. But we boy, me and Everton and Shelby and Noel, we get chase all the time. Don't matter if you small like Lasco, you still get chase. One time, a security guard catch Lasco and hold him down inna car park and beat him bad-bad. A foreign white woman, she come over and she tell the security to leave that boy alone. The security say, "Ma'am, you don't understand dem boy. Dem bad, dem bad, them bad so 'til. Dem must beat like mule or donkey. Ghetto pickney *must* beat." The white woman say she going call the police, and the security, he laugh. "Lady," he say – him stop call her Ma'am now – "the police will beat him harder than me. Dem boy, dem t'ief and cause pure trouble. Management say we must run dem *every* time we see dem."

There is a white man with the white woman and him say she must stay out of what don't concern her. The woman say it concern her; this is a chile being beat up. The man say they on holiday, don't know about things in Jamaica, come away, Lawra, or some name like that, come away, him say. All the time this going on, Lasco him just stand there, him don't cry. Him tough, Lasco. Where him come from make you tough like coconut. Him mother name him after powder milk, then she take him to Maxfield Park Children Home and leave him. Him run away from there before he reach ten. I know something bad-bad happen to him, but I don't know what.

Me, now, I try make sure security and police never catch me. If them catch me, I bawl livin eye water and beg them not to beat me. Me say me hungry. Me say me need money for school shoe for my little sister. Most time them don't trouble me. I know one security name Sinclair. Him say him like me because I mannersable, always say, *Good mornin* or *Good evenin* and call him Sir. Sometime him will give me a ten dollar or a twenty dollar, if him have them in coin. Plenty shop only want paper money now, say not takin coin, especially not the red coin, the ten cent and twenty-five cent. But enough coin will buy patty and soda over at the gas station; so Sinclair, him give them to me if him have them. Him say him get a boy-chile 'bout my age, but I know him think I is nine or ten. I small. I am twelve last birthday.

Sometime I get coin from boy who pack inna supermarket. They hustlin to take bag a food to car and drop the coin-them. I find them stuck inna asphalt. I have to careful how I pick them up, if the supermarket boy see me, them will beat me and report me to security. They hate us car park boy, even though some a them was car park boy before.

Lord, me hungry. Sinclair not on duty tonight. Best chance I have is stayin round here in the shadow, behind expensive chiney restaurant, and wait 'til movie house let out. Plenty rich people go to movie and when them come out, them don't like see young boy inna car park. This don't work every time, because when it late, uptown people scared and go to them fancy car quick-quick. Car park a dangerous place for them.

You have to pay mind to the movie showin too. Uptown people like movie 'bout love, they don't come out for show with kung fu or plenty black people. They come for certain kinda black people, like that one Morgan Freeman with all the mole on him face, or Denzel, or that nice-nice gal Halle Berry. Wesley Snipes, Eddie Murphy – now, uptown people don't come to see them so much. This movie tonight is about some kinda sun, a Tuscan sun, never heard a that. I think plenty uptown people will be at this movie.

Uptown people can be black, brown, white, chiney, coolie or syrian. All a them have cell phone nowadays. Them start phonin soon as they come out of the movie and then them don't see us car park boy. Woman-them look at us, though, except the very young one. The best kind a woman is not too young, white or chiney, the kind that look like she have pickney already. Syrian woman have hard heart, always tell you get a job. Black woman now, them hard to read. Some a them look sorry for we, but some just get mad.

Foot bottom hurtin. Barefoot on hot asphalt all day is hard. Need two pair a shoe. Have only one pair and Mumma say it can only wear go school. When school over, shoe come off. Then Mumma send me to plaza to beg. I like this plaza, Sovereign it name, because the boy-them are small and you don't have to fight. One day, I did go down by Half Way Tree and one big boy beat me 'til I vomit. After that I stay here in Sovereign Plaza, even though the pickins slim sometime.

Movie lettin out now. People laughin. That good; mean them not thinkin 'bout gunman on them way to them car. You have to think about gunman all the time – them everywhere – like rat, lizard, cockroach, mosquito.

Trick is not to scare people, so them have to see you comin. Sometime that make them turn back and walk down a different row of car, but you have to take you chance, for if you surprise them, they angry for sure.

I get up and walk out a the dark. I pick a woman and a man to beg. Would be better if the woman was by sheself, but uptown woman don't go to movie alone. The woman is right age, a brownin, not so young. She wear jeans pants and a T-shirt with writin on it. When I get close, I see the man is young, maybe her son. Him more fair than she.

"Good evening, Miss, Sir," I say. "Beg you some money for school."

"No, thank you," the uptown boy say, quick-quick, and him push the woman to one side. But she see me and she stop.

"What you doing out here so late?" she say.

"Miss, have to get money for school."

"What's your name?"

"Miss, Dexter," I say. Is my pet name. My real name is Raymond.

15

"Where your parents?"

Too much talkin now. How it work, if them don't give you money right away, prob'ly not going to. People from the movie walk 'round three a us. People look. Shoulda ask some other woman.

"Miss, don' know my father; my mumma, she at home with the other pickney."

The woman make up her face and look vex. "How old are you?"

"Nine," I lie. Better them think you young. I don't even tell teacher at school my right age.

"Where you go school?"

"Miss, Papine Primary." Another lie.

"How many brothers and sisters you have?"

"Miss, one brother, one sister." Want to get away now. This woman not going give anything and other uptown people leavin. I hear car door slam and engine start up. Look like tonight is night for hungry bed and beatin from Mumma. It rough.

"What you do for fun?" the woman say. For fun? This woman strange. I know I must not tell her about jumpin on back a pick-up truck at traffic light and t'iefin a ride from downtown, or cuttin up seat on the bus with Lasco knife. Must not tell about the time police corner me and Everton and make we climb one chainlink fence. While we up there, them lick us with a piece a two by four and them laugh. After – this is the fun part – we stick ice pick inna them car tyre. Must not tell how we find one old can a spray-paint and write badwords on the wall a the First Methodist Church in Jacob's Pen, or pull down poster for dance we car park boy can't go to.

"I play draughts with my brother," I say. Draughts better to tell about than domino, even though domino need more brain and countin. Uptown people think domino for rum head and wut'less corner boy. "We make a board from old cardboard and use bottle top for men. I teach him, my little brother – me, I is the best draught player around."

The woman smile a little. The boy say, "Come Mom, it's time to go." Him pull her hand. So is her son. Him wearin the new kind a high top sneaker. The woman just stand there. The boy shake him head and start take out a wallet from him back pocket. *Yes,* I think. Maybe him will all and give me a hundred dollar. I look at him shoe again. They new, but not new-new. A little old, cool lookin, you know. Is shoe like that I want. Prob'ly never will get though.

"Where you live?" the woman say.

Now I frighten. What she want know for? "Miss, Bell Town," I lie. Bell Town is a next community to our own.

"If I want find you, how I find you?" the woman say.

"Miss, just ask for Miss Arleen. Everybody know her. She my mumma. We live top a steep hill, near the bus stop." Lie upon lie.

The woman nod her head, yes. She step forward and she make up her face again; this time I know is because she smell me. She put her hand under my chin and she make me look straight-straight at her. "Do me a favour," she say, as if she talk to a big person. "When you grow up, don't send your children to the plaza to beg."

"Yes Miss, for sure Miss," I say, word-them all jumble up. Don't like to look at her. At school, teacher say you don't show respect if you look straight at a big person. I frighten a these two, want to get away. Maybe the boy is older than him look and is police.

The woman take her purse from a little school bag she carry. She put five hundred dollar in my hand. Me can't believe it, no way at all. Nobody ever-*ever* give me five hundred dollar. "Miss, thank you; Sir, thank you," I say.

"Go home," the woman say.

I think about this woman sometime. I sorry she can't find me, because I tell lie 'bout where we live. Maybe she woulda help; you hear such things happen. Maybe I shouldna lie. That five hundred dollar last one long time. Mumma, she smile when I bring it home. 'Course – this a the bad part – now she expect it again.

SAHARA
Summer Lion

"I'm gone, Mom!" Carl yelled, going through the front door. "I took a thousand dollars from your purse!"

"Wait, Carl! What time will you be home?" I walked quickly to the door, which Carl had left open in his hurry to leave. *A thousand dollars*? I wonder if he's on drugs? Carl was almost at our gate and already had his Walkman on. I'd have to run if I wanted an answer to my question. Just then the phone rang. It was Carl or the phone. He was almost sixteen. It was Monday – that meant tennis after school and he'd drive home with Mark. I would find out about the thousand dollars later. I locked the front door and hurried to the telephone.

"Hello?"

"What's happening, Sar?" It was my friend and business partner, Lydia.

"Nothing much, Lyds. This is early for you."

"Are you coming into the restaurant soon?"

"By nine."

"Could you be there a little earlier? Londel wants to make his callaloo dish for lunch and I'm expecting Kemar to bring in the callaloo at eight-thirty. You know if we're not there, he'll just go and flog it in Coronation Market."

"Sure, I'll try."

"Thanks, Sar." Lydia sniffed. She must be crying again. "How was the movie?"

"Sweet. Carl hated it."

"Well – what did you expect? It was *Under the Tuscan Sun.*

How come Prince Carl went with you at all?" Lydia and Carl don't get on – it's one of the few areas of tension between us. She thinks I'm way too soft on him.

"He's buttering me up because he wants an iPod to replace his Walkman. Says he's a social pariah because he's still using a Walkman."

"So – was anyone there?" Lydia said, sniffing more audibly. What she meant: was her ex-boyfriend Paul there with his new, twenty-two-year-old model girlfriend named after somewhere in Africa – Zimbabwe? Kinshasa?

"No, Lyds, Paul wasn't there." I knew why Lydia was calling – first, to find out if I'd seen Paul and secondly, because she wouldn't be at work on time. She hadn't been at work on time for months. "But let me go now, we'll talk later," I said. "Gotta run if I'm to be in Liguanea by eight-thirty."

"Okay. Let's have lunch then." This is our joke – we never have lunch together, because we're generally running around with lunch orders.

"Sure," I said. "What time will you be in?"

"Dunno, Sar." Lydia sounded choked; sniffing was progressing to full-blown crying. Fucking Paul. Fucking men. Mostly I was glad I no longer had one.

"By ten." I held back my sigh. Lydia hadn't been pulling her weight at Summer Lion since the break-up.

We'd been friends since prep school. She'd come up to me after my father left, while the rest of my schoolmates were still treating me as if I had a communicable disease, linked her arm through mine and said, "Come and play jacks." We walked onto the verandah of our prep school where girls sat in circles like fallen flowers, their uniform skirts spread around them. "Move over, Rebecca," Lydia said, to the most popular girl in school. I'd loved Lyds from that moment.

I had to hurry – no time to clean up our small Mona house. Carl had left his dirty plate on the floor again. I locked up, checking the windows at the back more than once. The patio furniture was piled up in a corner of the kitchen – there had been a recent spate of robberies in Mona. More or less everything left outside was being stolen – garden hoses, furniture, buckets, clothes on the line, potted plants. I just hoped my car wouldn't be next. It was an old VW, the yellow paint fading, but it did the job and a new car was out of the question. I hoped its battered appearance made it unattractive to thieves.

Outside, the sun blazed down. It was March, dry time. Fires burned every night on the hills behind Mona and what passed for a lawn in front of our house was brown. My neighbour was burning garbage again. There were water restrictions and dust hung in the air. As I drove out, I made a mental note to catch some dishwashing water to wash the car on the weekend – I could barely see through the windscreen.

Summer Lion – the vegetarian restaurant owned by Lydia and I – was a short distance from Mona right in the middle of Liguanea. It was a great location. Lydia owned the land; she'd inherited it when her mother died. She sometimes received offers for the real estate, but so far hadn't been tempted. The only problem was parking, but as many of our clients walked or used public transport, the small parking lot hadn't affected us too much.

I was the restaurant manager; Lydia the cook. I had loved coming up with the concept of Summer Lion – the thatched huts under an enormous guango tree, the communal seating, the concrete floor with imprints of leaves set into the cement, the faintly applied lion silhouette on our menus and wall hangings. We changed the colours every year, the menus every day and we used only Jamaican produce. Over the last few years this had become a challenge – globalization meant it was now easier to buy seedless grapes than mangoes from local vendors.

I was responsible for the buying, the staffing and the accounts. When I told people that Lydia "just" cooked, she'd scowl and say Summer Lion would have failed in the first year without her. It was true – she was a genius in the kitchen, read cookbooks like novels and her recipes were all originals. We kept our menu limited and our prices low, so we had a mixed clientele of working people in Liguanea and those who arrived in monster vehicles, affecting grassroots cool. They came because the food was good, plentiful and cheap, but complained about the lack of air conditioning and the shared tables.

As usual, Liguanea was choked with traffic. At the Matilda's Corner traffic lights, a young boy came up to my open window and shoved a grubby bit of paper at me. "For school," he mumbled. I fancied his eyes searched out the location of my handbag, which was safe on the floor in the back. "Sorry," I said. "Can't help. Go to school, son." He cut his eye at me and sauntered off to another car. The streets of Kingston were often full of children – children erupting from schools, children walking three abreast in the road, children begging. I thought about the boy last night after the movie. He'd looked so young and it had been so late. I'd got an impression of bright eyes and intelligence. I wasn't sure why I'd given him money – I didn't usually give children money – it encouraged them to be on the streets. I'd even asked where to find him – why? Bell Town, he'd said. Bell Town wasn't far from Liguanea.

It was three before I sat down at the computer. I tallied up the day's sales, glad it was over. We didn't open for dinner so my days were intense, but short. The restaurant was doing well, but would never amount to wealth. I would be thirty-three in a few months and sometimes middle age seemed way too close.

"How'd we do?" Lydia said, coming up behind me.

"Pretty good. The otaheiti apple/lime juice was a hit – we ran out."

"Let's have our tea."

This was our ritual. We never had lunch, so when the lunch rush died off and before we closed, we sat and had a cup of tea and a slice of whatever bread Londel had baked – banana nut, pumpkin, sweet potato, carrot. We also offered a tea of the day – today it was lemongrass. We carried our tea to the hut near the trunk of the guango tree where it was cool and furthest away from the traffic fumes on Hope Road.

"You okay, Lyds?"

"I guess. Just wonder when the pain'll stop."

I was silent. There was nothing to say. Paul had gone and that was that. He'd been cruel and Lydia was hurting and there was no way out but through.

I cast around for something else to talk about. "I gave five hundred dollars to a boy in the car park after the movie last night."

"That's a lot. Whyever?"

"Dunno. He was sweet – big eyes and a bright smile. Felt bad, Lyds. He was out there begging and Carl and I were coming from the movie, where Carl probably ate more than he does in a week."

"There's a million of them, Sar."

"I know. I found out where he lived."

"*Why*?"

"Dunno. Thought I might try and help."

"Are you nuts? What could you possibly do for this child? His mother probably has a violent criminal for a baby father and you'll be the next one found in a gully with your throat cut."

"I know. He was a nice looking boy, that's all. Respectful. Hopeful."

"Miss Sahara?" Londel called from the kitchen window.

"Yes, Londel?"

"Kemar come back – say we shorted him for the callaloo."

I sighed. This was a weekly ritual with Kemar – he claimed the carefully weighed callaloo had been wrongly tallied and an outrageous sum was still outstanding. He usually got a few hundred dollars out of me. "Soon come, Lyds," I said, getting up.

"Take your time. Wouldn't want my wallow interrupted." One of Lydia's many saving graces – she has a wry sense of humour.

DEXTER
Going for Water

"Get up, Dexter! You going late for school." Mumma say that to me every mornin. It still dark outside and I don't want come out a bed, but plenty things have to do before we can leave out for school. Dance in Jacob's Pen keep us up whole night. Except Lissa – that chile can sleep!

"Marlon?" I say to my brother. "You ready?"

"Long time." Marlon always like look better than me. Soon as Mumma touch him shoulder inna mornin, him get up. Him don't give no argument about going to get water. I walk past the cot him sleep in and smell piss – Marlon still a wet him bed. We stop talk about it and every day, Mumma just put old shower curtain on him cot and hang him sheet out on the line to dry.

I pick up the bucket. Marlon already have him plastic bottle. Me, I been carryin the bucket long time now – since I ten. When Marlon reach ten, him will carry the bucket too and when Lissa reach five she will carry a plastic bottle. Maybe then we can carry enough water so we don't have to go to standpipe every day.

Outside, Dallas Mountain over the river is huge and black, but the sky gettin light behind it. Rooster over by Ma'as Ken makin whole heap a noise. We better hurry. We go through the zinc gate onto the road and I start run. "Wait!" Marlon whisper. "Not so fast!" Marlon 'fraid a gettin water. Him don't like the dark, stony road; it easy to fall down, easy to walk into things, plus, him 'fraid a duppy. Sometime we hear the noise a patoo make – *whahhg* – and then him *really* 'fraid. Old-time people say when patoo call out, it mean death, but that is bare foolishness.

23

Start see other pickney on the road now; all boy-them. You hardly ever see girl go to catch water inna dark – sometime them will go a evenin time. Girl could get rape, so they only go to standpipe if they can go with them older brother. All a we wearin house clothes; tear-up vest and old shorts. All a we barefoot. I leave Marlon behind – want to get to the standpipe first so don't have to wait long. Pay no mind to him callin for me to slow down. Him will catch up.

The standpipe is tall – smallest pickney can't reach the top. So long time ago, somebody lick off the tap, and it run water day and night. The water make a big pool under the pipe and then run down the side a the road. Don't make no sense to wear shoe to standpipe, 'cause we have to stand in water and mud.

Only two pickney at standpipe. Good. That mean no long wait this mornin.

Busta Markham first; him bucket nearly full up. Next is Curtis Chambers with two bucket – him a big boy for thirteen. "Yow, big man," I say, very respectful. I stand behind Curtis. Other pickney start comin out a the dark. Some stand in a line, but most a them just stand around, waitin for a chance to fill up them bucket.

Marlon come. "What you leave me for?" Him breathin hard and I can see him vex. Marlon have to tough up.

"Why you so fraidy-fraidy?" I say. "You walk down this road every day a life. If I never run, we not near the pipe all now."

Busta Markham pick up him bucket and walk off. It heavy for him; he hold it with two hand and take small steps. Water spill. Busta live far and up a hill – wouldna like to be him. At least where we live is close to standpipe.

Curtis second bucket halfway full when we hear commotion on the road. It more light now; I can see the face of the pickney waitin for water, can hear nightingale singin inna bush. I know what is comin. Marlon squeeze close to me and I make sure he hide behind my back. Four big boy walk past all a we and go up to Curtis. I know two a them: Rayton Roberts and Donny Wilson. Other two come from outside Jacob's Pen, so I see them around, but don't know them name. Them laughin and skylarkin.

"Move over, bwoy," Rayton say to Curtis. "You inna mi way." Rayton don't have bucket to fill up; him just come to make trouble.

"Come out a my face, rass hole," Curtis say, but even though him sound tough, I know him just want get away, even with one bucket not full-full.

Bam, bam – Rayton kick over Curtis's two bucket and the water wash over him foot. "You wet me up, bwoy, you mus' pay for dat," Rayton say. Nobody say anything. We all prayin Curtis don't bother answer Rayton.

"Suck out you madda," Curtis say, but him say it quiet. Is like he know him have to say something like that, but him know it going get him beat up. The word them not out a his mouth good when Rayton pick up one a the empty bucket and clap him across him face: *whap*. Curtis stagger and fall, but him not hurt – bucket light. Him not hurt *yet*. All four a the big boy come and stand 'round him where him sit on the ground.

"You wan' water, bwoy?" Rayton say. "See water over dere." He point at the puddle a muddy water under the standpipe. "You wan' water, you going drink it like di donkey you is."

Curtis don't move and then Donny draw a knife. All a us pickney make a sound together and draw back. Nobody run, though. Donny lean down and put the knife to Curtis's throat. "Drink di water like di donkey you is, bwoy, or mi going stick you like goat."

Curtis start cry. Is the worst thing him could do. Rayton and Donny laugh and call him batty boy and mumma boy. Them drag him to the puddle and push him face down inna water and mud. Them throw him bucket-them far inna the bush. Then them go back up the road.

Sun over Dallas Mountain now. Rooster stop crow. Curtis stand up like a old man, him face fulla mud and shame. Him turn and walk down the track inna bush to find the bucket-them. I am near the standpipe and I put my bucket under the water and watch it fill up slow-slow, splashin over the side because pipe too tall. Pickney come closer and push to be next one at the standpipe. Marlon so close, him skin stickin to my back. All a we late now.

SAHARA
A Small Life

"I'm home, Mom! What's for dinner?"

I'd read all the articles about the selfishness of teenagers, but still it drove me crazy when Carl acted his age.

"I'm starving. Is it steak?"

"Fricassee chicken," I said.

"Again? I wanted steak."

"You used to love fricassee chicken."

"Whatever." I heard him moving around, opening windows, throwing his bag down, turning on the TV, collapsing on the couch. I debated insisting he help with dinner. It would only lead to an argument. "How was school?" I called out. There was no answer. I started frying the chicken.

Sometimes I think my life has amounted to nothing. I'm an only child, born late to a Baptist preacher father and primary school teacher mother. My father was an English missionary – he came to Jamaica as a young man and met my mother in rural Trelawny. They moved to Kingston to escape the members of my mother's family, who were scandalized by her marriage to a white foreigner. I know little about my parents, really. My father abandoned us when I was eleven – one day he left the house for work and he didn't come back. My mother haunted our house in her nightdress and our maid, Salome, walked me to school. I went to bed when told, but after my bedroom door was closed, I sat, hugging my knees, watching for the sweep of headlights across our lawn. The headlights of my father's car. Four months later, my mother was diagnosed with lung cancer and I stopped waiting for my father. My mother was dead in less than a year and I never heard from my father again. I know about loss.

After my mother's funeral, which I hardly remember, Aunt Gladys moved into the Mona house with me. She was my father's sister – a loveless woman who'd never married or had children for good reason – she hated everybody. I had no idea why she'd left England to come to Jamaica, since she loathed the place, but there were photographs of her at my first birthday party, so she'd obviously been in Jamaica for many years. She'd lived in an apartment not far away and she rented it out when she came to look after me.

Aunt Gladys and I struggled through our enforced association – she did her duty, put food on the table, supervised the maid and the gardener, saw I did my homework, took me to the doctor through recurrent bouts of tonsillitis. I called her Ma'am, said grace at table, cleaned my plate at dinner and kept my hair plaited. We spoke to each other in short, respectful sentences. I thought I was becoming invisible and checked the skin of my arms and legs for the first signs of bones showing through. I cried myself to sleep at night at first, but no one appeared to sit beside me on the bed and stroke my hair. I learned that displays of grief are useless without witnesses.

I tolerated Aunt Gladys until the day I brought Lydia home after school. Lydia was black. We ran up our front steps, holding hands, laughing. Aunt Gladys stood in the doorway, her face stiff. I already knew that face – it was the one she used to confront low-class Jamaican behaviour, the deplorable antics of "those people". Lydia and I stood before her and I introduced them, as I'd been taught. Aunt Gladys inclined her head and stood aside to let us go inside the house. "I'll have Salome set another place for dinner," she said, her voice tight with disapproval.

Lydia was no fool. "I have to go home before supper," she said.

"Indeed," Aunt Gladys said.

That night at dinner, my aunt made it plain that Lydia was unwelcome. The words "black" or "Negro" were not uttered,

27

but I should understand Lydia was unworthy of my attention. My father had made an incomprehensible choice of wife. She could only do her best in these unfortunate circumstances, but it was likely I would come to nothing – how could I, with those genes? My dislike turned to anger and then to fear. I was yoked to this woman; I was an orphan with no other relatives. I fantasized about travelling to Trelawny – Warsop, was it? – and finding my mother's family, who would welcome me into a nurturing rural life. I imagined a small wooden house with a view of endless hills. I looked up Warsop on a map, but could tell nothing from the word. I gave up my fantasy of escape and paid for the roof over my head and regular meals with obedience.

When I was seventeen and just out of school, I met Carl's father, Lester Longmore. Lester came from old money and I was hooked in a heartbeat – ensnared by his white skin, his good looks, his elegance, his clothes, his manners, his air of entitlement. We used to meet at Carib Cinema and neck in the smoke-filled, dirty back rows – even now, I find the smell of cigarette smoke erotic. Lester distracted me from contemplation of my future – what would I do? There was no money for university and no plan. Aunt Gladys didn't even counsel a desirable marriage.

In no time I was pregnant and Lester's horrified family had shipped him off to England. I didn't hear from him until Carl was nearly one year old – and then all that arrived was a plain white card with a gold border and a cheque. I tore them both up.

The day after my nineteenth birthday, I suggested Aunt Gladys should go back to her apartment. I told her I could no longer stand her cold contempt. She accused me of ingratitude and called me a slut. "Then you'll be well rid of me," I said, summoning some gumption. I hardly saw her after that – in my mid-twenties, she showed up unannounced at the house and told me my father had died in Africa. I could see she imagined him among multitudes of black female flesh and the thought was unendurable. She herself died last year and I didn't go to her funeral.

My parents' gifts to me were simple – a good early education, a head for figures, some artistic talent and a modest house in Mona. When Carl was four months old, I got a part-time job at a real estate firm doing their books. My salary was just enough to pay the maid, who looked after Carl, and buy food.

When Carl was nearly three, Lydia dropped out of the University of Florida where she'd been studying literature. She came home – said she couldn't stand the racism in the US, was bored with needing to have an opinion about everything she read and all she wanted to do was cook. She brought a present for Carl – a soft ball, suitable for a baby's crib. She dangled it over his head and made cooing noises. It was way too young for him and he turned his back on her.

"I'm starting a restaurant," she said. "You know that land my parents left in Liguanea?"

"The one with the guango tree?"

"Yes. It has a broken down old house on it; I'm going to make that the kitchen and build huts in the yard. It's going to be a vegetarian restaurant."

"A vegetarian restaurant in Jamaica? I don't think that's going to work."

"It'll work. The food will be fantastic; we'll give it a Rastafarian theme and it will be the last word in cool."

"We?" I said.

"We. I have the land and some money. You can do the books and manage the place. I just want to cook. It'll be flexible, so you can look after the baby, no problem."

"Carl," I said.

"What?"

"Carl. The baby's name is Carl."

"I know. Carl. Well, what do you say?"

I got up and hugged her. "What'll we call it?"

"Dunno. Something with lion in the name. Lions are very Rasta."

I looked outside – it was the height of summer. "Summer Lion?" I offered.

"Brilliant!" Lydia said.

Two years ago, Lester had moved back to Jamaica with a second wife – I'd completely missed the first – and baby son. He got in touch, and Carl wanted to see his father and half brother. I stayed out of it. I suspected Carl wanted his father to finance his college education. I asked no questions about his visits or their relationship. I knew Lester ran a lucrative law practice and that was about it. I didn't want to see him.

I'd never married; not that I'd given up on the thought. Oh, there had been men I told Carl to call "Uncle", but most were put off by my single motherhood and left as soon as they decently could. I had no social status, little money, and my only child was halfway out of the house. No, I didn't like to take stock – my life was small and growing smaller with each year.

"Is dinner nearly ready?" Carl called from the living room. "Why can't you start cooking earlier?"

I started chopping vegetables and didn't answer.

DEXTER
Nightingale All Age

My school is Nightingale All Age – a big-big school on Molynes Road. The school not name after the bird, but some nurse that help soldier-them inna big war one long time ago. It have buildin with two floor and class keep in one long room with three class going on same time. Between one class and the next class is a blackboard and teacher write on it, one teacher on one side, next teacher on the other side. Most time we can't hear what the teacher say. Blackboard is old and shiny and chalk slip over it screechin, screechin; make our blood run cold. Get used to it, though. Most writin too light to see anyway. Some old poster on the wall, cobweb inna the roof, pile a dirt and sweetie paper in the corner. Most a the year, it so hot that if you try write in class, your arm stick to your exercise book.

I sit in the back; teacher always put question to pickney in the front row. Is even harder to hear what teacher say from the back. Traffic make plenty noise and shift student a run up and down outside, yellin and carryin on. I use to be on afternoon shift, but now I come on early shift. The ride on the bus harder on mornin shift, but I think afternoon shift has more noise. Ghetto pickney has nowhere to go inna day, so it don't matter which shift you on; you go a school same way and school don't have place to put you.

Teacher-them hate the shift system; I hear them talk about it all the time. Them say is Michael Manley cause it; he a Prime Minister we did have, people either love him or hate him. Him dead awhile now and people still a fight about him. Far as I understand it, Michael say school should have shift system so

31

more children can use the same buildin. Sound like a good idea, but it don't work.

Today we havin a substitute teacher, one big fat lady name Mrs. Beckwith. Never seen her before – our regular teacher is Mrs. Barnes. Mrs. Beckwith wearin a blue blouse with button down the front. Her blouse is too tight and top button keep poppin open and we can see her big breast-them. Boy them are laughin, especially boy inna back, like where I am sittin, and we all waitin for more button to pop.

"Students, today's lesson is about the slave trade. How many of you know anything about slavery?" Mrs. Beckwith say.

Petrona Gardner put up she hand quick-quick. Nobody in the class like Petrona; she too curry favour and lickey-lickey. She sit in front and always know answer to the teacher question. Mrs. Barnes, now, she don't let Petrona answer every question; she pretend she don't see her hand wavin around in front a the class. But Mrs. Beckwith, she just come to Nightingale All Age and she don't know 'bout Petrona.

"Yes, young lady?" Mrs. Beckwith say. She don't know our name-them, like Mrs. Barnes woulda know.

"Miss! English people go to Africa and buy black people and put them on a ship. The ship come to Jamaica and bring a whole heap a black people to work on sugar plantation. They take them away from them family in Africa and don't pay them to work. That is the slave trade."

"Very good. Anyone has anything else to add?" Lotta hand in the air now. Mrs. Beckwith still don't notice her top button open. Silbert Walcott sit beside me and him laugh and cover him mouth before di laugh come out, so him sound like him chokin.

"Yes? You there at the back? Yes, YOU. Apparently you have something to say? What is it?" Mrs. Beckwith lookin at me.

"Me, Miss?" I say. "Not me. Don't have anyting to say."

"Stand up, boy. Come up here to the front of the room." Plenty pickney a laugh now. I shame. Don't know how I get into trouble so easy, even when I not doing anything. This is why I don't like school – too much angry teacher, angry pickney – too easy to get inna trouble. I go to the front a the room.

"What's your name?" Mrs. Beckwith say.

"Miss, Raymond."

"Raymond what?"

"Miss, Raymond Morrison."

"What you laughing about in back of my classroom?"

"Miss, not laughin. Was listenin."

"If you weren't laughing, who was?"

"Nobody, Miss."

"Don't chat foolishness, boy. Somebody was laughing. If you don't tell me who, I'll send you out of the room."

Fine with me. It strange what teacher try to frighten you with. It more cool outside and I will watch the boy-them kick ball on the field across the way, look at the Blue Mountain and think a being out a school forever.

"Miss, nobody laughin, true-true. We all listenin to what you sayin about slavery," I say.

Mrs. Beckwith lean down to me. Now I am close to her, I can see her second button is nearly outta the hole. Don't let it pop while I am up here; for sure I will get the blame. I see a little sweat runnin down between her breast and can even see the edge of her kerchief, that she tuck under her brassiere. Why she don't wear clothes that fit her? She smell a carbolic soap and chalk.

"Alright, Rayton…"

"Raymond, Miss…"

"Raymond. Since you were listening so carefully, tell us all about the slave trade."

I look at the floor and wish I was in some place different – any place. Any place not in front of class with fat Mrs. Beckwith in front a me. No way out a this but to talk.

"Well, Miss, is like Petrona say. White people go to Africa and get black people. I hear say they buy them from other black people, but me, I don't believe that. Them put them in chain and take them to the coast a Africa where big ship wait. Them tear off them clothes and take them away from them family and put them in bottom a big ship. Then the ship take them all the way across the ocean to Jamaica. Some people say the first place the ship stop is Jamaica and that is where them let off the most troublesome slave. Other people say Jamaica was the *last* place ship stop; and slave left alive is the strongest. People say that is why Jamaican people have plenty-plenty attitude."

"Go on."

"Well, Miss, them crowd up the slave inna bottom a the ship, they was inna the dark, them never seen a ship before much less go on one. Some a them don't even see the sea before. Ship rockin, everybody a vomit. White people talk to them in language them don't understand; they don't even understand what other black people say, because them come from different-different tribe. Plenty a them die, get sick, the white people beat them, some a them get throw inna the sea for shark to eat. The one that live until them get to the West Indies, them get sent to plantation to cut cane. If them do anyting wrong, them get beat by slave master, some get hang. That is the slave trade."

Classroom quiet now. Pickney lookin at me, not at Mrs. Beckwith shirt. "You may go back to your seat, Raymond," she say.

"Miss! Thank you, Miss."

Mrs. Beckwith turn her back to the class and start write up on the board. She write: "The Middle Passage." She dust off her hand-them and put the chalk back in the box on her desk. She turn around. Petrona hand still in the air.

"Yes? What's your name?"

"Petrona, Miss!"

"You have a question, Petrona?"

"Yes, Miss. The white people…"

"You mean the slave traders?"

"Yes, Miss. They take children to the ship-them?"

"They did."

"Why, Miss?"

"It was the slave trade. They took whole families, but if any member was weak, they were killed."

"Why, Miss?" Petrona never know when to shut up.

"You making mischief, Missy?" say Mrs. Beckwith and I

34

know is because she can't answer Petrona question. I think a being a boy on a slave ship, inna dark, nobody I know near me, hearin people cry and vomit, not knowin where the ship going. Must a been rough can't done.

"*No*, Miss!" Lickey-lickey Petrona *never* make mischief.

"Alright then," Mrs. Beckwith say. She turn to pick up the chalk and her second button pop open. Whole class start laugh and slavery is forgot.

SAHARA
An Orange Notebook

I cleaned the house on Wednesday nights. I cherished the illusion that this left my weekends free for exciting activities. I'd not had a nanny growing up – my father had decreed my mother was to stay home and take care of me. We did have Salome, who came in to clean, cook and do the laundry, and a gardener named Basil. This continued for a while after my father left and my mother died, but no one could get on with Aunt Gladys for long. She treated Salome and Basil disdainfully, speaking very slowly as if to children. She corrected their English and searched their bags when they were leaving. They were issued with their own cutlery and crockery, kept on a high shelf in the kitchen. They were not allowed to use our eating utensils. I remember those neat piles – Salome and Basil each had a plain white dinner plate, a dark blue side-plate, and a mug with stripes. A knife, fork, spoon and a large plastic glass. They were not allowed to rest these utensils in our dish drainer – as soon as they were used, they had to be washed, dried and restored to their place on the high shelf, in case they got "mixed up". Salome and Basil soon left, to be replaced by Roslyn and Kirk, Verona and Bedlam, Patrice and Morgan. We shrugged off household staff like old clothes.

After Carl was born, I wanted to look after him myself. But I had to work and working meant leaving him with Aunt Gladys. I could not abide the thought of my son being influenced by her worldview, so I hired a nanny – a young woman, my age, straight from the country, from Trelawny. Her name was Margaret and I believe she loved Carl as soon as she saw him. Now, I look back on her devotion to my son and I realize it took me months to ask her about her own children. Eventually we met them – a boy and a girl, a pigeon pair, as we say. Every now and then, she'd bring them to the house to play with Carl, but they never came to his birthday parties.

Margaret left when Carl was ten – she'd met a man and was moving to Negril. I tried to replace her, but it didn't work out – a series of helpers, as they were by then called, were lazy, dishonest and unreliable. By the time Carl was thirteen, I decided we could look after ourselves. So on Wednesday nights, I cleaned.

I liked it, actually. I had come to love the Mona house, even though it was almost too hot to live in during the summer months. The house had a flat roof – good for hurricanes, but bad for reflecting heat. Once, cobwebbing, I stood on a chair and laid my hand flat against the cement roof. It was hot to the touch, radiating heat around my head and shoulders. A ceiling fan just moved the warm air around.

The house was set on a large, flat lot, mostly lawn, with a privet hedge around the perimeter. When I was growing up, the hedge was low and you could see over it. Then, the house had aluminium louvres and no window grills – now, the hedge was eight feet tall and all the doors and windows were caged in with metal. My parents had added a small patio at the back and planted fruit trees – Julie mango, lime, orange and an ackee tree. The trees were large and gave the house privacy, although my neighbour on that side, an older woman called Sadie, disliked the trees and was constantly asking me to cut them down. "They positively invite thieves," she whined. It was true – in mango season my back garden came alive with boys stealing mangoes.

The house itself was unremarkable, three small bedrooms, a living/dining room, small porch, two bathrooms and a kitchen. Terrazzo tile floors. After Aunt Gladys left, I painted every room a different colour, tore down the dingy drapes and lace curtains, bought and refurbished flea-market furniture, hung my collection of carved calabashes, tried to give the boring rooms personality. People who visited often said, "Wow!" as they came through the front door.

I started to clean. Carl was out with his father – they went to a movie or for dinner about once a month. I wondered if he'd have to sit through *Under the Tuscan Sun* again. Probably not. Lester would have taken his new wife to that one.

When I was finished the routine cleaning, I decided to tackle the third bedroom. It had once been Carl's nursery, then a small office, now it was little more than a junkroom. It would be nice to have a proper guest room, or even a library.

I went into the room and opened all the windows. It was dark outside. One thing I didn't like about Mona houses – they were low to the ground. Anyone could walk up to the windows and see inside. I imagined a dark face with shining eyes, details indistinct in the night and a gun pointed at me through the window grills. It happened. Only last month Sandra McIntyre on Gerbera Way had been held up at her gate. I shook off the bad feelings and started to make a pile of things to be sent to the Salvation Army.

Two hours later, the room looked much better. There was still a large box of papers and notebooks from my days as a real estate agent to go through. Really old stuff that I should probably just throw away without looking at it. I was tired and wanted to stop for the night. Carl would soon be home. Maybe we could sit on the couch and have a cup of cocoa together. No, if I didn't finish this now, I would never do it.

The box was full of nothing. Old bank statements. Birthday cards. Bad photographs. Invitations to weddings. Cockroach eggs and lizard droppings. Diaries. School reports. A three-ring binder of essays. Why hadn't I just thrown it all away years ago? Then I found a bright orange notebook and idly flipped through it – shopping lists, clothes I wanted, doodles. Pages where I'd written "Sahara Longmore" over and over, practising signatures. Pages where I'd written "Lester Longmore" above "Sahara Lawrence" and crossed out all the letters common to both names. I racked my brain about that and remembered – you then counted all the remaining letters, chanting "he loves me, he loves me not" and whatever you ended on was supposed to be the truth. I'd done it many times, as if our names might

38

suddenly sprout new letters and a different answer. I counted again – he loves me, he loves me not. On the last letter, I said out loud, "He loves me not."

I didn't find a date until the last entry in the book – the year Carl was born. I was seventeen and pregnant and in the orange notebook I'd made a list of all the things I wanted to do before I died. Go on the Orient Express. Visit Venice. Climb Mt. Kilimanjaro. Learn Spanish. Play a musical instrument. Write books. Read all of Shakespeare. Live in London. Get married. Have two children – a boy and a girl. See the animals in Africa. Go to the Grand Canyon. Help people. I didn't remember making the list or wanting those things. At the end of the list, I'd written "CHANGE THE WORLD" in decorated capital letters followed by eight exclamation marks.

I wanted to cry, but heard the door slam and I knew Carl was home. I wiped my eyes and got up to greet him.

That night I couldn't sleep. I lay in the dark, listening to Carl move around. Eventually, his room fell silent. Surely the night noises were louder than usual – dogs barking, trucks racing their engines, distant sirens. I thought about my stupid list – I might as well have written: "Be an Olympic gymnast." This was childish; I was privileged in comparison to many. I'd made my choices, my life was nothing to moan over.

I thought about the boy in Sovereign Plaza after the movies. What had been his mother's name? Arleen; that was it. I wondered again if I could help. Lydia, naturally, had dismissed the idea, and it was certainly risky. But I could try, couldn't I? At least I could attempt to find him and see where he lived, what his mother was like. I began making plans in the dark for a boy I'd spent five minutes with. Finally, I fell asleep.

DEXTER
Mad Like a Dog on Full Moon Night

Is late. I at Sovereign again; this time in front a the pharmacy talkin to Sinclair. Him tell me how the police lock up Lasco last week for t'iefin a cassette from the game arcade. Sinclair say him police friend see Lasco at the station, handcuff to a window grill. Then Sinclair look over my shoulder and say, "Evenin Ma'am?" I look 'round and the brownin woman from the other night after the film show stand there, lookin at me. This time she by herself.

"You don't live in Bell Town," she say to me. "I went there, I looked for you. I asked for Arleen but no one knew Arleen with three children at the top of a hill. Why you lie?"

I shame. Dunno what to say. Sinclair listenin. "Miss, I afraid you was police," I say quiet-quiet, lookin down at the ground.

"Come talk to me," she say. She walk over to the step and sit down *braps.* She touch a place beside her. "Sit," she say.

This woman definitely mad like a dog on a full moon night. She want me, *a black ghetto boy*, to sit beside *her*, a uptown brown woman, on front step a the Plaza! If is not Sinclair on duty, other security woulda run me already. I frighten, but I want see what this crazy woman do next. I sit.

"I would like to meet your mother," she say. "I would like to help you go to school, pay school fees and buy books and shoes. Would you like that?"

Shoe! Is all I hear. "Yes Miss, yes Miss, thank you, Miss."

"But," the woman say, "probably you have to leave your mother and go to boarding school. You know what that is?"

"Miss, when boy come from country to Jacob's Pen, them

40

board with people in the community. You talkin about school where pickney sleep."

"Yes. So Jacob's Pen is where you really live?"

"Yes, Miss."

"Anyway, I have a friend on the Munro School Board. I've talked to them and they'll take you in September. I want to talk to your mother about it."

I nod my head, yes. I hear 'bout Munro. Boy at my school talk about it, say it in the country, in St. Elizabeth, and how the wind blow 'til the tree all bend down in one direction, how teacher beat the boy-them and how the water to bathe in cold like ice. But I hear say you get food three time a day on long table. Seem like boy get beat no matter where them is, but other things sound good. I never see myself in such a place, though. "Come," the woman say. "Drive with me to your house."

She drive a little yellow VW, the old kind, not fancy like the SUV most uptown people have. Whole heap a book and paper on the front seat. She put them in the back and tell me to get in. Could be she a teacher. She don't talk. I wonder if she can smell me, like the time she touch me. "Miss, what is your name?" I say.

"Sahara Lawrence."

Is a funny name. "Miss Sah-hara?" I say.

"Yes." She smile. "Like the desert."

We pass Bell Town and go to Jacob's Pen. They tell us at school why some place in Kingston called "Pen" but I forget. Something to do with old-time day and pig farmin.

We live at the bottom a one hill, near the bus stop, in a board house some white people from foreign build. Marlon father, him did help the white people build it because they say someone from Jacob's Pen have to help, or no house. Marlon father say is him house after that and Mumma and him fight. We don't know where him is now. We glad him gone; him behave like hog, beat everybody mornin, noon and night.

"Miss, stop here," I say. People lookin from behind them window and over zinc fence. Mumma come out; she carryin Lissa. The uptown woman get out a her car while I still try open door on my side. I don't hear what the woman say to Mumma right at first.

"… I can get him into Munro and I'll look after his schooling. He'll come home in the holidays, but I think it's important for his education to get him out of this environment," the woman sayin to Mumma.

Mumma don't say anything. I know she figurin out "this environment" business. She don't ask the woman to come inside; she don't want the woman to see that we t'ief light and shit in a hole in the ground out back; she don't want her to see where we wash, using bucket and rag, standin on a slippery flat rock; she don't want her to see the cardboard under the zinc roof inside to catch leak.

"Miss Arleen?" Miss Sahara say. Look like she a mannersable woman; lot a uptown woman woulda just say Arleen.

Lissa start fuss and Mumma give her a soother to suck on. Mumma thin, you can tell she don't eat plenty. She hardly ever put Lissa down. "Well, Miss Sa-hara," Mumma say. She can't say the name right. The uptown woman must of introduce herself. "For true I woulda like Dexter go school. Him bright. But we woulda miss him 'round here." She don't say is me bring home most a the money. She not going tell the uptown woman that.

"Well, think about it," the woman say. "Talk to Dexter about it. I'll come back in a week and you can tell me your decision."

"Yes, Missus. Thank you, Miss Sah…" I know Mumma hopin the woman will give us another five hundred dollar, but she don't. She just say goodbye and go back to her yellow car. She don't take me back to the Plaza, so I going have to walk. If I don't go, we don't eat tonight.

Mumma never talk to me about boardin school. Nobody have to say anything and I don't tell anybody, not even Lasco or Sinclair. The week go by fast-fast and is Saturday mornin and I know the woman will come to hear Mumma decision. I wake up early and I climb up the hill behind our house and I hide inna macca bush. Sun go up and day is hot and my stomach make noise – not even sugar water I drink since mornin. Macca bush scratch and I smell garbage fire. I see river over the way; water is low this time a year. The yellow car drive up and Miss Sahara get out. She carryin something in her hand. Mumma come out a the house and the two a them talk. It don't take long. The woman go to her car; she still holdin the bag in her hand. Then she stop. She turn 'round and go back to Mumma. She take something out a the plastic bag and even from inside the macca bush I can see what she bring: is a brand new draughts set. She give it to Mumma and she go back to her car and she get in and I watch the yellow VW drive away until I can't see it no more.

SAHARA
A black plastic bag

"Carl? Can you help me with the groceries?" It was Saturday morning and Carl was inside the house, getting ready to go to Lime Cay with his friends. There was no answer. "Carl?" I shouted, from the verandah.

"Okay, okay, I'm coming!" My son came out of the house, dressed in beach clothes. His legs surprised me these days – they were a man's legs, hairy and muscled. His body was still not a coherent whole – his shoulders and arms were skinny – but you could see he was going to be a solid man. His face had a smattering of pimples in among the freckles and his hair needed cutting. He'd started shaving a few months ago, but only did it intermittently.

"Have you got a hat?" His pale skin burned easily.

"Mom! God!" He started taking the bags of food out of the car.

"Leave that one," I said, "it's not for us."

"Who's it for then?"

"Some children."

"What children?"

"What time are you leaving?" I wanted to distract Carl; didn't want to explain or think about the bag of food I'd bought for that boy and his family.

"What children, Mom?"

"You remember that boy we met after the movie a couple of weeks back? In Sovereign car park?"

"The one you gave five hundred dollars to?"

"Yes."

44

"What about him?" Carl stood facing me, hands on hips. He was getting angry.

"Well, I looked for him. Couldn't find him at first, but then bucked him up again at Sovereign. I took him to his house and met his mother. I talked to her about sending him to boarding school, but when I went back to see about it, he was gone and his mother said no."

"And how were you going to pay for boarding school for this yout'?"

"Don't talk to me like that, Carl. I wasn't going to pay. I talked to Guy Petersen; you know him, he comes to the restaurant every week. He's on the Munro School Board and he said they'd consider taking him in, depending on his grades."

"So what – you're taking food up there now?"

"I thought I would. It's only some basics." Just then, Carl's friend Mark drove up in his car and blew the horn. Carl waved and ran back into the house to get his bag. Conversation over.

Mark lowered his window. "Hi Mrs. Lawrence," he said. I didn't tell people about my unmarried status and neither did Carl. We'd never agreed on this; it had just happened.

"Hi Mark. When will you guys be back?"

"Maybe four. But don't worry, we'll be fine." Mark was from a wealthy family and had the smoothest of manners. I didn't trust him an inch.

"Drive safely. Do you have your phone?" I said to Carl.

"Y-e-s, Mom," he said, drawling out the words. "And a fucking hat," he added, under his breath, brushing past me. Let it go, I thought. He went through the gate, banging it behind him.

As it turned out, I didn't take the food to Dexter and his family that weekend. I wasn't sure I should do it. I'd bought the food on impulse, remembering how thin Dexter's mother's arms had been, wrapped around the baby girl. I'd seen another boy peeping from around the door of the wooden house, which was mostly hidden behind a zinc fence. I didn't know if there was a man involved and Lydia's warning was a fair one – any man could be violent. Maybe I was getting into something I'd

45

regret. And if I started, wouldn't I have to take food there every week? Why wasn't the mother working?

On Monday morning, the plastic bag with the food was still on the kitchen counter where I'd left it. I put it in the car – maybe I'd give it to one of the traffic light boys. Or maybe to the one-legged man on our street corner.

I took the food home with me on Monday evening and back to work on Tuesday. On Tuesday afternoon, after work, I set out for Jacob's Pen.

I left Hope Road and drove towards the river. I knew the general direction, but wondered if I'd find the wooden house without Dexter's instructions. I dodged potholes, goats, wrecked vehicles and a fire – someone had thrown an old tyre over a dead animal and set it alight. The black smoke billowed across the road. The streets were choked with garbage and grey, greasy water pooled in the potholes – sewage, I assumed. I kept my windows rolled up and the air conditioning strug-gled. I passed Bell Town and went on towards Jacob's Pen. The place looked bombed – buildings were windowless and de-faced with political graffiti. The rich ones in Jacob's Pen lived in unrendered concrete houses, half constructed, with steel emerging from flat roofs – a second floor planned, even though the ground floor was unfinished. Dirty children stared, the youngest naked from the waist down. I was afraid. Suppose I had a flat tyre? Half-dressed men with muscles like rope would emerge from the shadows and demand money. Of course I would give it to them, along with the bag of food, but perhaps they would not be satisfied and would decide to have some fun with the uptowner who was stupid enough to leave her place.

But I found the Habitat for Humanity house near the bus stop. It was right beside a six-a-side dirt football field; the only wooden house in the area. I parked the car, got out, made sure all the doors and windows were locked, climbed up a short, stony path and banged on the zinc fence.

A voice called out, "A who dat?"

"Sahara Lawrence," I said. Arleen opened the gate and came out, the baby still on her shoulder.

"Yes, Miss?"

I wondered how old she was. Probably late twenties, but she looked forty. She kept her mouth half closed as she spoke, so it was hard to understand her. I could see she had teeth missing. Her hair was unkempt and she wore a washed-out dress and stained apron. The baby seemed well nourished, though.

"Where's Dexter?" I said. I felt embarrassed and didn't know how to conduct myself. Should I talk to this woman, find out about her life? Should I go inside? No, she hadn't invited me. Should I just give her the bag of food and go?

"Still a school, Miss. Marlon come home, but Dexter not here yet." A younger boy peeped around the zinc fence. He didn't come outside, but stayed there, half hidden behind the fence. His clothes were ragged and the one arm I could see was thin and scratched, as if by prickles or a barbed wire fence.

"I brought you some food," I said and gave Arleen the bag.

"T'ank you, Miss. T'ank you. We grateful for true." She did not look at me, but then the boy ran out from behind the fence. He took the bag from his mother and set it on the ground, squatting beside it. His knees were scabbed and dusty. He looked inside the bag, moving the groceries around so he could see everything. He looked up at me and his eyes shone. "Mackerel," he said to his mother. "Bully beef. Oats. Baby formula." He stood up and took a step towards me. And then he put his arms around my waist and hugged me – awkwardly, as if he feared rejection or a blow. I touched his shoulder and, to my shame, wondered what I might catch from this boy. He let me go and stepped back. "T'ank you, Miss," he said. He picked up the bag with both hands and struggled through the gate into the yard behind him. He might have been eight and already he was the man of the house.

DEXTER
Big Trouble Now

It hot-hot inna classroom today. Grade 5 teacher on the other side a the blackboard teachin Language Arts. My teacher, Mrs. Barnes, she teach Science. She my most favourite teacher, she young and neat lookin, always wear different colour skirt and white blouse. She wear silver earring and a thin silver chain around her neck with a cross on it. She smell good too, if you go close to her. Rest a Nightingale All Age smell bad; smell a pickney who take only sponge bath, hot weather, garbage, black smoke from car and truck on the road, shit and piss.

Is not because we careless why school smell a shit and piss. Bathroom out by the playin field a dark, nasty place. Toilet never work; always full up and stink. All a we stop go there since last year, when two girl get rape by man from the community. I never go school that day, only hear about it after, but seem like Sophie Peterson and Lavanga Kircaldy go bathroom together and two cokehead man wait for them, rape them right there on the wet, nasty concrete floor. School close for two day and I never see Sophie or Lavanga again. We hear the man them is friend with the area don, so nothing happen to them. After that, girl at Nightingale All Age don't go bathroom; school stop clean it and boy stop go too.

School put up a sign this year. When we come back in January, a big black and white sign is right at the entrance: "No urinating or defecating in corridors." Most a we never know what that mean, but Principal tell us is shit and piss. Him don't say "shit" and "piss"; him talk about "going to the bathroom in the corridor". We don't say anything, but we still not going to the bathroom over on the playin field, no way. It easy to piss behind the Paul Bogle buildin anyway, no teacher ever go there.

Mrs. Barnes talkin about temperature today, something about Celsius and Fahrenheit and thermometer. Some children sleepin with head on them desk. All a we find it hard to sleep inna night, too many people inna small room, noise inna community from dance and boom box, gunshot. Sometime is only at school we sleep.

I think about the uptown woman with the funny name – Sahara. I remember Miss Blake in Science tell us about Sahara desert in Africa. Maybe the uptown woman come from there, but she talk like a Jamaican with good education. I think about going to boardin school and food three time every day on one long table. I think about new shoe. I think about the big boy in Sovereign who call Miss Sahara "Mom". I wonder if him go a boardin school.

"Dexter!" Mrs. Barnes say loud. She know my pet name. She standin right next to me and I jump. I smell her flower smell.

"Yes, Miss!"

"You're not paying attention. Please tell me the boiling point of water on the Fahrenheit scale."

I look down at the desk. I shame. Pickney start laugh. Silbert Walcott poke me inna back and say, "Dunce bwoy!" I don't know what happen, but next thing I know, me and Silbert a fight on the floor. He on top a me, his breath smell awful inna my face, I kick over a desk. Everybody scatter.

Is easy to get into a fight. Sometime I just get mad and hate everybody and must hit something or die. Silbert is bigger than me and him punch me inna stomach and I feel sick, but him too close to hit me hard. I know Mrs. Barnes tryin to get us apart, but she small, and we on ground and she can't reach us good. Other pickney yellin, "Lick him Silbert! T'ump him, Dexter!" More desk turn over, everything is pure noise and confusion. I see a pencil on the ground, I pick it up and I stab after Silbert. Him let out one scream and roll off me and start bawl, "A dead now! Him stab mi, him kill mi for sure!" I get up, and sit on

49

Silbert chest. I going *kill* him with beatin. By the time I done with him, him going know stab with pencil nothing at all. Then two strong hand hold me from behind and haul me off Silbert. "You boys are animals," Mr. Reckord say close to my ear. He the Principal. Big trouble now.

Don't want go home. Mr. Reckord give me paper for Mumma, he say she must come to school to see him or I will be expel for fightin. Mumma not going come school. The only time she ever come school is first day. She take me first day to Grade 1 and she take Marlon first day to Grade 1. After that, never.

Walk down Hope Road, away from Jacob's Pen. Don't know if Marlon hear about fight. Prob'ly somebody tell him and he will get home before me and then Mumma wait for me tonight with the belt. It rough, bwoy, rough.

Walk past Jamaica House with it huge lawn, turnin brown. No rain fall in awhile. Far back from the road, I see the white house where the Prime Minister have office – him don't live there. It big enough to hold a t'ousand people.

Think about Lasco. Wonder what happen to him. I don't see him since the day I meet Miss Sahara again at Sovereign, the same day Sinclair tell me Lasco get arrest for t'iefing a cassette and police chain him to the window grill. I woulda like see Lasco now – him get so much beatin in him life, he carry scar upon scar. Him don't worry 'bout trouble.

Maybe I should pray. Teacher tell us about God in school. We have to pray plenty-plenty at Nightingale All Age. I never use to mind all the prayin, but then I see one picture a Jesus in a Bible story book and him is white; him even has blue eye and soft hair. That couldna be Jesus? But so teacher say and the Bible storybook full a white people, angel and Moses and Noah and all a them white-white. After that, I never believe God care about me; that He know me in trouble at school and if I pray, He do something to fix it. What God going do anyway? But maybe I wrong and just in case, I say inside my head, please God, don't make Mr. Reckord throw me out a school.

I reach Half Way Tree. Is middle day and the sun so hot asphalt a melt. Taxi and bus and car all mix up inna the square.

I look to see if the clock tower a tell the right time. No. Still sayin six o'clock. The only time it tell the right time is about two week last year when some foreigner fix it. Is some history thing; foreigner say clock must look after. Big argument bust 'bout whether them can use digital clock or have to use old-time clock. Argument don't sort out yet, so clock still wrong.

I find a bench and sit down inna park. It name for Mr. Nelson Mandela from South Africa. He did come to Jamaica one time. They put tree in this park but no grass; is bare concrete everywhere you look. And garbage, plastic bottle and fast food paper and Styrofoam lunch box. Plenty goat inna Mandela Park – the goat-them love all that garbage. The bench is dirty with bird shit and sticky stuff I hope is soda. I start think about Miss Sahara and I watch traffic and look for a yellow VW. It look like hardly anybody have a yellow car. I see a windscreen boy flash the water in him bottle on a car just when the light change. Him see me watchin him and walk over to me.

Mandela Park is where I did get beat up that time when I leave uptown Plaza. Whole heap a street boy and man live in Mandela Park or roundabout. Better look like I have someplace going or them going think I come to box bread out a them mouth. Lot a street boy is crack head or smoke plenty-plenty ganja and them prefer fight to eatin.

"Yow, yout'. What you lookin at?" him say, standin too close. I see him is not a boy; maybe him could be twenty. Him clothes tear up and him so dirty, he black like coal inna jerk chicken pan. Him empty what water leave in him bottle in my lap. One a the lime inna the bottle fall out, bounce off my foot and roll away. This windscreen man ready for a fight and him waitin to see what I will do after him wet me up.

"Nah look at anyting. Respec', bred'ren, nah badda you. Just waitin on di bus fi go back a Jacob's Pen," I say. My pants wet and people will think I wet myself. I want kill him.

"Bus to Jacob's Pen on odda side a di park," him say.

I stand up. *Dont say anyting.* Him big; him will win a fight – easy. "Respec'," I say again. The windscreen man take a step back and I see him muscle-them relax. Him touch him fist to mine. The smell a him heavy, like it alive.

51

"Standpipe over dere," him say and he point up Hope Road. "Here. Take dese – I gone. You keep what money you mek." Him give me the empty bottle, two cut lime still inside, and the scraper. "Give di scraper to Umroy when you finish."

"Wait!" I say. "Why you givin me this? What you want from me?"

"Nutt'n. See all di yout' dem a clean windscreen? Dem all work for mi. Plus mi got 'nuff plastic bottle an' scraper. A nuh nutt'n. Mek a nanny, g'waan 'bout you business."

"Blessin, big man. Show mi Umroy again?"

"Him." The windscreen man point to a madman, sittin on the edge a the dry fountain.

"*Him*?" I say. "Di madman?"

Windscreen man don't answer. Him walk off inna the traffic. Taxi have to brake up hard not to hit him. Taximan lean out a him window and cuss him dog rotten. Windscreen man don't even look at di taximan.

Dark. Time to go home. I did wipe a few windscreen, get enough to buy a patty, no drink though. Mandela Park have no water. When the government did build the fountain, the madman-them start bathe inna it so the government take out the water. Now people throw garbage inna fountain and blue paint peelin off. I did try to give the scraper and plastic bottle to Umroy, but him look at me like I am a duppy. I leave the scraper and bottle beside him on the fountain; don't want no argument. Patty and long day and trouble dry inna my throat. Start walk home.

Stream a car on Hope Road, everybody inside, window roll up. Long line a red light headin up the road, like the eye-them of a thousand rolling calf. A bus pass me and stop. Plenty people come out, start walkin into Ranny Williams Centre. Something must be keepin there tonight. A dance, or maybe bingo, or even a church barbecue. The people dress up, talkin to each other, laughin. Some a them have pickney with them; the woman-them hold the pickney hand. The girl are all dress up. The night is warm and I feel sticky, like I did roll on the ground in Mandela Park, roll inna the things people throw away. Over the way at Ranny Williams, the light fall out a the window onto the dry grass, and inside I can see table with white tablecloth. I hear music. When people see me, walkin the other way, them separate around me like a river round a rock. I run to catch the bus and I jump on it, usin the last a the windscreen money.

Mumma in bed with Marlon and Lissa a watch TV. The room is hot and smell a fryin. My stomach roll over; sorry I not home when Mumma cook. Ghetto steak and syrup water much better than patty and no drink.

"Bwoy, where you been?" Mumma say, gettin up. She a reach for the belt already. "What you mean to come here this time a night? You fightin in school? After you have no sense." Look like Marlon tell her what happen.

Her voice loud up. "Marlon, carry Lissa inna back room."

"Mumma…" I say. I want tell her what happen, but don't know how. *Whiss*, the belt make noise inna the air and I duck. It catch me on my neck. Is good, she have buckle in her hand, no murderin this time.

When she finish, Mumma put down the belt. She breathin hard like she run somewhere. "That woman come by today," she say, like nothing just happen between us.

"Which woman?"

"The woman in the yellow car, Miss Sah-arah, whatever she name."

Mumma breathless from beatin me; now I breathless too. "True?" I say. "What she want?"

"She bring food. One big plastic bag with mackerel, corn beef, corn meal, rice, flour, sugar, saltfish, condense milk. She say she comin back."

SAHARA
A beach full of starfish

"Lyds, did I tell you about those kids up at Jacob's Pen?" We were under the guango tree as usual. Sweet potato pone and cerasee tea today.

"I don't know about kids – you told me you'd given a boy money after the movies one night and tried to get him into Munro, but he went missing and it didn't work out."

"Yeah, that's right. They live in Jacob's Pen…"

"They?"

"His mother, a brother and a sister."

"No baby father?"

"Not so far. But I don't really know. Anyway, here's the thing. I bought some food for them and took it up there yesterday. And now I don't know what to do."

"Not following. What is there to do? You took them some food; that's nice. So what?"

"I dunno. The brother hugged me up. They're children, Lyds, and they're hungry and probably only being half educated and how come that's just how it is? How come we just accept it? How would we have turned out if we'd never had enough to eat and lived in a board house?" My words fell over themselves and sounded stupid, even to me.

Lydia shrugged. "Sar, I don't know what to say. Yes, it's sad, we all know that. But what can you do? What can any of us do? Probably all that can be done is what you did – take a basket of food. Maybe take another one at Christmas. Why are you agonizing about this? Plus you know it's dangerous in those places."

I was silent. *Those* places filled with *those* people. I didn't know why I was obsessing about Dexter and his family. I kept thinking about the way the younger boy had looked through the bag of food and then looked up at me as if every one of his dreams had just been delivered in a black plastic bag. I kept seeing his knees and the scratches on his arms, kept smelling his skin, boy-sweat and dirt, kept seeing him stagger up the path holding the bag like gold.

But there were thousands of boys like him. I was not rich and I had a child of my own, who needed things too. Of course, the things Carl needed were of a different order. An iPod. Fashionable clothes. Steak, instead of chicken.

"Maybe I got it wrong about the boarding school," I said.

"Huh?"

"Well, doesn't seem like the mother works. I bet the bigger boy, Dexter, brings home the money. So if he went off to school, the whole family would starve. Assuming there's no man, of course."

"There's probably a man – but he's probably not bringing in any money."

"True. Maybe what I should do is try to get them into a good prep school in Kingston."

"How in the world are you going to do that?"

"Remember Gail Jarrett from school? Married somebody Carpenter?"

"Sure – runs a prep school. Holborn Prep, I think."

"Exactly. I bet I could talk her into letting the two boys in."

"Well, maybe you could. But how're you going to pay? Prep schools aren't cheap."

"I know." I pushed away my plate, most of the pone uneaten. It was too heavy for a hot afternoon. "How're you doing, Lyds?"

"I'm okay, I guess. Bastard called me last night, asked if I'd found a pair of his jeans. Told him I used them to line the garbage bin, since I figured he wouldn't be needing pants again."

I laughed. "What did he say?"

"Cussed. Said I was overreacting and why couldn't I be civilized. I wished him the clap and hung up."

"You're definitely feeling better."

"I guess. But I'm still in a rage. Or bawling. I mean, I know, good riddance and all that. But I still miss him." Her eyes filled with tears. Why had I brought this up? I reached across the table and patted her hand.

"Hang in there. It'll pass."

Lydia shrugged. "Anyway. Back to these children. I think you should be careful. You're going to get involved and there's going to be all kinds of trouble and you won't be able to back out of it so easy. Leave it at the bag of food. I mean, what can you do about children in Jamaica? Not a damn thing."

"You know the story of the little boy and the beach full of starfish?" I said. Lydia shook her head.

"Well, there's this beach with a whole pile of starfish washed up on it and a little boy and his father are out for a walk…"

"Some country other than Jamaica, obviously…" Lydia said.

"Listen. So the little boy goes over and picks up one of the starfish and puts in the sea. But there are thousands of them and the father says to the boy, *Son, you're not going to be able to help all of them. You're not going to be able to make a difference.* So the little boy picks up another starfish and puts it in the sea. He says to his father, *I made a difference to that one…*"

"That's a fairy tale, Sar," Lydia said, flatly.

DEXTER
Head Tough Like Coconut

Mumma comin school with me. She read me letter from Mr. Reckord. Some long word inna it, like *"incorrigible"*. Don't know what it mean, but know it not good. Letter say I lazy and don't apply myself and show attitude to teacher. Is not true. Me, I could be incorrigible, since I don't know what that is, but definitely not lazy. Up every mornin before six, go with Marlon to standpipe to get water, big bucket to carry. Stand in line with the other pickney; big boy come and make trouble, beat up somebody most day. Only good thing about five-thirty is it not hot yet.

In Jacob's Pen, about ten big boy wear khaki uniform like them go school, but they don't. Rayton and Busta part a that crew. Them too old for school, but nobody say anything, everybody 'fraid, maybe them have gun already. Some mornin them come on school bus – them mornin always the worse kinda mornin.

Don't show attitude to teacher neither. From beggin in Plaza, I learn how to be mannersable. Always call teacher Miss and don't look at them face. Mr. Reckord say I don't apply myself, but I don't know what that mean. I go school, sit at a desk, try to hear, even though it so noisy. Maybe him talkin 'bout homework. Sometime teacher give us homework and is true, I don't do it, but is because it really hard at home, no desk, one light, nobody to help.

I get up extra early on the mornin Mumma comin to school, before she wake. Wake up Marlon too. Him vex with me, him don't have to say it, I know him think I give pure trouble. Last time I get inna fight at school, I sit on the step a the Paul Bogle buildin, mouth bust, and Marlon come up to me. Him say, "Why you have to fight? Why you don't stay out a trouble?" Him spit did fly, him so angry.

"This your fault," Marlon say now, gettin out a bed. "Serve you right if you expel."

"Shut you mout', what you know? Wait 'til you big and boy t'ump you and anyhow you don't do nutt'n, every odda boy call you a batty man. You will fight."

Not so many pickney at standpipe this mornin; it a Friday. Plenty chile don't go school on Friday, don't know why, just how it is. Country pickney say is because market day is Friday, but no market inna Jacob's Pen. Always some pickney not going to school, whatever day it is. Some day no money for lunch or bus, so pickney take it in turn; today I go school, tomorrow you go school.

No big boy at the standpipe either. Feel better, even though Mr. Reckord still ahead. Maybe today will turn out okay.

Water pressure low. Bucket take one long time to fill up. I wait until it right to the top. Sometime, on day the big boy come, them make you stop with bucket only half full. That mean you sure to get slap from Mumma. 'Course, when you walk up the hill, water splash out a the bucket, no matter how hard you try to hold it level. Plastic bottle whole heap easier to carry than bucket.

When we get back, Mumma boilin pot for tea, Lissa fussin on her shoulder. Stove make the room extra hot. Sometime show on TV is in country where it cold, where it have snow, and I think I woulda like that. When I lie in bed at night – I sleep in small room at back, Marlon, Lissa and Mumma in the front room, Mumma and Lissa in one bed, Marlon in small cot – sometime I think about snow. Think it must soft like cotton, cool like water. Think you can dive inna it and it will close over you and inside is quiet and white-white. No time to think about snow now. Will never see it; never leave Jamaica.

Mumma face make up, she angry too. House full a anger.

Well, Mumma more 'fraid than angry. Mumma hardly leave Jacob's Pen after Lissa born, don't think she could find school alone. Don't know why she don't want to leave community – I know she come from country, but she never want go back. She spend lot a time in our house; don't understand that either. If I lock up in there all day, like when tropical storm come in summer time, it so borin inna that one and a half room, I want to get out bad-bad.

This is what is in our house. Front room – one three-quarter bed. One cot. One cardboard barrel where clothes keep. One little gas stove with big gas cylinder. One nice dresser Mumma say she find on the side of the road before I born and her uncle fix up. TV on top of that. TV is very small and show only black and white picture. I shame of that and never tell anybody at Nightingale All Age is only black and white TV we has. Small igloo in another corner. Sometime Mumma tell Marlon to buy ice and some chicken neck and back from Ma'as Ken. Then we get chicken three day runnin, but that don't happen plenty. Calendar from last year and picture a Jesus on wall. One lamp on dresser near TV. That is where we steal the light. Marlon father – him a 'lectrician – he take light from public service pole on that side a the house. We use to have to watch out for public service van inna community lookin for people stealin light, but they hardly come Jacob's Pen any more.

In the back room, where I sleep, one small bed. One table with Mumma sewin machine. One stool. When I see Mumma sew, I know it hurt her back because she don't have a proper chair. Some night she have to sew when I tryin to sleep. She take the light from the front room and bring it in my room and I watch her back bend over the machine. Is a old machine, always a break down.

"Go and bathe," Mumma say, when we bring water. She done bathe already, must a use last a yesterday water. She still in nightdress, though. It barely six o'clock, but I know if we want get school by eight, we have to leave out in half hour.

Nobody in our house can tell time good; no clock or watch is there. I know six o'clock because a the clock in Half Way Tree

59

and twelve o'clock, but not sure about the quarter to and the quarter past. In Jacob's Pen, time tell in different way – like, I know when Ma'as Collins down the way start up his car, is after six. Ma'as Collins run taxi and he always leave out at little past six. Seven at night is TVJ news. Midnight is when Ma'as Collins come home.

School bus, now, you can't tell time from that. It come any time. We never use to have school bus, but a while back government say children must go to school in them own bus. Before that, bus driver never like take school children because we pay low fare. Bus 'ducta stand at the bus door and shout out, "No schoolers!" Then I get to hear how a 'ducta push one schooler off a bus and she fall down and bus run over she head. Plenty road block that time. People go on TV, politician say is terrible tragedy and talk about discipline and accounta something – them things politician always say. After that they put in school bus.

School bus is worse, though. True, 'ducta don't throw us off, but school bus come any time, so it easy to late for school and it crowd up with pickney. Some mornin pickney a climb in through the window-them, since is only one school bus come to Jacob's Pen. And then if the big boy come… Them come on the bus, no matter how full it is, them touch fist with the 'ducta, him don't dare say anything, them throw small pickney on the ground, take away them school bag, lunch pan, lunch money. Whatever them want do, them do.

The three a us drink tea with condense milk and Mumma give Marlon and me one fat piece a hardo bread to share. It stale and make hard round ball inna my throat. Marlon and me sit on the big bed, Mumma stand up, drinkin her tea, breast feedin Lissa with one hand. Lissa nearly two and she still a breast feed. She the only one a us fat. Mumma, she don't eat nothing.

"How long it tek go school?" Mumma say.

"Depend," I say.

"On what? Don't give me you ginnaltalk, bwoy!"

"Not givin you any ginnal talk, Mumma! Depend on which bus we go on, what time it come. Prob'ly won' let you on

60

school bus, so we have to tek regular bus from Mountain View."

"You go school every day, you must know how long it take!"

"'Bout a hour," I say, givin up tryin to tell the truth. I don't go school every day. The bus could take half hour, could take two. "But we should leave out soon as everybody tidy."

The three of us dress. I have three khaki uniform; one clean, one dirty, one dryin on the line out back. One a them too small now, pants short, waist tight. Is the small one I has to wear today. Marlon only have two uniform, some day him wear dirty uniform. Teacher give him hard time about it.

Not all teacher is like that, though. Take Mrs. Barnes – she always ask why you a wear dirty uniform, if you have lunch money, why you late. If you tell her the truth, she don't punish you. Not every day, but sometime she give you money out a her purse, give you her sandwich, sometime just a icy mint. Mrs. Barnes *see* the pickney she teach. Most teacher don't see us at all, at all.

We walk over to Betsy Smallwood house, so Mumma can leave Lissa. Miss Betsy is one old woman in the community, old-old, hard to tell how old. She live 'cross the way from us and she and Mumma is friend. She fat and her hair white and she have hair on her chin and her chest. She don't go out to work. Community say she have son with big position inna private sector and he send money, but don't come visit because him shame a his mother and Jacob's Pen. Could be true. Miss Betsy house make of concrete, have three bedroom, alusteel roof, carpet on the floor, Courts furniture, legal light. Most people in Jacob's Pen don't have those things. She like children, so she take community pickney inna her house in the day for a small money. Miss Betsy was English teacher way back when school was elementary school or some such thing and she have speaky-spoky voice. Is she tell me how to speak soundin out my "h's" and how to be mannersable. "Say child or children, Dexter," she say. "Not pickney." I still say pickney though.

Mumma knock on her door and call out, "Miss Betsy! M'awnin!"

"Comin, Miss Arleen. Hold on one minute; the kettle on the stove."

The door open and Miss Betsy stand there. She wearin a apron and have a towel over her shoulder. "M'awnin, Miss Arleen," she say.

"Miss Betsy, you can keep Lissa for me? I have to go school with the boy-them. Dexter in trouble again for fightin." Lissa holdin on tight to Mumma neck. She don't like it when Mumma leave her. I look at my foot, don't want any argument with Miss Betsy.

"Lord, your big boy in trouble plenty! You must be sparin the rod, Miss Arleen. I done tell you plenty time – ghetto pickney *must* beat – them head tough like coconut, them ears hard, them skin like leather." Miss Betsy reach out and box me on the side a my face. *Don't answer, don't say anyting, keep look down.* Never hurt much. "What wrong with you, boy? I know you since you a baby; you never use to give trouble."

"Miss Betsy, I dunno what wrong with him," Mumma say. "I try with him, Lord know I try, but him fight and get into trouble every minute." I don't say anything. Make them go on talk, we going late for school if them go on run up them mouth.

Miss Betsy reach out for Lissa and she start cry. Mumma give her to Miss Betsy. "We back by lunchtime," she say.

"Don' worry, Miss Arleen. If you late, I give Lissa some oats porridge."

Three a us walk to the bus stop – not the one near where we live. Regular bus don't come to that one. Sun up now and day is hot. Walk up the hill, no sidewalk, so taxi driver blow horn after us because we inna the road. Brown dog and goat walk with us. Dog thin, goat fat. Goat don't have trouble finding things to eat; one time, I even see a goat lick inside a condense milk tin, lick it careful, so it don't cut him tongue.

When we reach Hope Road, plenty-plenty children a wait for the bus, nobody inna line. At school they try make us form line for everything; it never work. Always big boy come and push them way in. I see Tesfa Morgan and Cheryl Jobson and Tamara Hardy – all a them go to Nightingale All Age – but today they see we is with Mumma and they don't say nothing to me. Prob'ly them know 'bout fight.

No shade to wait. This bus stop tear down long time, and anyway, couldna hold all the people. Is not only children waitin, big people going work a wait too. Everybody face make up and miserable. Everybody hate bus. Bus is always full-full, everybody sweat, sometime a girl will cry out to big man and say, "Take you hand off a me!" Everybody will go on like nothing happen. Some day I feel sick because the bus a swing 'round corner, and I have to hold on to my schoolbag to make sure nobody take it, and my hand middle start sweat, and a rag tag man in the back a smoke and the bus smell a diesel and people, and the bus radio blast out music like a jackhammer, word-them full a killin.

Mumma don't know nobody at the bus stop. She stand at the edge a the crowd, holdin her bag in front a her. She wearin her dress and good shoe. Dress is nice, have flower on it, but I know is not proper clothes, not like the kinda clothes women who go to work in a office wear. Even in the heat, them woman wear skirt and blouse and jacket and stockin. Them woman don't look straight at Mumma, they look at her from the corner of them eye.

Sometime I feel sorry for Mumma, like today. I know she do her best to look after the three a we. Mumma sew 'til her finger cramp and her eye run water. She don't eat so we will have food, she clean, cook and try keep us safe. When gunshot fire inna Jacob's Pen, when crew a fight or is election time, she tell us to hide under the three-quarter bed and keep quiet. She put her body between us and the door. We all know wall a wood house can't stop bullet. One night Marlon say, "Mumma, don't gunman know we hide on the ground? Maybe they shoot at the floor? We should hide inna the roof!"

'Fool-fool!" I did tell him. "How we going hide inna the roof? Nowhere up there to hide, unless you a lizard!" I know Marlon feelin hurt because I call him fool-fool, I know everybody 'fraid, everybody heart beat fast, everybody want throw up what we eat. I know Mumma frighten Marlon coulda be right about the under-the-bed hidin place.

This is what everybody inna ghetto know: If anybody want kill you, white man, big man, policeman, area don, schoolmate, politician shotta, anybody – them will just do it. Nobody can stop them and after, nobody will care. You can think man who do murder will be arrest and put in jail and you, the person who is dead, will be in heaven lookin down on them in jail with a whole heap a batty man, but that is not how it will go. Man will kill you like a cockroach for reason no bigger than a domino game and that is the end – the end a everything.

SAHARA
Roast breadfruit

"May I speak to Mrs. Carpenter, please?" I said.

"Name, please?"

"Sahara Lawrence. An old school friend. She'll know."

"Please hold on. I'll see if the Principal is free."

"Mrs. Lawrence?"

"Yes?"

"Mrs. Carpenter is asking if she can call you back. She has a parent with her at the moment. What's your telephone number?"

I supplied all my numbers, wondering if Gail Carpenter would call back. We hadn't known each other well in high school; she'd been part of the black power set – a scary clique of girls with Afros and dashikis. I remembered the time Gail came rushing into our Sixth Form classroom and shouted, "They've expelled Walter Rodney!"

"Who's Walter Rodney?" I'd asked.

"Roast breadfruit," she'd snarled at me, meaning black on the outside, white on the inside. I remembered how I'd wondered whether or not I was in fact black on the outside. I knew I wasn't black on the inside.

I hadn't thought much about race until high school. At our prep school, most of the children were light skinned, although few were truly white. There were a sprinkling of black-black kids like Lydia, a few Chinese ones, some Lebanese, one Indian. A couple of expatriate children, speaking with accents. The teachers corrected anyone who spoke in patois. We understood using patois meant you were low class.

It was different in high school. Classes were much bigger, for one thing, and girls came from all over Jamaica, from all kinds of backgrounds. My all-girls high school was full of black girls, some coming from primary schools. They were louder and fatter than the prep school girls and often in trouble for wearing too short skirts and prohibited jewellery. Many had made-up names like Tameesha or Florenda. A few had African names.

In Sixth Form, the black-black girls started to wear their hair natural and berated those who straightened their hair. If a browning prefect sent a black girl to the back of the line at break, the black girl would raise her fist in a black power salute at the prefect's back.

I was wary of the black power girls, scared of their intensity, annoyed by the incessant talk of slavery and a whole bunch of isms – colonialism, imperialism, racism, tribalism. Move on, I thought – this all happened too long ago to matter. I was sorry for two English girls in our class, who were called Backra Misses and addressed with exaggerated subservience. The black power girls ignored the brownings, who were not black enough to be part of their set, but too black to be called Backra Missy. The brownings disliked the black girls and made fun of their looks – their large backsides, broad noses and fat lips. The brownings called the black-blacks Zulus.

By then, Jamaica was independent but when we recited our national motto, a version of the American *e pluribus unum* – "Out of many, one people" – nobody believed it. One of the black power girls wrote "Out a one whole heap, 'nuff" on the blackboard before school one morning. She did it in front of everyone and threw the chalk down afterwards. Our form teacher, Mrs. Ellis, came in and said, "Clean the blackboard, girls." She didn't ask who had written the new motto on it.

We had a French teacher who once went around the room, commenting on everyone's grooming and appearance – the black girls got the worst of it. I remember the only girl whose appearance met with Madame's approval was one of the English girls, a freckled redhead with really short hair. "Look at Bridget," Madame said, while Bridget hung her head. "Neat hair, not sweaty, pressed shirt. I want to see all of you looking like Bridget."

Gail Carpenter called back the next day and sounded happy to hear from me. "What're you doing these days, Sahara?"

"Still with Lydia, running the restaurant."

"Oh yes, that place on Hope Road. Summer something. I've been there a few times, but I'm a carnivore," she laughed.

"Summer Lion," I said.

"That's right. Summer Lion. So what's up? What can I do for you?"

"I need to come and see you, Gail. About some children."

"O-kay," she said. She sounded cautious. I suppose if you're the Principal of a prep school, you must get people wanting to see you all the time about "some children". I knew prep school places were highly sought after – parents often had to book places for their children at birth. Holborn Prep was not the most desirable prep school in Kingston, but I'd heard it was a good one.

"When suits you?" I said.

"Let me look." I heard pages turning. "What about next Tuesday, the 14th? Ten o'clock?"

"That's fine. See you then."

"Look forward to it," Gail said, but the note of caution was still in her voice.

DEXTER
Community Service

"Come in, Missus Morrison," Mr. Reckord say. Him don't know Mumma last name is Jones – I name Morrison after my father. We stand in the corridor outside the Principal office, under sign about urinatin and defecatin. "You wait there, Raymond. I expect to see you right there when I want you." I shame. Student pass by, some a them laugh at me. I feel same anger that cause me to fight with Silbert Walcott buildin up. My head feel like a pot a gungu pea-dem, boilin up.

Children all inna class now, except a few straggler. Children always late at Nightingale All Age. One time Principal put in a fine system, if you come late, you have to pay fifty dollar. Children have to give over them lunch money for fine and so then they start steal from a vendor on corner name Miss Dulcy. Miss Dulcy tell her baby father that Nightingale student a steal from her when her back is turn. Baby father wait outside for a boy in Grade 9 name Boston Petersen. Don't know why them think Boston steal the pack a cheese crunchie – true, him run around with a crew in Nevada and him tough-tough, but nobody know who steal the cheese crunchie. Coulda been any hungry chile at school.

Anyway, the baby father – I hear him call A.K. after AK 47, you know what kinda person *him* is – him wait for Boston one day and chop him hand clean off. Him left hand. A.K. stand over Boston where him lie on the ground, tell him he lucky him don't chop off the right hand too. One taxi man take Boston to University hospital. I hear say Boston don't even bawl out when A.K. chop him. Boston still at Nightingale All

Age now, they let him repeat Grade 9, which hardly anybody ever get to do. I see him playin football sometime, no shirt, his stump hand hold away from him body, like it still hurtin him. Him is all muscle and damage.

"Raymond?" Mr. Reckord say. "Come in now." I go inside Mr. Reckord office which is air condition. Make you shiver first time you go through that door, air is cold and clean and all school smell gone. All the same, don't much like the smell of air condition; it don't smell natural, but when you go inna that office, sweat start dry on you skin.

Is a small office, plenty book on shelf and school trophy. Mr. Reckord not a tidy man, so paper and things all 'bout. Two chair is in front of desk, Mumma sit in one, she cryin a little. She shiverin in the cold. I want touch her, but I don't. Not in front a Mr. Reckord.

"I've spoken to your mother, Raymond, and she tells me you're a good, decent boy and that you look after your brother and sister. She says you don't get into any trouble, go straight home after school and work with your books," Mr. Reckord say.

"Yes, sir, Mr. Reckord," I say. Is not true, but everybody, includin me, want to believe it.

"I want to be fair to you," say Mr. Reckord. "I don't believe it will serve any purpose to expel you. But you're going to have to do community service. For a week, you have to clean up the school grounds."

I been lookin at the floor, but now I look at him straight-straight. I *want* to say: You want to fair to me, Mr. Principal? Then ask me what happen. Ask me why me and Silbert fight. Or ask me what "community service" going to mean. How pickney going laugh after me, call me garbage man, labourer, how sun hot and place behind school buildin stink so bad your eye run water.

What I say is: "Thank you, Sir. I glad not to expel."

"Not to have been expelled," say Mr. Reckord. He want us speak proper English, even though plenty time I know him say things wrong.

"Alright, Mrs. Morrison, Raymond, we will consider this

incident closed." Mr. Reckord stand up. Him feel good about himself now. Him chest a little puff out, him lean forward with hand on desk. Him a Principal. Not a big-big man, but bigger than me and Mumma.

"Sir?" I say.

"Yes?"

"Silbert – him have to do community service too?"

"Yes, he will." But Mr. Reckord frown. This is not for me to ask, it is for him to decide and me to do what him say. Him think I showin him attitude.

"Come Mumma," I say. Time to get out a Mr. Reckord air condition office before he change him mind and expel me for fightin.

In the school yard, Mumma say, "How mi going get home, Dexter?" She wipe her eye with her kerchief.

"I take you, Mumma. Don't worry. Bus will most likely take long to come, but it going empty now."

SAHARA
Holborn Prep

I drove to Holborn Prep on Tuesday morning. I'd persuaded Lydia to come to the restaurant early – lied that I had a dentist appointment. I hadn't wanted another lecture about the children. I told myself it was only an exploratory visit. Quite likely Gail would tell me there were no spaces at Holborn Prep for several years and that would be that.

I parked in a shady car park outside a chainlink fence. There was a large gate, with a smaller one cut into it, manned by a security guard. "Good morning," I greeted him. "I have an appointment with the Principal."

"Name?" he said.

"Sahara Lawrence." The guard nodded and opened the small gate.

The schoolyard was pretty – several large trees around a grassy playing field, brightly painted classrooms, an open auditorium over to one side. There were no children in sight, but I could hear the thrum of voices. As I walked up to a door labelled "Office – Knock and Enter", I heard children laughing from a classroom down the corridor. I knocked on the door and opened it. A blast of cold air hit my face.

"Good morning," said a young woman, sitting at a receptionist's desk. "Can I help you?"

"I'm Sahara Lawrence. I have an appointment with Mrs. Carpenter."

"Oh yes. Please have a seat, Mrs. Lawrence. I'll tell the Principal you're here." I sat on a chair in a row below the front window. There was a glass case of school trophies along one side of the room. On the other wall, there were framed paintings done by children. Each frame had a small plaque with a child's name on it. There was a real orchid on top of a peach and grey filing cabinet.

A woman came out of the closed door to my left. She wore a designer suit, hair styled, gold jewellery – probably in her mid-fifties. Either a donor or a grandmother. I was wearing my restaurant clothes – Kente print tunic over a long black skirt with sandals and a headtie. Perhaps I hadn't dressed up enough. Perhaps I looked too Rasta. I was nervous.

Gail Carpenter followed the well-dressed woman out of her office. She looked completely different. In school, she'd been on the track and field team; her sport had been hurdles. She'd been lean and wiry and in her black power phase, her huge Afro had overwhelmed her slight body. Now she was square through the middle and the Afro was gone. Her hair was creamed and set and the only echo of her black power phase was in a pair of huge hoop earrings.

"Sahara! Great to see you. Come on in," she said. I followed her into her office.

"Have a seat." She stood behind her desk for a minute, shuffling papers into a file and putting the file into an out tray. "Can I get you anything?" she said, sitting down.

"No, thanks. Are these your children?" I said, pointing to a framed photo of a boy and a girl.

"Uh-huh. Aisha and Madu. How's your son?"

She remembered my early pregnancy. "He's well. Going into Lower Sixth at Campion in September."

"That's great. He must be more a companion than a son."

There was a silence. We hadn't been friends; there was no point in this chit chat. Gail had done well for herself – probably still married, two children, a successful school. "I'm sure you're busy, Gail. I need your advice."

"Sure. What about?"

"Well, I met this boy. A whole family, really. And I want to get them into a good school. I don't know how to go about it. I thought you might be able to help."

"How many children are we talking about and what ages?"

72

I realized I wasn't sure about their ages. "Three kids. The oldest says he's ten, but he could be a bit older. The second boy is maybe eight. And the girl is a toddler, two, maybe two and a half."

"Are the boys not in school now?"

"Yes, they're in school. Nightingale All Age. But you know what those places are like, Gail. I wanted to send the older one to boarding school, so that he wouldn't be sent to beg, and I spoke to Munro about it. It didn't work out because he was bringing home the money. Then I thought that maybe the way to help would be to get them into a prep school, where they'd get a good education."

Gail raised her eyebrows. "So these are, what, your helper's kids?"

"No. I met the older one begging in Sovereign one night after the movies. I took food for them, realized it wasn't just him. Asked the mother if I could help, she seemed receptive, but like I said, the boarding school thing didn't work out. Can you help, Gail? If I were to get the money, could they come here?"

"Don't know what to tell you, Sahara. We're full to bursting. I have a waiting list of twenty for September. There's a nursery school on the premises you could talk to about the toddler; I think they have space, but I just don't see how I can help with the two boys."

I stood up. I was embarrassed. I remembered Gail calling me "roast breadfruit". "Thanks for seeing me. I just thought I'd try. Take care. It was great to see you," I stammered.

"Wait, Sahara. Don't go yet. Let's think about this some more. Have a cup of coffee with me?" Without waiting for an answer, she walked around her desk and opened the door. "Miss Sheilds? Could you bring us two cups of coffee, please? Condensed milk?" she asked me.

I sat down. "Black with sugar," I said.

DEXTER
Havin sex on TV

"You ever see blue movie on cable TV?" Lasco ask me. We sittin on the sidewalk, beside supermarket in Sovereign Plaza. I catch up with Lasco at last. Is a Sunday afternoon, uptown people comin back from Lime Cay, trying to catch the supermarket before it close. Me and Lasco watch them come out a them SUV and BMW, face red from sun, walkin funny cause them drunk too much rum. Them go inside and buy bread that just bake or a six-pack a Red Stripe. If them have pickney, one a them stay inside the air condition car with the pickney-them. Uptown people has fun on a Sunday. Some a them go church, but after that, them go country, Lime Cay, out to Port Royal to eat fish, visit each other. Inner city people don't do that so much; them go church, cook Sunday dinner, sweep up, do washin, lick a six a domino. Maybe one time a year poor people go on church trip to Dunns River.

Me, I never leave Kingston yet. Been down to the waterfront, seen the sea. Never been in it, though. Them say Kingston Harbour dirty, but boy swim in it all the same. Don't know how to swim.

"No," I tell Lasco. Not sure what him talkin about. Think blue movie have something to do with people havin sex. Don't seem like such a big thing to me, easy to watch people havin sex. When Marlon father was around, him and Mumma have sex in three-quarter bed. We pickney pack up inna small bed in back room. Them make a whole heap a noise. Not supposed to look, but I look.

"You know Boston go a your school? Wit' di one hand? Him

74

have cable or dish at him house, blue movie channel anyhow. Him say come over tomorrow after school, him granny gone country, we drink Red Stripe, smoke weed and watch. You wan' come?"

Lasco don't look good. Him did tell me how him steal the cassette for true, police find it in him bag, one brownin boy tell the owner man on him. Lasco say when him see the brownin boy, him going kill him. Him say the police handcuff him to a window grill inside the station and leave him there whole day, only let him go to piss under the ackee tree outside. Him sit with hand over him head, chain to grill, from mornin to night. Him say him hand still hurt sometime.

I did ask him how come Babylon let him go, since them find the cassette. "Them never wan' keep mi," Lasco say. "Just have to do someting cause a owner man. When night come, them don' have no place inna cell for mi, no food, so one corporal, him take mi out back and gi' mi some licks. Easy licks, yout'man; licks like you Mumma mighta give out. Then him say if mi don't stay out a trouble mi soon dead. After that, him let mi go."

Not sure I want go with Lasco to Boston house. Sometime I 'fraid a Boston, but I bored too. Tired a Plaza, tired a Mumma, Marlon, Lissa, Jacob's Pen, Nightingale All Age, tired a everything. I tell Lasco yes, me will come with him. Have some money from early beggin. When we finish at Boston house, I come back to Plaza. Sunday night better for beggin than Sunday daytime anyway.

Boston live in Nevada. Nevada is one bad community, always inna news. Man dead, road block, girl rape, police brutality, everything. New MP now, him tryin to clean it up, him take down the zinc fence and put up concrete wall; pay artist to paint picture of waterfall and sea and mountain on the wall-them.

Bus take long to come on Sunday. Me and Lasco wait, not too many people on the street. Bus come after maybe one hour and we get on. Lasco hail up the bus driver, call him Rocket. Lasco know every single bus driver inna Kingston. Him never pay fare, far as I can tell. "Dis a mi frien' Dexter," say Lasco and

Rocket nod him head. Him don't smile, don't say anything, don't ask for bus fare. Him smoke a giant spliff and music a play loud enough to make you mad. Only two church sister sittin in back. You can see them want to say something about the music, but don't dare. Me and Lasco sit up front, far away from them.

"You no 'fraid a Babylon wit' dat spliff, big man?" Lasco say.

"Dem all downa stadium, some match a keep dere," Rocket say. "Anyway, dem know mi, bred'ren, mi and dem is awright. Did hear say Babylon lock you up; a true?"

"A true. But dem jus' give mi some licks and let mi go, nutt'n serious."

Rocket turn up the music more. It so loud I can feel it inna my chest. Rocket drive fast on the empty street. One old lady hold out her hand at a bus stop, but him drive past. I look behind and see her, bend over her walkin stick, watchin the bus leave her.

Bus stop inna Nevada and we get out. Nevada not so different to Jacob's Pen – it crowd up, noisy, and man on street look at you hard. It scary in a community not your own. In Jacob's Pen, now, me know people, the bad man-them – me know Idi Amin and Tomahawk and Merciless. Them don't trouble me most a the time; most them will do is send me go shop for them. Maybe me fool, but I don't think anybody kill me in Jacob's Pen on purpose. True, I could dead by accident, like if man a shoot up the community and bullet come through the wall a our house. That could happen, it happen all the time. Here in Nevada, because I don't know the man-them, them could shoot me because them want to, don't like how I look at them, walk on the wrong side a the street. Anything.

Lasco greet the man-them, though, very respectful, and them look at us hard but let us pass. We turn off on a small lane, plenty garbage and goat shit pile up, look like garbage truck never make it to Nevada. Walk between broke house, leanin every which way. Some house still have zinc fence – look like MP only move the zinc fence on the road where people drive.

We come to one house with a high zinc fence, can't see over it. High fence good – mean people can't know your business so easy. Zinc fence also mean Babylon can't see in.

Lasco knock on a piece a zinc set up like a gate and call out to Boston. The gate open and Boston stand there, no shirt, baggy pants, barefoot, with him one hand. Him look over Lasco shoulder and see me and I can tell him not happy I there. Don't know about Boston. Even though him so big and muscle up, sometime I think him a batty man. Just the way him look at you sometime.

"Respec', bred'ren, this yout' here is Dexter. You know him from school," Lasco say. Him not dealin with any argument. Lasco only come up to Boston shoulder and him thin as yard broom, but Lasco is the one not to mess with.

Boston stand back and let us in. Dirt yard, clothesline, mawga brown dog. House made a concrete, good to keep bullet out. Roof look good, one of them small satellite dish on top. Not even cable, but dish! Me hear say that give you one hundred channel to watch. Prob'ly everybody inna Nevada hate Boston family, unless everybody get to watch dish too.

"Where you get di dish, big man?" Lasco say.

"Mi Auntie Hazel live in foreign, inna New York, she send it come. All di time it stop work – bloodclaat white people in America block di signal. If it block, wi have to buy card from a man over on di gully bank. Been down a long time now, only come back two day."

Boston house is dark. Small piece a carpet on floor, furniture pack up the place, big TV on a table. Him don't ask if we want anything. Him sit on the couch and turn on the TV. We sit beside him and him flick through the channel-them, cowboy on horse, nature show, basketball, man a fight, gunshot a fire, airplane crashin, white woman a plant flowers in front a one small, pretty house, like you see in a storybook. Boston stop going through the channel when him find what we come to see – people havin sex on TV.

Is hard to believe people do all what them do in front a camera. White woman, black man, two woman, a whole pile a man and woman together. Man hood big like donkey; if that is how hood suppose to look, me will *never* have sex. Man suckin woman – can't say it. For sure we will go to hell for watchin this, but I can't stop and my hood hard like rockstone inna my pants.

Three a we watch blue movie until night. Lasco and Boston smoke a spliff. I take a small drag, but don't suck it in because it will make me cough and them will laugh. I know all a us want sex. I sure Lasco and Boston have it anytime them want. Me? I 'fraid to ask a girl. I 'fraid a disease and the girl gettin pregnant; worse – I 'fraid she laugh after me. Want to rub myself. Hard to do that at home with Mumma there, have to take a rag to bed with me and wait until late inna night.

Boston lean forward and say, "Have to stop soon. Di old lady soon come." Him not lookin at me, him a look at Lasco. I feel something bad going happen. Boston turn off the TV and turn on a small lamp. The light shine on him face from down underneath. Him face is all shadow and black skin. I scared a him now, even with him one hand. Lasco turn to me and say, "Yout'man, mi stayin here awhile. You go back a Sovereign."

Want to go, but want to stay too. Feel 'fraid, but excited, like before a race on sports day. Imagine what it feel like inside a woman, like on TV. "G'waan," Boston say, quiet-quiet. I stand up and leave them on the couch.

Outside, it pitch black night and Nevada is no place to be.

SAHARA
Some expatriate Jamaicans

"That was a long dentist appointment. Did you get an injection?" Lydia said. There was never any point in lying to her.

"Okay, okay. I didn't go to the dentist. I went to see Gail Carpenter."

Lydia shook her head. "Later for that. Right now the lunch orders are backed up and Londel is in one of his moods."

"Sorry I was so long," I said and headed for the kitchen, where dancehall music was pounding. Londel turned up the music whenever he was upset. I cast my eye over the order slips and picked up a tray of drinks for table five. The ice was already melting.

The lunch rush was over quickly. It was one of those rare days in June when black clouds gathered over the mountains and it looked like rain. The lunch crowd looked anxiously at their watches and no one lingered. The breeze dropped and the light dulled, but the rain stayed in the hills.

"So what did Gail say?" Lydia asked, as we sat down under the guango tree.

"At first she said no. No space. Recommended a pre-school for the baby girl. But just as I was about to leave, she called for coffee and we talked."

"So? Will she take them?"

"She might. She gave me forms to fill out. I need to get their birth certificates and their last school reports. Holborn Prep has a special ed class that has space. How they work it is the special ed kids get all the help they need in small classes, and then they mainstream them with the other kids for a few hours a day."

"Sounds pretty good. What about the money part?"

"She gave me some names of expatriate Jamaicans – people living in New York and Toronto. They formed a group to help pay school fees for Jamaican children. I have their e-mail addresses and phone numbers. She says mostly these people are worried that there's no one here to supervise, so if I agree to keep an eye on the children, I might find someone willing to help."

"What're you going to do?" Lydia said. She wasn't eating her bun and cheese.

"Why aren't you eating?"

"I'm on a diet. Don't change the subject – what're you going to do?"

"I'm going to try," I said. Until I said those words, I hadn't decided anything. Lydia made a sound of exasperation, but didn't say anything more.

The rest of it proved surprisingly easy. The first overseas Jamaican I contacted, Josephine Blanchard, said she'd love to help. She couldn't afford to sponsor more than one child, but she offered to make contact with other people. Within a week, two other donors had been lined up. They wanted to pay fees to the school directly and that was fine with me. They agreed to pay all the tuition costs, as well as books and uniforms. The children would write monthly letters to them. Of course, their school reports would be provided. One of the women – they were all women – said she was planning a visit to Jamaica that Christmas and would like to meet the children then. I called Gail Carpenter and told her I'd found the money. "Bring in the paperwork, then," she said.

DEXTER
What Miss Sahara Don't Know

"How much you get tonight, boy?" Mumma say.

"Just over two hundred dollar." Not a bad night at Sovereign. After me leave Nevada, me glad to get back to the car park at Sovereign with it bright light and big car and uptown people. Less than two hour and I beg enough to go home.

"Give it here. Marlon, you go Ma'as Ken and get a tin a mackerel and some flour." Marlon get up and take the money. He like going shop – is him do most a the shoppin for Mumma. Mackerel and flour dumplin for supper.

I lie on the bed in the front room to watch TV with Mumma and Lissa. "You smell renk, boy, go wash," Mumma say. *Don't say anyting.* I tired; tired unto dyin. I want Mumma say a kind word to me, just one single deggey-deggey kind word. Is me bring home the money, after all. I get up and go out inna the dark to find the bucket and rag. See people havin sex in my head, wonder what Lasco and Boston do after I leave them. Don't want think about it. Don't want Lasco to be a batty man. When I get to the bucket 'round the back, I see hardly any water leave. The rag hang over the side of the bucket and it smell bad like a dead animal swell up in the street.

From behind the house, I hear a car drive up. I only wearin brief; can't go look. I hear a door shut and the sound a somebody walkin up to our house. I hear a knock on the zinc gate. I hear Mumma voice and I hear another voice and I hear the squeak a the zinc gate open. Wonder if is police or Mr. Reckord come for me.

Dress quick, skin still damp. Throw nasty rag into the

bucket. Run round the side a the house and go through the back door. And I see the brownin woman, Miss Sahara, standin in our front room, holdin two plastic bag. Mumma stand in the door to the back room, Marlon hide behind. Mumma holdin Lissa.

That is how it start and that is how it go on all summer. Every Sunday evenin after that, Miss Sahara drive up in her yellow car, bringin two bag a food. She come inna the house and she sit on the big bed and she ask us things, like, what book we read (none), how much Mumma make for sewin (is different every week), why Lissa still breast-feedin (is free), how much school uniform and shoe we have (three uniform for me, two for Marlon, one shoe each), if we play football or cricket (both a them).

After about four Sunday pass, Miss Sahara find out Marlon can't read. She ask him to read from him story book and him smile and take the book, because him want impress her. Him love Miss Sahara, him jealous is me find her, and is me she pay attention to first. Him think me don't deserve Miss Sahara. Marlon know how some day I don't go school, how I say I at Plaza but really I go downtown with Lasco – him even know I go to Boston house that time. Marlon go church with Mumma and after him come back, him say I am the devil. Me, I laugh, but I wish him did look up to me.

Marlon pick up the story book and start read, fast-fast, all a word run together like one long word. When Marlon did start school and learn how to say the alphabet out loud, him did think "el-em-en-o-pee" was one letter. I had to tell him the sound mean different letter. Him did hit me and start cry.

"That's very good, Marlon," Miss Sahara say. "You must be an excellent student." She wrinkle up her face in a way we get to learn mean she don't like something. She take the book out of him hand and she look through the page. "Here, read this page for me." She give him back the book.

Marlon look at the page and don't say anything. Him eye shine. Miss Sahara sit close to him and put her arm 'round him shoulder. She look at the book with him and point at a word.

"Read that word for me," she say. Marlon don't say nothing. "Try," she say, her voice soft. Miss Sahara should be a teacher. She have patience.

"Tee-aitch-ee," Marlon say, but he don't know them three letter make a word. Me not too surprise. Lot a children at Nightingale All Age can't read. Lot a them do just what Marlon do, learn readin book from front to back and can say it out loud.

"Can you add and subtract, Marlon?" say Miss Sahara.

"Yes, Miss," he whisper.

"Show me." She reach inna her bag and take out a little notebook and pen. She write a sum on the paper and give it to Marlon. Him look at it, but he don't take the book or pen from Miss Sahara. Him hold him head down again, because him don't know what the sum mean.

"Marlon," I say. "Mumma give you a hundred dollar to go shop and you get two bag a counter flour. How much change you bring home?"

"Sixty-two dollar fifty," Marlon say, quick-quick.

"How much is a bag of flour?" Miss Sahara say to Mumma.

"Eighteen dollar twenty-five," Mumma say.

"That's right, Marlon! That's amazing. You did the sum in your head. That's called mental arithmetic." Marlon look confuse; him don't know what Miss Sahara just say, but him know she happy.

Is a whole set a things Miss Sahara don't know. Like, every ghetto chile go shop from them young – them all can make change. Them can add and subtract in them head, but when them go school, most a them don't know how to take the number out a them head and put it on paper. She don't know we don't have book, well, maybe a romance book or a religious track, but no book-book, like library. She don't know about bus, about big boy inna the community, she don't know how teacher shame us, she don't know how it dangerous to live in Jacob's Pen.

All a we look forward to Miss Sahara visit on Sunday. At first, she bring only food, not special food neither; just regular food, mackerel inna tin, flour for dumplin, bully beef, coconut oil, soap, sugar, Milo, rice, a bunch a skellion, maybe some callaloo. Then she start bring ten bag a cheese crunchie which is good for school, three chocolate bar, ovaltine biscuit, bag a icy mint. Some Sunday, she bring sock for me and Marlon, not new sock, not fittin us good, but sock all the same. She bring T-shirt and belt and washrag and new toothbrush. Is like Christmas every Sunday evenin. We thankful, but still wish for new shoe and clothes straight from a shop.

We all stay home and wait for her, Marlon 'specially. Him climb up the hill behind our house, sit on a rock and wait. Him have sponge bath early and change into him one set a good clothes. Every Sunday night, him wear him good clothes for Miss Sahara.

She get easier with us as time go on. At first you could see she never know how to talk to us, never know if she could sit on the bed, and nobody say much while she there. But all summer she come, every Sunday night, not always the same time, but before it get too late. By seven the latest, we know Marlon going come runnin down the hill and say, "She a come!"

Miss Sahara tell Mumma she must stop smoke, 'cause it a waste a money. She tell Mumma Lissa must stop breast feed and must get toy to play with. Miss Sahara bring toy for Lissa and she angry when next time she come back, toy-them break. None a we know how to say that is not that we careless why we break them, we just not use to toy and don't know how easy them is to break. She tell Mumma I must not go to the Plaza and she tell Mumma she is not to beat we. That whole summer me stay in Jacob's Pen, play little football, go down by Rocky River with Jacob's Pen boy, even go to church with Mumma and Marlon. Miss Sahara bring football and basketball hoop and domino and jigsaw puzzle and book. She start stay long when she visit and she make Marlon copy out him letter and him begin to read simple word, like "cat" and "mat" and "the".

We eat better than I ever eat in my life. Even Mumma gettin fat, her clothes tight and bust out a they seam. Lissa try talk and she laugh every minute. People inna the community start visit when Miss Sahara come. Them knock on the door and look at this uptown woman sittin on the bed teachin Marlon him letter. We don't like it when they come; we think them want take Miss Sahara from us.

Then one Sunday night, right after Independence weekend, one night so hot only Mumma wearin a shirt, Miss Sahara come late, near eight. She come through the door, one arm around Marlon, him both hand tight around she waist. "Dexter, you want to bring the bags from the car?" she say to me. Me, I know I am too big for her to hug, but I wish she would touch me. Most me get from her is a squeeze on my shoulder.

I run down to the VW; one door leave open. Miss Sahara don't think people going steal from her. I pull out two bag – that make three tonight – shut the car door, and go back inside. I don't like miss any part a Miss Sahara visit. True, sometime she angry about things we don't understand, like, she don't want Mumma to throw partner, which is how everybody save money. She ask Mumma why she don't put her money inna bank instead of inna partner. "You don't get any interest from partner and they can steal your money," Miss Sahara say. We know partner can steal – it happen to Miss Lurline who run the rum shop, but we don't know what is this interest she talk about. What we know is – security guard going run us if we go to the bank in Ligueanea.

Miss Sahara want know if Mumma read to we. Mumma say she can read, but not too good, since she only go primary school. Miss Sahara get the look that mean she don't like that.

She don't want anybody father or new man eatin her food. In the beginnin, she ask after my father and Marlon father and Lissa father. She don't like it that we all have different father. She don't like it that they all gone away, but she definitely don't want them to come back neither.

I put down the bag-them over by the stove. I hungry tonight, it late, and I want to open supermarket bag and see what is in there. Coulda eat fried chicken. Miss Sahara don't bring those kinda thing, though, is mostly tin she bring. One time she did bring chicken neck and back when Mumma ask her. She don't like if you ask, so after that, none a us ask for anything.

"How was your week?" Miss Sahara say.

"Fine, Miss!" we all say together. Most time we don't know

how to answer Miss Sahara question-them. One week in Jacob's Pen same as the next one – noise at night, sweat in bed, early wake up, get water, drink tea and chunk a hardo bread, wash up, get dress, look for something to do, or go school. Sit on rock down by the river, play a little ball. Keep a look out for the big boy, crew member-them. Week is fine when nobody get beat up, rob or murder. Week is fine when we get enough food.

"Well, I have some good news tonight," she say to Mumma. "I've got Dexter and Marlon into a good prep school." Miss Sahara is sweatin a little. "Perhaps the boarding school wasn't a good idea, but this is a nice school in Kingston, so the boys will be able to come home at night. They will help Marlon catch up with his reading and get Dexter through his G-SAT exam, so he can get into a high school. They have a preschool too, so Lissa can go. Some overseas Jamaicans will help pay the fees."

Nobody say anything. Never seen the inside a any prep school. Me, I really too old for prep school; Miss Sahara don't know my right age. Wonder if them have food on a long table, three time for the day. Maybe a play field with grass.

"Aren't you happy?" Miss Sahara say, lookin around at all a we. "I went to a lot of trouble to organize this." Her face make up bad-bad and I know say we have to talk quick-quick or she stop visit, with her three bag a food and treat. "Yes, Miss, yes Miss," I say in best Plaza way, "thank you Miss. We very happy to go prep school." I know Mumma thinkin about lunch money and uniform and bus fare and book and football gears and she *know* it not going happen.

Miss Sahara get up and open one a the bag and I sorry to see is not food in there, but some other things – pen and pencil and notebook and readin book and some T-shirt, too big for any a we. My stomach hurtin and Lissa start cry. Miss Sahara sit with Marlon and make him copy out his letter, one at a time. First time I want for her to go. Not forever, just now. I want her go now so we can get something to eat.

SAHARA
Realities

Driving down from Jacob's Pen on Sunday night, my cellphone rang. I was later than usual. I'd started to relax with the children, no longer wondered where to sit, what to say, how to behave. Sometimes we even laughed together, genuine laughter, not the kind they put on to please me and the kind I used to hide my nervousness. "Yes?" I said.

"Where are you? Why aren't you home?" It was Carl. He sounded angry.

"I'm on my way," I said. "Ten minutes. Is something wrong?"

"No, nothing's *wrong*. Not what you mean, anyway."

I sighed. "I'll soon be home."

"It'll be too late."

"What'll be too late?"

"Nothing!"

"What'll be too late?"

"Mark and Kimberley are at Village Cafe. I wanted to go, but they'll be gone by the time you get home."

"Well, it's a school night anyway," I said.

"So what? I'll be in college next year!"

"I'll soon be home, Carl. We'll talk then."

"Whatever."

I parked the car and hurried to our front door. It was unlocked. Carl was slumped on the couch, channel surfing. He didn't look up as I came through the door.

"The door was open," I said.

"So?"

"So, it's dangerous, Carl! Anyone could come in and you'd be the next statistic, the next robbery gone wrong. You want me to treat you like an adult, but you behave like a child!"

"I'm not the one behaving dangerously!"

"What're you talking about?"

"I'm leaving the door open in *Mona* and you're in *Jacob's Pen* at all hours – *that's* what's dangerous!"

I went into the kitchen. I was hungry and afraid Carl was right. He followed me. "I'm talking to you!" he shouted.

"Don't shout at me, Carl. I know you're upset that I wasn't here to take you out with your friends, but don't shout at me, okay?"

"I'm not shouting. But Mom, you're going to regret this, honestly! You don't know what ghetto people are like. You should see how they behave in school – the girls are slack and the boys have knives. They're always in trouble."

"Carl, doesn't it bother you?" I said. "No, don't give me that look. Don't you *see* it? Don't you see the boys at every traffic light, barefoot and dirty? Don't you read the newspapers? Doesn't it strike you how lucky we are – how lucky *you* are?"

"Me? Lucky? How am I lucky?"

"Look at your advantages…"

"Oh, God, not the advantages speech…"

"Well, look at you. You're in a good school, got enough to eat…"

"I gotta go. I've got homework…"

"Why shouldn't I try to help the Jacob's Pen children? How well do you think you'd manage your life if you'd never, ever had enough? If you'd gone to bed every night hungry and had to fight every night for space in a bed?"

"They bring it on themselves! Why don't they work hard at school? Why don't they get jobs? Why do the girls get pregnant before they're sixteen…"

"Like me?"

"No, not like you, you always think everything is about you! At least you didn't abandon me… ghetto women have dozens of children for men they'll never see again."

"You can't blame the children for that."

"Look at all the helpers we had – always late, always stealing! Why should I feel sorry for any of them?"

"Carl! It's not nearly so simple. How've you come by these opinions? Do you think you'd be any better if you were poor?" My voice shook and I knew I was near tears.

Carl leaned against the kitchen counter and dropped his voice. "Okay, so poor people don't have an easy beginning. But I promise you those Jacob's Pen kids are not going to take advantage of any opportunity you give them. They're going to get into trouble and fail their exams and the end result is going to be the same – they'll be criminals on the street, a lot of money will have been spent on them and you'll have bawled a whole heap. That's if you don't get slaughtered up there one night."

"God! How'd I raise such a cynic?"

"Like I said, I've got homework."

"Wait. Carl, your attitudes are *racist*. It makes me so sad."

"Mom, it's got nothing to do with colour. Yeah, poor people are mostly black in Jamaica, but there're lots of successful black people. Black people run this country. Look at the government. I have black friends at school."

"Not many. Bugs, you're black yourself. You're hating yourself!"

I saw him flinch. "I'm not black and I don't hate anybody. I told you, it's nothing to do with those children being black. It's to do with where they are from, their *class*, their *attitudes*. Anyway, you'll see. I'm gone to study."

"If you helped someone less fortunate, made a friend of a boy like Dexter, maybe it would do something for *you*."

"Something like what?"

"Make you kinder, more thoughtful. I don't know. You're hard-hearted, Carl, and I wish I knew why."

"I'm gone," he repeated, turning away. I reached out and held his arm, but he shook me off and went to his room. He was only fifteen; I had to remember that.

I poured a glass of water. I was no longer hungry. I walked around the house, checking the doors and windows, turning off the lights. I went to bed but lay long into the night, thinking about my pale-skinned son hating everybody, even me. He frightened me – he sounded like Aunt Gladys but he often told me he did not remember her. She was in his genes. And what about me with my own half black, half white genes? How did I really feel about the three black Jacob's Pen children and their feckless mother? Was I saving them, or they me? If I was being honest, I feared Carl was right about the children and although I hated what he said, I knew in my heart I felt the same way. I fell asleep only when morning began to seep through the cracks in the louvre windows, tight shut against the night.

DEXTER
With the Slow Children

"What you doing out here, Dexter?" Miss Sahara say.

"Nutt'n, Miss. Was playin ball before; now me just waitin." Summer nearly over and me sit on the wall behind the football field; it give a good view a the road into Jacob's Pen and I can see the yellow VW comin from far. Marlon wait for Miss Sahara on the hill behind our house – him say he can see the car before me. I don't always wait outside for her; but today the evenin is nice and cool. We been havin good rain; gentle rain, the kind a rain that is not hard enough to wash away dirt or flood out the people livin too close to the river.

Miss Sahara walk across the muddy field. She not carryin anything, except her little backpack. Maybe she don't bring food tonight and she come over to tell me she not comin back again. I going to jump down, but she say, "No, stay there. I'm coming up beside you." She put her backpack on the wall and jump up. This woman different for sure – one uptown brownin woman sittin on a wall in Jacob's Pen! Her shoe-them mud up and the top a the wall wet.

She don't say anything, just sit there. I start think about her boy, Carl, who I don't see from the first time I meet her. I feel like I have to say something.

"Where your son go school, Miss Sahara?"

"Carl? Campion. Why?"

"Nutt'n. Just wonderin." Is the best high school in Jamaica. When CXC result come out, Campion always have most student pass. "He play sports?"

"A little tennis. Do you want to go to a better school,

Dexter? Or do you want to stay at Nightingale? Do you have friends there?"

Don't know what answer Miss Sahara want. Some part a me want go to a better school; most a me want to be *out* a school. But all a me want Miss Sahara to keep bringin food on Sunday night, so I know we must go school. I pick easy answer. "Mi have friend at school, yes. But mi best friend don't go school."

"*I have a friend* at school…" Miss Sahara correct me. "Tell me about your best friend."

"Him name Lasco. Him a street boy; him hang out at Sovereign too."

"*His* name is Lasco, *he* hangs out at Sovereign…" Miss Sahara say. "Doesn't sound like such a good friend to have."

"Him have a hard life, but he a good boy."

"Hmm. So, what about the new school? Are you happy about it?"

"Yes, Miss." Decide not to tell her we think it not going happen.

"It's nice up here," she say. She look out over the community, down to the river. Sun is settin behind us and smoke from cook fire hangin in the air – no breeze this time a day.

"Miss?" I say.

"Hmm?"

"Your son. Carl. Him – *he* – ever get in trouble at school?"

"What kind of trouble?"

"Any kind a trouble."

Miss Sahara shift the way she sit on the wall. "I suppose. He's had detentions. Is that the kind of trouble you mean?"

Not sure what is a detention. "I mean, like, gettin into fight-them, that kinda trouble."

"No, Carl hasn't got into fights, Dexter. Fighting isn't good."

I don't say anything. Can't imagine a school without fightin.

"Well, school soon start," Miss Sahara say. "We have to go and get uniforms and shoes. Maybe this Saturday." She jump down from the wall and stumble a little when she land. She brush off her jeans pants and pick up her backpack. "Come. Help me with the bags in the car."

September come and the first mornin for new school. What a confusion. We wake up late, don't know why. Maybe is because Miss Sahara say she comin for us in her car and we know that can't take as long as bus. She make sure and tell us she is not doin this all a the time; just the first mornin. Lissa is comin too. Since August, Mumma been takin her off the breast, getting her ready to go school. Me, I never hear of three-year-old going school, but Miss Sahara say is not proper school, is nursery school, and the teacher-them will show Lissa toilet trainin and social skill. Miss Sahara say the nursery school is on the same compound as the prep school, so we can go see her in break if we want.

We so late we don't even have time to catch water, so not much washin for anybody. Lissa start bawl as she open her eye. Marlon more frighten than me – him know him can't read. Even though Miss Sahara teach him some word over the summer, him know other children will be much better. Him think teacher will beat him and make him stand outside the classroom and send him go Principal office.

We dress in new uniform. Even if school is terrible, it worth it, 'cause we all get so much new things. Week gone, Miss Sahara take us and buy three set a uniform and shorts pants – she say is for something called PE. I ask her what is PE and she say, Physical Education. She say we will get school T-shirt on the first day. We get sock and new belt and two kinda shoe – brown shoe for everyday and crepe for sport. We get brief and vest and school bag and lunch pan. We get book and pencil and crayon and Bible and a fat book call a dictionary – one book with plenty word, page upon page a word.

That shoppin take one long time. Mumma, she come along with Lissa and we have to go plenty shop for everything. Some place you can see the shop people lookin at us strange, like, what is this *uptown* woman doin with them *ghetto* people? I pay them no mind and Miss Sahara don't seem like she notice the people in the shop.

Last shop we go to is in Sovereign. Feel strange to walk 'round and not worry about gettin chase. Me and Marlon walk close-close to Miss Sahara. We walk fast and Mumma and Lissa get left. Without them, nobody look at us. When me and Marlon with Miss Sahara, we not ghetto people any more. I see one security watchin Mumma and Lissa. I start walk quick-quick.

Owner man in Sovereign shop look at me like him see me before, but him can't remember. Him is the same man that own the game arcade, the man that cause Lasco to get beat that time. Did hear say him own plenty shop. Me smile at him and stand close to Miss Sahara. She start talk to him and tell him what she want and the man don't look at me any more.

When we finish, Miss Sahara ask if we hungry. She shoulda know better. We go food court. It early for lunch and only two people eatin. She take us to a place that sell oxtail and white rice and butter bean, or stew chicken and rice and peas. Me, I wish we could go to one a the fast food place up the road, Burger King or Kentucky. All a we get the stew chicken and it wonderful for true – a big piece a chicken and plate pile high with rice and peas, yam and dumplin. We want soda, but Miss Sahara say no, soda is not good, and she buy limeade. Mumma don't eat much. I know is because she hardly ever see so much food on a plate and don't know about the knife. We only have fork at home. When we eat chicken at home, we pick up piece and eat it, but we can't do that here. Can't tell what to do from watchin Miss Sahara; she order red pea soup. We do the best we can. Marlon pick up chicken leg – leg! – not neck and back – Miss Sahara look away. She don't say anything though.

We all dress now, on first school mornin, Mumma in her flower dress. We drink tea but we all too frighten to eat. We have lunch pan but no food inside. "Mumma, you think we should put some food inna lunch pan?" Marlon say.

"Don't bother me, Marlon," Mumma say and kiss her teeth. But she cut two thick slice a hardo bread and give we. We can't get the lunch pan open, but then Marlon work it out. Inside is a little igloo for drink and a plastic look like it for sandwich. We put the hardo bread in the plastic. Mumma find two bag a cheese crunchie and we put that in as well. Is the first time this prep school business look like it real. You hardly see pickney going all age school with a lunch pan – only maybe the young-young ones.

Lissa still fuss. She say, "Down! Down NOW!" She really start talk since Miss Sahara tell Mumma must read to her. 'Course, Mumma don't do it every night like Miss Sahara say, but she do it sometime.

"She here," say Marlon. He stand by the front door watchin. "She here. Come before she get mad."

We go outside and pile inna Miss Sahara car, Mumma in front holdin Lissa and me and Marlon in back. "Everybody ready?" Miss Sahara say. She smile, but I can tell she thinkin bout something else. "Marlon, where's your school bag?" she say. Marlon look behind him like the school bag going jump on his back. "Come on guys, we're going to be late! You should've been ready for me!" She upset. Marlon scramble out a the car, I think him going cry. He run up the hill, but the house door lock. Mumma pass Lissa to me in the back seat and she start one piece a bawlin. Can't imagine how Lissa going get left at school, Mumma been carryin her since she born. Mumma get out and run to the door, stumblin on the path. She dig in her bag for the key and open the front door. Marlon go inside and get him bag and them come back. Marlon get in first and climb inna back and then Mumma get in front. Miss Sahara car small, but it a Escalade compare to school bus.

School we a go to is call Holborn Prep – on Holborn Road, off Trafalgar. Bus trip going to be easy – straight up Mountain View, straight down Hope Road and then walk over. But traffic bad-bad this mornin – always bad first mornin a school. Miss Sahara car is air condition, but it don't work too good and all a we sweat, but not like in bus. We drive past people walkin out a Jacob's Pen. Me feel shame that I drive and they walk, but I feel proud too. Maybe they going hate me for being in Miss Sahara yellow car, all the same. Put my head down and hope no one see us. Fool-fool. Is bare foolishness hopin that. Everybody inna ghetto know everything. Them know say we going prep school from the day Miss Sahara say it.

Miss Sahara listen to the radio; is a talk show I hear of but never listen to call *Morning Talk*. Plenty big man talkin and some big woman too. Them always talk about things nobody understand, *balance a payment* and *fiscal defeat* and *informal secta*. Sometime – after a killin – them talk to "community member from a inner city area" on the show – that mean ghetto people. When them come on, them mix up them word and you can hear plenty confusion behind them, other people makin noise, baby a cry, truck engine revvin. The big people on the radio show, you can hear what them drive and what them wear inna them voice. Them say, "We must all pull together," and "We are all responsible," and them talk like them respect inner city people, but is not true.

You can never figure out what it is all about, the killin. If is a police killin, you hear say the dead man never do nothin, him a bathe inna him yard only wearin brief. If police not involve, you hear is a fight over woman or what them call "turf". Me, I dunno what is this turf. Seem like people a fight for one dirty street corner over another.

It a serious thing, though. At Nightingale All Age, some pickney mother can't come school cause gang war don't let them pass a certain street. Old people say it start with politi-cian, when political meetin mash up with people throwin stone and bottle. Then politician give young man gun and them become like soldier man. After that, no more stone and bottle. After that, pure gunshot. Old people talk about civil war one time, between all the political party-them. People who support one political party must leave whole area of Kingston or get kill.

Jacob's Pen – now it was a land lease place. That same Prime Minister everybody love, Michael Manley, him give land to poor people for growin food. Old people say everybody love that. But instead a farmin, the people sell off every bit a the land and Jacob's Pen don't have not even one piece a dirt leave that could grow a patch a callaloo. People not supposed to sell the land and now the government say everybody who live in the land lease part a Jacob's Pen is a squatter.

We drive in a gateway. It full a car. One security directin traffic. Don't see any children walkin inna school by themself. All the car drive inna small car park and stop. Uptown woman get out, them dress in grey or black suit for the office, or some a them wear clothes for exercise. I see them kinda clothes on TV, tight pants with cris-cris running shoes. Not so many man droppin off them children. Woman get out a them car, children come out, one or two children the most, and the woman walk into school holdin children hand. I think a Nightingale All Age – even the young-young pickney come school by themself. Most that will happen is big pickney bring them. I see some other car not stoppin in the car park, but drivin up to a big chainlink gate. Young woman – must be a teacher – stand up there and when the car stop, she open the door and children come out. Them look glad to see her. I don't see any children cryin, even though is first day a the new school year, and some children must come school first time today.

Miss Sahara drive into the car park and stop. "Okay, let's go, guys," she say. "Don't forget anything." When we all stand outside the car, close together, she look at us and smile a little. "You all look great. Don't worry, they'll look after you here and you'll learn a lot. Nobody will be unkind to you."

We go through the small gate cut inna the big chainlink one. First thing I see in the school is a big, grass play field. A little bit a dust near the middle, but only a little. Everything paint up nice – even tree have trunk paint white. Classroom block are only one storey high; each one look like a separate little house with door and window. Them join up, a course, but them still look separate. Cover passageway run outside and I see a pile a bright blue shelf outside every classroom. I see a boy go up and put his lunch pan on shelf and run off, callin to him friend. Plenty lunch pan already put there. Wonder how they stop children from t'iefin other children lunch. Coulda never do that at Nightingale All Age – end a the first day, every lunch pan gone.

Miss Sahara stop near the top a the outside passageway and knock on a door. "Enter," someone inside say. We go in and is cold, like in Mr. Reynolds office. Air condition. But this room is not a Principal office, is a room with four chair and a table with magazine on it. A lady sit at a desk in the corner. "Come in, come in, and shut the door," she say. "We want to keep the air conditioning inside. Mrs. Lawrence?"

"That's right," Miss Sahara say. "And these are the two boys, Dexter… no, Raymond and Marlon. Say good morning, boys."

"Good morning, Miss!" Marlon and me say.

"'Morning. Welcome to Holborn Prep. My name is Miss Gordon. And this is…?" she say, a look at Mumma and Lissa. I surprise Lissa don't cry.

"The children's mother, Miss Arleen Jones and the baby of the family, Lissa. I'm taking her over to Young Minds," say Miss Sahara.

"Why don't you do that now?" the lady say. "I'll get the boys settled in their classes. Then come back and we can do the paperwork."

"Okay, thanks," Miss Sahara say. "Boys, go with Miss Gordon. She'll look after you."

"'Bye, Mumma," Marlon say. Him voice scratchy, like him gettin over a cold.

"G'waan," Mumma say. She not lookin at us. I wonder if she going cry. *Don't make her cry and disgrace we.*

Miss Gordon take us back outside. "I'm taking you both to Special Ed," she say. "I understand you have some catching up to do. After this term, we'll assess how well you do and put you into the right grade." Don't know what she is talkin about; don't know what is this Special Ed. She walk fast; her shoes go click on the concrete. "Miss Gordon, Miss Gordon," children call out.

"Good morning, Ingrid. Good morning, Bradley. Did you have a good summer?"

"Yes, Miss!"

Four boy run up and down on play field. "Michael! Patrick! It's nearly eight o'clock. Go to your classes. You know you're not supposed to be skylarking now," Miss Gordon call out.

"Yes, Miss!" one boy say. All a them look 'bout my age, but tall and heavy, like them use to good food. Them is uptown children; you can tell that. Them is all brownins, some light, some dark. None a them is black.

We pass classroom and I look inside, lookin for black children. I do see some, but not plenty. I see one whole heap a white children, *white-white* children, with blue eye and yellow hair. Never seen so many in one place before. Girl are pretty-pretty. Some wear ribbon in them hair. Boy wear khaki uniform like we have on; girl wear light blue tunic over white shirt. In some class, children is wearin white shorts and different colour T-shirt with "Holborn Prep" write on front. Must be the PE uniform Miss Sahara talk about.

Right at the end a the classroom block, we see one little house by itself. Not even concrete passage go right up to it – it in the far corner a the playin field under a big common mango tree. It paint yellow and dark blue, like the rest a the school. A low, white picket fence run around some flowers bed outside this little house. It pretty. A boy inna wheelchair sit there. Him look like him don't have muscle; him hand hang over the arm a the wheelchair, one foot touch ground. Him head fall forward and it cotch up on a tin can on a shelf that join up to the wheelchair. Him hair black and stick up and him skin whiter than any skin I ever see. The boy see us comin and he smile. Him eye cross. Him look like a duppy. What him doing here? Him shoulda be in a madhouse or children home.

"Hello, Felix," Miss Gordon say.

"Hel-lo, Miss Gor-don," the boy say, draggin out him word-them. Him is hard to understand.

"These are some new boys, Felix, just starting school today. This is Raymond and this is Marlon. Raymond's pet name is Dexter – is that right, Raymond?" She don't wait for me to say anything. "I know you will look after them. Say hello to Felix, boys."

I vex that Miss Gordon think this wheelchair boy can look after we. Them must really think we has no use. But we say hello and then we follow Miss Gordon inside the little house. Felix stay outside. Suppose he can't move, unless somebody come for him. I see Special Ed house has ramp going inna classroom and on other side a the entrance, another ramp to play field. Must be so Felix wheelchair can get up and down.

Is cool inside. Same bright colour, same blue shelf for lunch pan inside classroom, not outside like rest a the school. Children sit at their desk, each child have his own desk. Not plenty children, I count them quick: seven. Four boy; three girl. Marlon and me will make nine and Felix outside, ten. But him coulda never be in class, him is fool-fool, can't learn. Then I see a girl, very fat, same white skin and cross eye – is a whole heap a them at this school! She colourin in a book, her head down, nearly on the desk. She don't look up when we come in. And then I understand – they put us with the *slow* children; that is what Special Ed mean. I feel shame more hot than I ever feel in my life.

SAHARA
Men and Guns

"So how's school going, Dexter?" We were sitting on the wall outside, watching the sky turn pink. I'd taken to arriving earlier at Jacob's Pen on Sunday afternoons and staying later. People from the community were beginning to greet me. I felt proud of this – I was beginning to belong. I was an uptowner who reached out. I no longer noticed the squalor. I'd salvaged some wood from behind the restaurant and Londel's brother, Patrick, had made two small desks. Now Dexter and Marlon had places to do their homework.

"Alright, Miss. School going alright."

"Do you like your teachers?"

"Yes, Miss. Most a them."

"What's your favourite subject?"

"Dunno. Everyting hard. Marlon doing good, though. Him readin fast-fast."

I looked at the wooden house. It had never been painted. Perhaps next weekend I'd buy some paint. I imagined a pale yellow with khaki trim. I'd bought a drum for water and it was sitting at one corner of the house, positioned to collect rain off the roof. Fewer visits to the standpipe for the children, I'd reasoned. I wondered if I could convince Arleen to take down the zinc fence. No, it was probably necessary. She'd started growing some callaloo in the small yard and there was even a skinny puppy in residence. I'd been lukewarm about the puppy at first – I wasn't sure I wanted to finance a pet. But Marlon loved the brown puppy and told me how he barked at night if anyone came too close to the zinc fence. The puppy's squeaky yapping would be no deterrent to a gunman, but I was glad it made Marlon feel safer.

"We should go inside and write letters to your sponsors," I said.

"Yes, Miss."

Half term had just come and gone. Whenever I visited Jacob's Pen, I looked at everyone's school books and it seemed the boys were making progress. Marlon especially was learning – I supposed he was younger, not so far behind.

"You're not still begging at Sovereign, are you?" I said.

"No Miss! From you tell me stop, me stop."

"*I have* stopped," I corrected. "Let's go and do those letters." I jumped down and turned towards the house. Marlon was sitting on the front step; I could just see him through the gate. He was watching us and I knew he wanted to be with us on the wall.

"Hey, Marlon," I said, walking up to him.

"Hey, Miss Sahara." It was cute, the way he copied my speech.

"Let's go and write letters to your sponsors." I reached out for his hand and he took mine and stood up. "Oh wait. I brought some nice stationery," I said. "It's in the car. I'll get it."

"I get it for you, Miss Sahara. Give me the key," Marlon said. He loved to get things out of my car, opening and shutting the door carefully.

"It's on the front seat. In the scandal bag." It was only the second letter we were writing to the sponsors. The first one had been a struggle. I planned to suggest the children draw some pictures as well, so I'd brought crayons and paper.

The boys sat at their desks. I noticed Dexter was outgrowing his already. Probably it had been too small to begin with. Arleen stood at the back of the room, as she often did, holding Lissa. I sat on the bed.

"Let's start with the letters and do the pictures later," I said. "Here's the paper. Do you have pens?" There was a silence.

"No pen, Miss," said Dexter.

"What happened to your pens? I've brought at least two packs here since the beginning of term. You boys need to take better care of your things."

"Yes, Miss Sahara," said Marlon. "But sometimes the big boy take our things from us."

"Shut up, Marlon," said Dexter, under his breath.

"No, let him talk," I said. "What big boys?"

"Nutt'n Miss. We lost the pen-them. We sorry," said Dexter.

"What big boys? Are you being bullied?"

"Marlon don' know what him talkin about, Miss Sahara. No big boy. No bullyin. Everyting fine. We write di letter." Dexter's face was closed.

They struggled. I had to tell them what to write in the end. They turned to drawing pictures with much more enthusiasm. Even Lissa joined in, sitting on the floor, colouring so hard she tore holes in the paper. "Not so hard, Lissa," I said. "Look. Like this."

I sat on the front step while the children coloured. The gate was open. People walked by on the road and many waved. "Good evening," I called out. "Evenin' Ma'am," they replied.

Could I live in such a place, live Arleen's life? The walls of the wooden house were so thin, too insubstantial to protect anyone from all that was outside. How much did a person really need? I'd never visited the outhouse at the back, where the family washed and excreted. It was a tiny shed-like structure made of zinc. The walls were not straight and the ground was always muddy at the entrance.

"We finish, Miss," Dexter said. I stood up. It was dusk and the light inside the house was dim.

"Bring the pictures here," I said. "There's more light." Marlon handed three sheets of paper to me and I sat down again on the step, holding the drawings at an angle so I could see better. The top one was obviously Lissa's – scribbles in many colours, with a few tears in the paper. She'd signed her name, though – "LISSA" in huge crooked letters. The nursery school was doing its work. Marlon had drawn some stick figures, a man, a woman, a house, a tree. He'd used only greens and blues. "Very good, Marlon," I said. "This is a lovely picture." He smiled and sat beside me on the step, resting his head on my shoulder. "I think you should take it back inside and sign your name."

Dexter had coloured his page black in wide strokes. On top he'd tried to draw in red and the colour only appeared in places. "Are these men?" I asked him.

"Dunno." He stood behind me, his face in shadow.

"You must know. You drew them."

"Yes, Miss. Men."

"And are these guns?"

"Yes."

"Why'd you draw men and guns, Dexter?"

"You tell him to draw someting from his life," Marlon said.

"Shut up, Marlon. Shut you mout'. What you know about anyting?" Dexter said. His voice was shaking.

"Don't talk to your brother like that," I said, weakly. "Are there men and guns in your life, Dexter?"

"No, Miss Sahara. No men and no guns. Is just a picture. You tell me to draw one picture and me draw it." He brushed past me, went outside and picked up one of the buckets. "Going a standpipe," he said and disappeared through the gate.

"Wait, Dexter…" I called after him, but he had gone.

I looked down at Marlon's head. He was so much easier to deal with. I held him closer. Marlon would do okay.

DEXTER
"Big Foot"

"Big Foot," the boy say, quiet-quiet, so no teacher hear. We inna line for assembly. My face get hot and me want t'ump him. *Don't say anyting.* I don't look 'round, but I know him laughin, him and him friend. From first day a school at Holborn Prep, I get call Big Foot. Marlon them call Baby Big Foot.

It happen because after that first mornin in September, when school let out, I see some boy a play football on the grass field. Want kick ball too. I sit on one a the bench under the guango tree and take off my new shoe quick – this is what Mumma teach me, end of school day, shoe come off. I only have two shoe after all. Before I meet Miss Sahara, only one. I run over to the boy with the ball and I tackle him, take away the ball. I feel like a doctor bird on that field – a hummin bird with shinin wings, can fly up, down, forward. Can even stay still in the air. Grass soft on my feet, not like the dirt and stone field in Jacob's Pen. Even the sun is warm here, not hot-hot. I zigzag my way down the field, the ball is my own – bird, butterfly – can't catch me.

A boy run from the sideline to try tackle me and I dally 'round him easy. I let the ball go from my foot, straight to goal. Maybe prep school not going be so bad after all. I run over and pick up the ball. "Look at this *barefoot* big foot ghetto pickney," the boy who tackle me say. He tall and handsome, a brownin with green eye like a cat. Other boy-them come up and they all laughin.

"Why you take off your shoes, Big Foot? You think this a *ghetto* school?"

Don't say anyting, don't say anyting, don't say anyting. I drop the ball and start juggle it on my foot – front, side, up high, down low. I know this boy vex because I did take away the ball from him.

"Come for it, nuh?" I say.

"I don't play with *ghetto* boys."

"Wha' 'appen? You 'fraid to tackle me, *red* bwoy?" Bounce, bounce the ball go. Other boy are quiet, standin in a circle.

"Take the ball from him, Travis," a boy say.

"Yeah. Take it from the Big Foot." Them all start say it together now, "Take it from the Big Foot, take it from the Big Foot." Want to hit the big boy so bad, so bad, want to turn Lasco on him, or Boston. He woulda stop laugh then for sure. But I keep the ball bouncin, from foot to knee now, foot to knee.

"Big Foot, Big Foot, Big Foot," all the boy-them say together. Them voice not loud, not like a fight at Nightingale, when pickney come from every corner a the school to see a fight. These boy don't want teacher to hear. I want to be back at Nightingale, even with the stony field and the stink a shit and the noise a shift children runnin up and down outside. Don't want to be here, on this pretty field with the big tree 'round the edge, all a them with them name print out on a little white sign. What kinda place put name on tree? The kind a place where them call me Big Foot.

"What's going on over there? Boys?" A Coolie man come over; him have a whistle 'round him neck. Mus' be the coach.

"Nothing, Mr. Malik," say the boy with green eye. "We're just having a game and watching the new boy – he's pretty good with a ball."

"What's your name, youngster?" the coach say to me. Bounce, bounce – I don't miss yet.

"Sir, Raymond." Bounce. Bounce. Knee, foot, knee.

"I'm the sports master, Mr. Malik. You look like you've played ball before. What school are you coming from?"

"Sir, Nightingale All Age."

"Big Foot!" somebody whisper.

"What's that? Somebody say something?" Mr. Malik look 'round at the boy still standin inna circle. I take my eye off the ball for one second, just to look at them face, just to see if there is any respect in them face – 'course, I miss the ball and it roll away. I shouldna look. They are lookin at me like I am dirt.

"Give me the ball, Raymond," Mr. Malik say, and I pick it up and give it to him. "That's enough for today. You boys go and wait for your pick up. Football practice is Tuesdays and Thursdays at three, Raymond. You come then, okay." Him must be a Coolie from India; him kinda hard to understand and him move him head sideway when him talk.

"Sir!" I say, but I know I will not go to football practice. Is not like the boy at Holborn Prep will friend me up 'cause I can kick ball. No, the better I play, the more them will hate me.

The boy all start to walk across the field and I see Marlon under a tree, watchin. Him sit alone. When the pack a boy-them pass him, the green-eye boy, Travis, say something to him. Even though I not too close to them, I hear it: "Baby Big Foot." Marlon hang him head and I know him eye start water. Marlon need to tough up; him cry too easy. Them soon start call him batty boy, you watch.

That is how it start at Holborn Prep. First day, is pure trouble we get into. We sit under a tree in break. When the children see our snack, just one piece a hardo bread and a pack a cheese crunchie, them whisper to each other and laugh behind them hand. The prep school children, them have peanut butter and jelly sandwich on brown bread and American apple and foreign box juice like Ribena and maybe even a cookie or a cupcake – not from a pack neither, home made. Them laugh at us at lunchtime too, when them see us try to use a knife and fork to eat school lunch. It spoil lunch for us – and it was a wicked lunch! Stew peas and white rice and callaloo and fry plantain.

We get into trouble every week because we come late. No amount of explainin how the bus late, how it crowd, how big boy throw us off *this* mornin, won't let us get off at the Holborn Prep stop *next* mornin, make teacher understand. We don't tell the teacher how nobody can tell time good at our house, and even when we learn, we don't have watch or clock. We get into trouble for not knowin what the bell mean, for not leavin the desk straight, for going inna library by mistake while teacher in there keeping a meetin, for not havin the right colour sock. It seem like we get into trouble for being born. I even hear say the mother a some a the uptown children go see the Principal and object as to how ghetto children allow into Holborn Prep. It don't matter what we learn – from beginnin to end, me and Marlon, we still Big Foot and Baby Big Foot.

Most day I hate being at prep school, with the slow children. But then some day, when I sit in a quiet classroom with Miss Gordon, and she explainin something to me alone, something I never did understand before, I feel like I can see over a giant concrete wall. When I learn something, I think about that wall fallin down, *erodin* like Miss Blagrove tell us in Science. And I see it in Marlon too – him begin to read fast-fast, as if him cannot get enough a readin. Teacher not the problem at Holborn Prep – them voice quiet, them don't beat we. Children a the problem.

As for Lissa, what a trouble to get her to school inna mornin! Bus not set up for small pickney like she. Me and Marlon take turn carryin her – by the time we get to school, our uniform wrinkle up and she bawl from heat and shovin. We get inna trouble for shirt not tuck in and we too sweaty. Teacher even ask us if we don't bathe inna mornin. It rough, man, every day rough.

I go see Lissa in break. By then she stop cry and she sit with the other children and do finger paintin or buildin block or play with some big letter in bright colour. "A!" she say, when I come through the door. "B!" She talkin plenty now and wearin trainin pants, not diaper any more. Miss Sahara did have to bring the trainin pants when the school say so. It don't look like Lissa havin it too hard at Young Minds nursery school.

Maybe she will be the lucky one a us – she will get a education. Me and Marlon, we so far behind, it not funny. We lie about how old we is. Miss Sahara suppose to get we birth certificate, but we give her wrong birthday and wrong hospital and we know registry office not going able to find we.

This education thing is like a race on sports day, with all the other runner one whole lap ahead, them runnin on grass track while you run on stone. You run and run 'til you heart want bust, but you will never catch those other runner, even though them don't run as fast as you and them not as strong. They just too far ahead and the stone under your foot too sharp.

SAHARA
A line at the end of the earth

"Carl came home last night and said he wants to change his name," I told Lydia.

"His name? What's wrong with Carl? What's he want to call himself? The boy formerly known as Carl? Or maybe he'll reverse the letters – Larc wouldn't be bad, I suppose." Lydia took a huge bite of a gizzada. Evidently off her diet.

"Not his first name, dummy. His last name. And stop being so sarcastic. Carl's a good boy."

"He wants to change *Lawrence*? Why? To what?"

"To his father's name, of course. Longmore."

"Good grief. Whyever?"

"Aah, Lyds, I dunno. We had such a fight about it. I mean, he came in with this bombshell and I just lost it and so did he. I told him he was an ungrateful little shit and he told me I had rendered him fatherless by giving him my name instead of his father's."

"Oh what total bullshit. His father rendered him fatherless. Not you."

"I know. But he wants his father's name now. I can say no, at least until he's eighteen, but what's the point?"

"Have you talked to Lester about it?"

"Of course not. We've hardly spoken since he came back. Well, he'll call the house sometimes and I'll answer the phone and we'll greet each other, but nothing more than that."

"You should go see him. Why should he just breeze back into Carl's life and take over?"

"But what do I tell him? Stop Carl from liking you? Be a

110

jerk? Go back to ignoring your son – my son? There's nothing to say, Lyds. We had a child together when we were little more than children ourselves and it turned out that all Lester did was supply the sperm. But apparently sperm counts."

"Well, maybe he'll pay for college."

"I don't even know if I want that."

"Don't be a complete idiot. Of course you want that."

I went home early that day, leaving the accounts, something I hardly ever did. It was November and the days were getting shorter. November was my favourite month of the year – the hurricane season was over, October rains had stopped, everywhere was green and lush. And the light changed from the flat glare of summer to the luminous glow of a tropical year at its closing.

Traffic was light and I got home quickly. I parked and went inside. I opened all the windows – something I hardly ever did in the week – and a warm light poured into the house. I put on the kettle and waited for it to boil, although I didn't really want another cup of tea. I needed something to do. Carl's cocoa mug was on the counter, swarming with ants. No matter how many times I asked him to rinse it and leave it in the sink, he left it all over the house. I washed his mug and watched the ants swirl down the drain.

I took my cup of tea outside and then realized all the patio furniture was in the kitchen. I put down the cup and dragged out a chair, setting it up in the shade. Grass quits flitted around, making their tick-tick-tick noise. The patio flagstones were mossy and the back garden looked unsupervised. One of the banana trees was bearing.

I thought about the fight with Carl. At one point, I'd found myself shaking a finger at him, as if the issue was uncompleted homework or playing ball in the living room. His eyes had narrowed, and I remembered thinking: this boy – my son, my only son – hates me. He hates me. He hates me for having him, for being his mother, for not being his father.

I thought about my own father. The thing I remember most about him was his voice – a cultured English voice that could have been on the radio or the stage, but was equally well suited to the pulpit. It was a solid thing, like a rippling blanket, which he could cast wide to the corners of his church or pull in close to wrap a sleepy child. I wanted to talk like him and for a while I did, until my schoolmates teased me. I remember his smell – cigarettes and the slightly mouldy smell of his church robes, which rubbed off on his street clothes. When we went to church on Sundays, I saw how the women in the congregation looked at him and I saw how he picked one of those women every Sunday and sent his sermon to her alone. I hated church. I hated dressing up in itchy, warm clothes with sashes and bows. I hated having to sit still for so long. I hated how the women came up afterwards and pressed my father's hands. I thought I would not go to church when I got older, but then I was afraid of going to hell. This was until my father simply walked out of the house one Monday, taking only his passport and the contents of their joint account, according to my mother. He must really have hated us, I concluded. A proper Christian would not have left his family. When my father left, I turned my back on the church. It was easier to blame his religion than his character.

So I too had been fatherless, for most of my life. And I'd brought a fatherless child into the world. As Arleen had done; not once, but three times. Could she and I be sisters under the skin, the difference between us only one of degree? Ridiculous. I'd looked after my child. Carl had never been sent to beg in plazas.

It was my father who named me Sahara. I once asked him why he'd named me after a desert. "Ah, my child," he'd said, in his preacher's voice. "I named you after a place without limit, with nothing but sky and horizons."

"What's a horizon?"

"The line at the end of the earth," he said.

"Have you been there?" I asked.

"Not yet. But I want to go. Bedouins live in the Sahara Desert."

"What are Bedouins?"

"Nomads. People who move around their whole lives."

"They don't have houses?"

112

"Tents. They have tents and they take the tents with them."
My father looked over my head and his eyes were unfocused.
After he left, I knew he had gone to the Bedouins.

I was named for a place without limit. But as I grew up, I
realized a desert was a place of empty sands that constantly
shifted and could easily kill an unwary person. A place where
the days were hot enough to fry an egg on a stone and the nights
so cold there would have been frost, if there had been any water
to freeze. The Bedouins were unwashed and uneducated and
the women were virtual slaves. No, I did not want to see the
desert.

My name was just my name. A person could call themselves
anything. I drained my cup and walked back into the house,
shutting the door behind me. I didn't remember the patio chair
left outside until I was in bed and then it was too late to get it.

DEXTER
Drownin in Shit

"Where you been, Dexy-bwoy? Mi buck up Boston down on di harbour ferry and him tell mi you stop go a school. You join up wit' Racehorse crew?" Lasco sittin on the back wall a Sovereign Plaza. I not suppose to be here. Miss Sahara say if she find out I beggin in Plaza again, no more school fee, school, uniform – no more bag a food on Sunday night. I bored on weekend, though. I tell Mumma me have school biology project and she just nod her head, like she know what is biology. Well, maybe she hear the word, but she don't know what it mean. I don't even know myself too tough, see it in a book; it have something to do with science.

I like science. I ask Miss Blagrove why the tree at Holborn Prep have funny name write beside their real name. She say is *Latin.* She talk for a long time about how old-time scientist start name all the animal and plant in the world, how there is a system for namin, with a order name and a class name and a species name and a family name, something like that. She tell me is like if somebody could look at my two name and know a whole lot about me, just from those two name. She say a scientist from China and a scientist from Africa who don't speak the same language can still understand each other when they use scientific name to talk about a animal or plant. Me, I like this – a set way a lookin at everything inna world, a way that one whole set a people, the scientist, understand. Miss say is *elegant.* Teacher at Holborn Prep know plenty-plenty word. Even student know whole heap a word.

I think a what my three name could tell. *Raymond* – my real name. It could say I born this side a the world, I am not Chinese, not Indian, not Russian, not Eskimo. *Dexter* – my pet name. This say I am not white; never met a white boy call Dexter. *Morrison* – my father name. This don't tell the right thing. This say my mother and father is parents, is marry, live in the same house, like on American TV show. Ghetto pickney need a new kinda last name that say – father gone away and everybody glad.

"You no hear me talkin to you?" Lasco say. I look at him. Him even more mawga, like a starvin mongrel dog on the street. Him have a cut on one cheek, just startin to heal. Him hair nappy, like it don't comb or cut in a long time. Him definitely look like somebody to be frighten of.

"Sorry, big man. I did hear you, just was thinkin…"

"*T'inkin…*?" Lasco voice scornful.

"Just thinkin." Before him can say anything, I go on, "I get send to another school, a prep school, down on Holborn Road."

"A *prep school on Holborn Road*? But hear dis now! How you manage dat?"

I glad Lasco not vex. Him smile, like him think it funny. But I not sure how him feel, you can never tell with Lasco, him take beatin in silence, but I know him hurt like everybody. "You 'member di uptown woman in di summer? I tell you 'bout her, she give mi five hundred dollar and then she start bring food to di house? Anyway, she get wi inna dis school, mi and Marlon."

"Whoy. You lucky, man. So, how it is? Di uptown pickney, dem must want spit on you." Lasco is a street boy, but him smart. Him know more 'bout the world than old people.

"Well, in some way it more easy than Nightingale, but some way harder. I in the same class with Marlon and whole heap a slow pickney there too. Them even have one boy inna wheelchair – him need help to hold up him head." I think about Felix. When children callin me Big Foot or I can't understand what the teacher sayin, I go and find Felix. Him always smile. Sometime him head drop off the tin can and I help him fix up himself. I get to like him. I glad that him end up at Holborn

Prep – no way him woulda last a day at Nightingale. The bad boy woulda drown him inna de toilet first week.

Lasco not interested in any boy inna wheelchair. Him look over the Plaza. "Anyway," I say, "them have one nice green football field and big tree all 'bout. Is a nice place. Teacher-them don't shout or beat we, but them have more rule than gravel inna river bed. But pickney-them *terrible* – call we name, laugh after we."

"So you bust dem backside," Lasco say. "Uptown pickney can't fight a ghetto yout'. You play football wit' dem?"

"Bwoy, dem no like you fight at dis school. Teacher say if you fight, you expel. Don't play ball. No gears and it just going make tings worse if mi beat dem."

"You have slave mentality, yout'. You not a man if you don't fight. Dem just a try downpress you."

I jump up on the wall beside Lasco, look 'round for security. Them not this side a the Plaza right now. A woman walk past; she hold two children by their hand; one boy, one girl. She look at us sittin on the wall and shake her head, but she don't say anything. Lasco don't move but I feel the anger in him, like steam inna pot with the top stuck down tight.

"Dis uptown woman," he say, "di one dat bring food? You ever see her house? She white?"

"Not white-white. A brownin. Never been to her house. She come up on Sunday night, bring food, look at homework, talk to we. What you want know for?"

"Nutt'n. Woulda like see her sometime."

"So come up Sunday night. Come 'bout six. You have to clean up though, she don't like it if you dirty. And Mumma nah let you in. You can find place to bathe?" As soon as I say it, I sorry. Where Lasco going get clean? Maybe he going beat me up now, push me off the wall, because I don't show respect by talkin about him being dirty.

But him just laugh. "I bathe inna di fountain at Emancipation Park; beg a shirt from the Baptist church on East Street. Mi will see you on Sunday night. Gw'aan now, security a come."

Confusion happen on Sunday night. Seem like some student at

the technical college near Jacob's Pen chase one car t'ief inna cesspool. Then them light fire all around it and every time the t'ief come up to breathe, them throw stone at him. Them stand on the other side a the fire and watch him drown inna shit. Police crawlin all over Jacob's Pen, lookin for these student. Don't know why, nobody from Jacob's Pen go to technical college. Is just because police want look like them a do something.

When police inna the community, nobody can go outside. You can get shot for nothin by police. You can be hangin clothes on a line, sweepin yard, carryin water. If you get kill by police, for sure them will find a nine millimetre on you – even if you naked. Plenty time we hear how a carload a police, maybe five a them, kill a unarmed man who attack police vehicle with a rockstone.

Don't know how Lasco or Miss Sahara going get here inna this madness. Hope Lasco don't bother – him the kinda person police will definitely shoot. "Resistin arrest," them will say. "Engaged in a shoot out." "Fired on the police, who were forced to return fire." Radio news say those kinda thing every single day a life.

Worry about Miss Sahara, too. Food low, but wouldna be the first time nothing to eat on Sunday night. I more frighten that she see how it really go inna Jacob's Pen and reverse her car and never come back.

Sometime I think about her when it too hot to sleep, or when rain crashing on the zinc roof and it too noisy. I wonder what she think she doing with us. She don't seem to like us too much – she always find something to complain 'bout. We go late to school too much, Mumma buy something Miss Sahara don't think we need – like, one time, Mumma get her partner draw and buy one Courts dresser from Miss Frankson over in Bell Town. The dresser not new or anything, but it is a place to put clothes, instead a in a cardboard barrel. But, Lord, Miss Sahara mad! She say partner don't make sense, why Mumma don't buy things that are important like book and clothes for the children. She don't understand about respect, how people inna ghetto disrespect you if you don't have certain things.

She don't like it that we t'ief light from public service, but she don't say how we is to pay the light bill. She say we watch too much TV – if TV on when she come through the door on Sunday night, she give a big sigh and tell Mumma turn it off. She always ask me if I go to Plaza because she definitely don't want me going there. But even though her words always seem hard, fact is, she come to see us every Sunday night. Few time she can't make it, she tell us the week before, and then she come another day. It don't seem like she respect us, but she want to help. She sit with me and Marlon and go through homework, most time she shake her head and you can see she don't think we learnin anything, but then next week she bring a lamp so we can see better, even though is t'ief light in our house. She bring little desk-them for me and Marlon. She hug up Lissa every time too – she don't touch me and she stop hug Marlon so much. I way too big for that, but I know Marlon miss her puttin her arm around him.

She talk to us too, ask us how we feel, how we doing. This hardly happen to me in my life – nobody want know how I feel. 'Course, we don't tell her the truth. We don't tell her children call us Big Foot and Baby Big Foot, we don't tell her how they laugh at our lunch pan, I don't tell her how sometime I want play ball – want the gears to do it, want to show the uptown boy what inner city boy can do. We tell her what she want to hear. Everything fine, Miss, we learnin so much, teacher them nice, nobody beat we. Miss Sahara, she take a set against beatin. She tell Mumma she must never beat we. Mumma nod her head, but she still beat we – another thing we don't tell Miss Sahara.

Miss Sahara think she can make us into uptown children. She think if we learn how to read and count, learn how to behave, get expose to *opportunity* – she always talkin about *opportunity* – make uptown friend, then we will be like uptown people. I sure it not going go like that.

I think about being a big man. I think about leavin school; maybe I make it through secondary school, so I leave at seventeen, maybe with a few CSEC subject. Before Miss Sahara come along, is true I woulda been out a school at fourteen with no subject. But what good the subject going do?

What job I can get? Packin grocery in Sovereign, washin car-them at the Texaco gas station in Bell Town – maybe the mechanic there, him like me, he let me watch him and after plenty-plenty year, I can call myself a mechanic. Could be I can get labourer job on a construction site, push wheelbarrow, carry water, learn how to mix cement, maybe masonry work, maybe even learn trade like 'lectrics or plumber. Biggest job somebody like me can get could be security guard like Sinclair, wait all day inna car park, or at the gate of rich people town house scheme. Lift a red and white barrier up and down. Earn extra money washin SUV and carryin bag a food into the cool house with tile floor and facety children.

Wonder what time it is. Marlon kneelin on bed, lookin out. Sound like police car leavin. Maybe Miss Sahara will make it. I hear footstep outside. Marlon say, "Who that? Is not Miss Sahara!" We hear a knock on the door, one loud knock.

"Who that?" Mumma say.

Marlon duck down from the window. "Is one a Dexter friend from Sovereign."

"What him doin here, Dexter?" Mumma say.

"I invite him. Him a frien'." I say. Another loud knock on the door. I wonder how Lasco make it through the police. "Let him in, nuh?"

"Mi not openin di door," Mumma say. "Next minute, it bring down police."

"Police gone," I say, but I don't know this for sure. I get up and open the door. Lasco standin there, dress in shirt and pants, hair cut, lookin clean. "Wha' 'appen," I say. Him come inside.

Right away I know is a mistake to invite him. We poor, but Lasco is something else. Him bad, desperate, I don't know. *Dog-heart*, people in Jacob's Pen call boy like Lasco. *Evil*, the church people woulda say. Bad thing-them will happen to him, already happen to him. Him will rob and rape and murder, and other people will try kill him too. Him could end up a area don, rich, drivin a Escalade, wearin cargo, people lovin him, but him will still die young and there will be a big funeral and politician will come. Or him could die tonight, tomorrow, next week in a shoot out. Lasco born to dead. When I see him in our house, is a different thing to when I see him in Plaza.

"This mi Mumma, Miss Arleen," I tell him. "That is Marlon and Lissa. Mumma, this mi frien' Lasco."

Mumma pick up Lissa; she always do that when she don't know what to say or do. Lissa say, "Down, Mumma! Want food." Marlon say hello to Lasco and go back up on the bed, start look out a the window again.

"Wan' go out by the rum shop?" I say to Lasco.

"Nah. Mi come see you." I remember what him say about Miss Sahara and I 'fraid for her. Maybe Lasco plan to rob her, take the thin silver chain from her neck, rip her earrin from her ear.

"She here," Marlon say. Him jump down from the bed and pull open the door and run to the yellow VW. Miss Sahara make it through all the police and confusion. She going bring her food and see Lasco. Maybe this is the last time we see her in Jacob's Pen; the last time we get the three bag a food on a Sunday night.

She come through the zinc fence. She have on jeans pants and a baseball cap and long-sleeve shirt. She look at the ground to make sure she put her foot right. It hard to see she is a uptown woman. She carry two bag. Hope she not going stay long tonight.

She come through the door inna the dim light. I surprise to see her face is wet. It not rainin; she cryin. "Did you hear what happened?" she say.

"We hear," Mumma say.

"It's too awful," she say. "Those were young people, teenagers. How could they watch a man drown in a cesspool? Why didn't they just call the police? Why is a cesspool open anyway?" She sit down on the bed and look around. She see me and give me the two bag. "One more in the car, Dex," she say. Is the first time she call me Dex. I like it – sound like a big man name. She wipe her eye with the back of her hand. Mumma put down Lissa and she run to Miss Sahara. Marlon sit beside her on the bed.

"Miss," I say, "this mi – *my* – friend Lasco. The one I told you

120

'bout." Miss Sahara look at Lasco and I see her eye get big. I look at him too, tryin to see what she see. A thin black boy, scar on him face, thick mouth. Him eyewhite shine. Him look like anybody wearin too-big shirt, baggy pants, old shoe. But him look different too.

"Nice to meet you, Lasco." Miss Sahara say, always mannersable. "That's an interesting name."

"Powder milk?" he say. "Not so *interestin.*" The way he say *interestin* sound like a insult. Miss Sahara put Lissa beside her on the bed and Lissa start cry. Mumma say, "Dexter, go for the bag in Miss Sahara car," and I know she think maybe Miss Sahara leave with the last bag still inna her car.

Miss Sahara stand up. "I can't stay long tonight," she say. "The police are everywhere. This mob killing was on the news; Carl will worry. Come with me, Dex, and I'll give you the bag. Nice to meet you, Lasco," she say again, and I know it is because she don't know what else to say.

Lasco follow me to the car and Miss Sahara walk quick-quick. She don't look down to see where her feet is going – she keep her eye on the VW like it is a prize. When she put key inna the door, she don't get it in right away. I know she frighten – frighten a the student who give man the choice a drownin in shit or burnin up, frighten a the police – maybe they don't see she is a uptown woman – after all, what a uptown woman would be doing in a place like Jacob's Pen on a Sunday night? She frighten a Lasco. She look at him and she see something everybody see, even though she don't know squat about his life. When Lasco stand at her shoulder, I see that him grow a little bit. Him not so short any more. Lot a ghetto children small. They say is because somebody jump over them head when them a baby and them downgrow. I still small.

Miss Sahara still tryin to get the car door open and Lasco walk up to her. First time since I meet her, I feel sorry for her. She in a place she don't understand, don't belong. I think of a science book at Holborn Prep tellin about all a the different-different place in the world, with all them different plant and animal. In Jacob's Pen, Miss Sahara is like cactus in rain forest, lion in snow.

121

She get the door open and get inna the car. "Dexter?" she say. Lasco standin between me and her, blockin the light. I walk 'round him and she give me the last bag. "'Bye," she say, "hope everything is okay at school." Her voice have a little shake in it and it full a leftover cryin. I take the bag and she shut the car door. She push down the lockin button. She look behind her and start reverse. I sure she not comin back after this.

SAHARA
A young man, beyond all redemption

I drove home as fast as I could and the traffic lights were with me. The driveway seemed darker than usual. I saw lights on in the house, knew Carl was home. I was glad, although he'd forgotten to turn on the outside lights again. I locked the car and hurried inside. Carl was standing just inside the front door.

"Hi," I said. "What's up? Are you waiting for somebody?"

"I was waiting for you. Why can't you keep your phone on?"

"Is it off? It must have died."

"It will die, Mom, if you don't charge it."

"Mmm. Why were you waiting for me?"

"I wanted to go to the movies and I needed you to take me."

"Mmm."

"Stop saying mmm. Where were you?"

"Jacob's Pen."

"Jacob's Pen." He was sarcastic. Then he seemed to see me. "What happened? You look upset."

"Nothing. Let's rustle up an omelette, I'll even put ham in your half, and then let's find some trashy movie on TV. I'm in the mood for something entirely without intellectual merit."

"Must have been a bad evening."

"Mmm."

I was surprised when Carl followed me into the kitchen, but had the sense not to remark on it. "Want me to do anything?"

My mood lightened. "You could chop up some onions and tomatoes."

"You do the onions. They make me cry."

"Okay. You beat the eggs then." It had been a long time since

123

Carl and I prepared a meal together. We used to make a game of it when he was younger. I chopped the onions and tomatoes and began frying them with a few mushrooms, well past their best. "Want a salad?" I said.

"No. I want french fries, swimming in oil and smothered with salt. With a steak. But I know what I'm going to *get* is an omelette and a salad."

The salad done, I poured the eggs into a frying pan and began adding everything else. Without being directed, Carl set trays and sliced bread, put the salad and some pepper jelly on the low table in front of the TV. Maybe he was going to be okay. I flipped the omelette and while it sat, poured two glasses of wine. A couple months ago, I'd agreed it was okay for Carl to have a glass of wine with dinner and the occasional beer. I slid the omelette onto a plate and cut it: a third for me, two thirds for him.

Carl channel-surfed, looking for a movie. I didn't object when the one he settled on had Arnold Schwartzenegger in it.

"So what happened up there?" he asked, pressing the mute button during a lull between action sequences. I knew he'd seen this movie at least three times.

"Where?"

"In Jacob's Pen. I saw your face when you came through the door. Someone trouble you?"

"No. But something happened at U. Tech."

"What?"

"Some students cornered a car thief and chased him into a cesspit."

"Serves him right."

"Then they set the grass on fire and watched the man drown." Carl didn't say anything to that.

"Is that why you were crying?"

"Partly."

"What's the other part?" Why was my son asking me these questions? Paying attention to me – something that hadn't happened in a long time. Perhaps he was working up to telling me something I wouldn't like.

"Oh, nothing much. Just met a friend of Dexter's who was really scary."

"Huh. Why was he scary? Did he threaten you?"

"No, nothing like that. In fact, I thought he'd cleaned up to visit me."

"You mean he came especially to see you? Mom, that's dangerous!"

"Yes. No. I mean, I don't know if he came to see me. I got the feeling he wasn't a frequent visitor. I'm pretty sure he's a street kid – very thin, but wiry and strong, scars on his face. He just frightened me, is all. He looked at me and… I can't explain it, son. He was just scary. A kid, a boy, a young man, beyond all redemption. The waste just made me cry. His name was Lasco…" I realized Carl had lost interest. He pressed the mute button again and the noise of the movie filled the room, automatic weapons, shouts of rage, screams of pain.

"I'm getting some ice cream," he said after a while. "Want some?"

"No. I'm going to bed. I'm tired. I'm so, so tired. You'll clear up? Soak the dishes or we'll have cockroaches. You left your mug on the counter again, by the way." As soon as the words were out of my mouth, I regretted them.

I went into the kitchen for my water, leaving all the supper dishes in the living room. It felt strange to do that. I walked behind Carl and dropped a kiss on his head. I checked the windows and the doors – leaving him to clear up was one thing, locking up quite another.

"Mom?" he said, as I walked down the passage to my bedroom.

"Uh-huh?"

"I'm sorry about the name thing. It was stupid. I didn't mean what I said."

"Me neither, Bugs. I'm sorry too. And you can call yourself anything you want. I'm glad you're getting to know your Dad."

"Really?"

"Really."

"Night, Mom," Carl said, turning down the volume on the TV a little.

"Sleep tight," I said.

DEXTER
Janga Inna River

Marlon come through the door and slam it hard. Is a Saturday morning, the next weekend after the U. Tech student drown the car t'ief. Police never find out who do it. No one will talk. People who talk to police is *informer* – them suppose to dead.

Bored. Want go to Sovereign, up to river, maybe down to Kingston Harbour with Lasco. Last Sunday don't seem so real now. Lasco not *dangerous* – I know him long time. Him have hard life, is true, but him not going hurt we.

"Wha'appen to *you*?" Mumma say to Marlon, when she hear door slam. She over by stove, pickin up saltfish, Lissa on her hip like always. "Open back the door – it too hot in here."

"Ma'as Ken dis me," Marlon say.

"What you do him? Ma'as Ken always like you. You must facety to him."

"I wasn't facety to him!" Marlon speak the best a us. He say *wasn't* and *didn't* and *his* and *hers* – him hardly speak in patois. "I just ask him for the corn meal and the tin a bully beef, like you want."

"So what him say? Why you say him dis you?"

"He say: 'So *Master* Marlon, I hear you going *prep* school down on Holborn Road. You start talk all speaky-spokey, like you is a big man. Soon you nah talk to di likes a mi. Tell your madda she better send Dexter next time if she want buy tings from mi.' Then I tell him Dexter is going to the prep school too and he kiss his teeth and tell me to *g'lang*."

"Is not a big ting, Marlon," I say from the bed.

"What you know? You *wasn't* – weren't – w*asn't* there! People

126

was around, Miss Melanie and that girl stayin with Miss Betsy – what her name? Shakira – they all hear and laugh after me." Marlon slam down the corn meal and the bully beef on the table and go inna the back room. You get mad in Jacob's Pen and there is nowhere to go, everybody livin on top a one another, all chacka-chacka, everybody fightin for space and food. Sometime we talk about how we is like crab inna barrel and is true, if you ever see a whole pile a crab inna barrel. Every crab try get to the top, every crab crawl on top a every other crab – crab at the bottom worse off. Sometime the crab at the bottom dead from the weight of the other crab, always climbin, climbin. Climbin, until the person who catch them throw them inna a big pot a boilin water. Every crab dead then.

I think about what Marlon say about Ma'as Ken. When this school business finish, where we going belong? Uptown people don't want us at school, not going to want us in any office job. And now our own people – people who know us from we a baby – don't want us around. I think about Miss Betsy son, the one who they say has big private sector job, how he send her money but never come visit. Him shame him come from inner city, him don't want nothin to do with it. Him a crab that escape the barrel *and* the boilin water.

I get up and stand inna doorway. "Yow, Marlon," I say. "Want go river? We swim, catch janga."

"*Janga*?" Marlon say, scornful. "When last you see janga in that river? That river hardly have water, much less janga."

"It have water now, we been havin rain. Come, make we go. It too hot here and borin."

Marlon come out a the back room. He not smilin but I can tell he happy I ask him to go somewhere with me. I feel bad – maybe I should mind Marlon more. He my brother after all, and old-time people say blood thicker than water. I think how we go to Holborn Prep and we never talk about it. Never talk about the boy who call us Big Foot and Baby Big Foot, never talk about Felix with him chin on a tin can, never talk about the teacher and the uptown children with them full lunch pan.

"Awright," Marlon say. "We go look janga."

River full a water, brown and white, full a small stone, runnin fast. It been rainin whole a last week – cold front, the radio say. People suppose to leave from "flood prone area". Where we suppose to go? Them chat pure rubbish on the radio some-time.

We take off we shirt-them and put them on a big rock to get warm, so we can dry when we come out. No other pickney is at the river, prob'ly they 'fraid a the deep, rushin water. I sit on a rock at bankside and put my foot in a shallow pool. Water cool. Sun hot and bounce off the surface a the river – have to squint my eye. Is quiet, just the sound a the water; rustling sound a lizard and rat in the bush and a bird inna cage somewhere around. Is hardly ever quiet like this.

Marlon walk inna river. Him lean over, put him hand under a rock, feelin for janga, even though him say none is there. I can see him is findin it hard, water strong, what with all the rain inna river.

Old-time people frighten a the river. Them say River Mumma live in the deep pool and bring down flood and disaster on the community. Don't believe this, but me can't swim, so me careful a the river.

"Watch out for deep water!" I call out to Marlon. When the river low, we know where all the deep pool is. But today, with water all muddy and churn up, is hard to see. River fall a little, though. I can see the water was higher before; behind me the grass and reed-them bend over and cover with mud.

I sit on the rock, put my feet inna water. Is peaceful down here by the river. Is nice to sit inna sun, watch it sparkle on the water, a look out for my brother. Maybe him *will* find janga. If him do, we will boil up a sweet-sweet pepperpot soup. Get callaloo from Miss Betsy garden and some scotch bonnet and maybe some okra from the corner shop in Bell Town – *not* Ma'as Ken. Mumma will make up spinner dumplin. Is one long-long time since I taste pepperpot soup. Spit come inna my mouth. Is only tea I drink since mornin.

"I find one!" Marlon shout. "I get one, I get one!" Him hold up the river shrimp and I see is a big one.

"Wicked!" I yell, over noise a water. "Bring it here and find more. We going make pepperpot soup today!" Marlon run over, stumblin on rock and hole in the river bed. Him give me one big, grey janga wrigglin to get away. "Wrap him inna shirt," Marlon say. "Come help me look, nuh?" I take the janga, feel it stickin my hand. I wrap it in my shirt and put the shirt under a macca bush, away from the river. Marlon run ahead, jumpin on rock-them, splashin through the water. Today he is just one happy boy, out on the river, lookin for janga. Fuck Mr. Ken, I say in my head, fuck him for makin Marlon sad. I hear it all a the time, a course, but I don't say it. Fuck Holborn Prep and the uptown people. *Fuck everybody.* Thinkin this make me feel good. Me, I am one crab that will make it to the top a the barrel.

In front a me, Marlon disappear without a sound. One minute him is runnin along, splashin in him wet-up, tear-up short pants. Next minute, nothing. No boy. River take him just like that. For one second, I think a the man drownin in the cesspool, that must worse than the river with just water, dirt and stone. Then I run after Marlon, headin downstream, callin out him name. My heart beatin like a M-16. Brown river water hide my brother. Him going drown. Marlon going dead and is my fault.

I see a place ahead with plenty big rock, where the river run narrow and strong. That is the place to wait. I run fast, but is hard, rock turn over under my foot, water try knock me down. I know I can't run faster than the river. I get to the rock and turn 'round, lookin for Marlon. I sorry for every time I curse at him. I don't see anything in the mud and spray. I stand with my back against the biggest rock, lookin down inna channel. It not so deep there. If Marlon come down that way, I will see him.

And I do see him, arm and leg going every which way, like a big spider, drownin, spinnin in the water. I grab for him, grab him elbow or wrist, I don't know which, and him slip out a my hand. I try again, my foot slippin. Any minute now, the river take two a we. I grab the waistband a his shorts. The river fight me for him, but I hold on, I hold on, and then he is in my arm-them, and I look inna him eye and see him is alive. Marlon cough and spit and start bawl. We just stay there, him and me, against the rock, holdin on to each other, the river crashin past.

We go back to the bank, very careful now, lookin out for deep water. Then I see Rayton standin on the river bank. Him have my shirt in one hand and the janga in the other. Him laugh after us and head up the path. *Don't say anyting.* Marlon start cry again, makin one whole heap a noise. Him shiver like him sick. The sun still shine on river, but the day gone dark. I dry off my brother with him shirt and him quiet down, stop cry, stop shiver. We go up the path, walkin slow to make sure we don't get near to Rayton.

So that is how it is. The river do still have janga, but none for we. *Fuck everyting.*

Telephoning Lester

"I think I'm going to meet with Lester," I said to Lydia.

"Good. Why'd you change your mind?" She was making sauce for curried ackee and she wasn't really listening.

"Well, the name thing, partly. Although Carl says he's changed his mind about that. I dunno. I guess Carl is seeing more and more of him and I guess I should stop pretending it isn't happening."

"Hmm. Taste this. No, not with a spoon, you can't just eat curry sauce like that. Put it on a cracker or something."

I found a stale piece of hard dough bread and dipped it into Lydia's sauce. "Lovely. Might need a bit more scotchie."

"Give me a piece of that bread," Lydia said.

I broke off another piece and she tasted her sauce. She shook her head. "No, I don't think so. It's got enough pepper." Lydia often asked me to taste her cooking but rarely followed my advice. She started adding the fruit of the ackee to the rich ochre sauce.

"I don't know how to approach it, though," I said.

"Sar. Later. We'll talk later. I have to pay attention to this, or I'll overcook the ackee. Go and make sure the tables are set or something."

I strolled around Summer Lion. Two students who worked part time were setting up for the lunch crowd. The concrete floors had been swept and each table had a bowl of dried leaves as a centrepiece. One early couple was sitting at the far table, drinking passionfruit juice and talking earnestly. Looking very clandestine. Except for the last table the students were working on, everything was ready. I wasn't needed in the kitchen and there were no orders to take yet. I sat down at one of the tables.

How to approach Lester? Should I simply telephone his office and suggest a meeting? Get Carl to ask him to the house for supper? No, not the house. Too much opportunity for him to cast a critical eye over my Mona place. What did I want to meet him for anyway? Carl had been seeing him for months and I hadn't become involved. If I was honest, I did want Lester's help with our son's college education, but my refusal of his cheque all those years ago was in the way. The plain fact was, without Lester's help, Carl wouldn't go to college. His grades just weren't good enough for a scholarship.

I thought about the night when the man had been drowned by students at U.Tech – students like the two girls setting the last table – and the way Carl had helped with supper. He'd been trying to comfort me, to make up for my evening. We hadn't talked about the Jacob's Pen children since then. It was best to stay off that subject.

Carl had gone into Sixth Form at Campion in September. He could do one year or two – entering college afterwards. I didn't know what was best – to let him do Sixth Form in Jamaica, or send him away to college early. And where should he go to college? American universities were so expensive. I'd heard Canada was cheaper. Of course, he could go to university here, but I kept thinking about the students who had stoned a man until he drowned in a cesspit. No matter how many years passed, or how much I thought I was used to it, when there was a big decision to be made, I longed for a partner, a lover, a mate. A father for Carl. Someone I could call now, and suggest he come to Summer Lion for coffee. He'd say he was having a beast of a day, but he'd get away somehow. And he'd walk in, complaining about the parking and the heat, lean down and kiss my neck and sit opposite me. "So," he'd say, taking my hand across the table, "What's on offer today?" And I'd jump up and get him a slice of grater cake or sweet potato pone and Londel's rich, organic coffee, and we'd talk about Carl's future. *That's a fairy tale, Sar.* Perhaps we needed fairy tales.

I'd call Lester this afternoon. Suggest coffee at the restaurant.

We'd talk in a civilized manner about Carl. I'd ask about his new wife and son. It would be fine.

"Excuse me? Hello? We'd like to pay?" I realized the couple in the far corner had been trying to get my attention for a while. The students had vanished.

"Of course. I apologize. I'll get your bill right away."

As I walked to the kitchen, I heard the man say, "You'd better leave before me. I'll call you later." If they were married it was not to each other. Fucking men.

After the lunch rush was over, I went to call Lester, then realized I didn't know the name of his firm. I would have to wait until I saw Carl later. This was procrastinating – surely a law practice would have the name of the lawyers in the title. I looked for a telephone directory, but someone had borrowed it. I called directory enquiries, but hung up after the seventh ring. It would have to wait.

"What're you doing in here?" Lydia said from the door.

"Nothing. Came to make a phone call, but can't find the directory."

"I've got it. Soon come."

"No – it's okay, I'll do it tomorrow," I called, but Lydia had gone. I looked out the window. It was only four, but the sunlight was softening already. Lester would probably have already left for the day.

"Here's the directory." Lydia dropped it on my desk with a thump.

"Shit! Look out for my papers!"

"Oh, we're edgy, aren't we? What's going on?"

"Nothing! Nothing. Can't a person have a bit of privacy?"

"O-kay, then. Excuse me for breathing. Yes, Ma'am, just coming," she said to a customer hovering in the other room. "The accountant appears to be on strike. I'll get your bill directly."

I gritted my teeth and started turning pages. And there it was, "Longmore and Wilson, Attorneys-at-Law." I dialled the number, feeling dizzy, hoping the customer would keep Lydia busy until I'd completed my call.

DEXTER
An Inappropriate Conversation of a Sexual Nature

The Principal Mrs. Carpenter come to Special Ed. five minute before break time. "Good morning, boys and girls," she say.

"Good mornin, Mrs. Carpenter," we reply, all together, like we singin a song.

"Can I see you for a minute, Miss Gordon?" she say to our teacher. The Principal lookin at me hard.

"Certainly, Mrs. Carpenter. Students, continue reading the story of Abraham and Isaac. We'll talk about it when I get back. Miss Cornell, look after everything," she say to the teacher assistant. No Nightingale pickney would believe ten pickney have two teacher. Miss Gordon go out with the Principal.

I put my head down and start read. Me, I am readin much better now. Not as much as Marlon, who couldna read at all. I could read before, but now I know more word. My writin better too. I like science best; don't like religious studies. All the old story a Bible people; don't have anything to do with my life. Plus I don't like church people in Jacob's Pen – them always cryin down hell and fire on people. And everybody know how them really stay – them go on like they is good, but them do bad things like everybody. Even Pastor Morecambe: everybody know him sex with young girl plenty time. He even breed a couple a them.

Today is story about Abraham and Isaac, how God did tell Abraham to kill him own son. What kinda thing is that? Remind me a the crew-them in Jacob's Pen. We have two crew: Rustler Crew and Racehorse Crew. Young boy belong to them, some as young as me. Sometime them fight and shoot up the whole place. Lotta story tell about them – how you have to do things to get in, like carry a gunbag or t'ief a car from the Parliament buildin or the Ministry of Finance car park – something dangerous. Like a exam to get inna school. That is why the Abraham story remind me a crew – God give Abraham one exam. Him have to do something bad-bad before God will like him. Him have to be *obedient*, like teacher at Nightingale All Age always tell us. Do what big people say. I don't like that kinda God.

Miss Gordon come back. "Raymond," she say to me, "go to the Principal's office now."

"Why, Miss?"

"Just do as I say. You're in enough trouble already; don't make it worse."

Trouble. What I do now? I did come late last Tuesday – bus never come to Jacob's Pen 'til quarter to eight. Friday I run along corridor and Miss Thornton did tell me to walk like the school rule say. "Running is for the sports field, Raymond, you know that," she did say. Never hand in English homework 'bout two week ago; it was a composition and I can't write composition. Never can think of anything to say. This one suppose to be about a day on the farm – well, I never see a farm, much less spend a day there, so how I suppose to write 'bout that? "You should have used your imagination, " Miss Gordon say when she ask me where my composition is. "Like Marlon did. See, he hasn't been to a farm either, but he wrote something. I'm going to have to give you a demerit."

But none a those things really bad. All a them happen before and I never get call to the Principal office yet. They must be want throw me out a school. Feel sick.

Walk over to the Principal office; everybody must know I inna trouble. Knock on the office door. Somebody say, "Come in." Go inside to bright, air condition room.

"Raymond," Mrs. Anderson say. She the bursar and she must know why I inna trouble. "Sit over there. The Principal will see you in a moment."

"Yes, Miss," I say. I sit. Anastasia Gilbert sitting in another chair, cryin. A woman in cris clothes sittin there too; must be

Anastasia mother. She cut her eye after me. Don't know Anastasia hardly; she in Grade 6. She a pretty girl, some part chiney, some part coolie, some part white. She have smooth brown skin, not too dark, and shiny black hair. She tall and thin and everybody say she going be top model at Pulse. Boy at Holborn Prep *love* her. Everybody say she and that boy Travis, the first one to call me Big Foot – them say him and her is *dey* – boyfriend and girlfriend.

She in the bus on a field trip we go on last week. Whole a Grade 4, 5 and 6 go to Hope Garden. Only time I ever talk to her is on the way back from Hope Garden; she come sit beside me in the bus. Make me feel special for a while, but then I figure out she and Travis have a fight and she just want make him jealous. She did ask me a few question; how I like Holborn Prep and if it different from my last school and if I make friend there and what we do in Jacob's Pen. She say she hear ghetto children – she correct herself right away and say, "poor, I mean poor children" – she say she hear we all watch blue movie on the weekend. I say yes, I see a blue movie. I don't tell her is only one time I see such a thing and I never like it. She start ask me what it like and then Travis stand over her and tell her to come back to where they was sittin. I not surprise when she get up and go with him. She don't say anything more to me. Is okay. Girl like Anastasia not for me.

Now, she sit across the room from me, her eye red from cryin. I wonder what happen. Anastasia don't look at me. Cris woman look at me though, mouth zip up tight, vein a stand out on her neck. She a coolie, she have long, soft hair. She wear a white dress with dark blue stripe; it look bright against her coolie skin. Her shoe is dark blue to match the dress and she have a gold watch and gold earrin. This is one stush woman.

The Principal door open and Mrs. Carpenter walk inna the room. "Raymond?" she say, like she don't know is me.

"Yes, Miss!" I say.

"Please wait inside my office." I get up and go inside and she shut the door, so I am alone in the Principal office. I hear the Principal talk and Anastasia mother too, but can't tell what they say. I don't know if I must sit down, so I stand there. Is a nice little office, very cool. Mrs. Carpenter have one a those computer desk with space for all the different part a computer, and she have a regular desk with pen and pencil in a cup and a picture of her two girl children. They must be big woman now. I wonder if they come here to Holborn Prep when them was small. I start think about Mrs. Carpenter children. Prob'ly them had their own room with spread on the bed and bookshelf and even them own computer. TV in the room and desk and plenty light to do homework. I never see a uptown person house yet, but I watch 'nuff America TV on cable, over at Miss Betsy or sometime Mr. Collins, and I see how them people live. I sure Mrs. Carpenter children use to live like that too. When they was small, Mrs. Carpenter prob'ly come in every night and read them story and kiss them good-night.

Is funny, when I think about being a uptown pickney, I always think a being a girl. Sometime I wonder if this mean I a batty man. Is really hard to think a Jacob's Pen boy in him own room in a uptown house. Them wouldna match; them would be like cactus inna rain forest, lion inna snow.

The only boy I think about being is Miss Sahara son Carl, even though him never come with her to visit. I only see him two time – one time, when they was comin from the movie at Sovereign and another time when Miss Sahara see me at Sovereign and drive me home. Him was in the car that time.

If I was Miss Sahara son, she would be in here with me now. She woulda put her hand on my shoulder, like she do sometime, while the Principal outside a talk to Mrs. Gilbert. If I was her son, Miss Sahara woulda be on my side.

The door open and Mrs. Carpenter come in. She shut the door and walk around to other side of desk. "Sit, Raymond," she say. I sit.

"I am very disappointed in you, young man," she say.

"Why, Miss? What I do?"

"What have I done," Mrs. Carpenter correct me. All the teacher at Holborn Prep talk like that. Sometime it hard to figure out a conversation when everything get say twice, one time wrong and one time right.

"What have I done, Miss?" I say, tryin to be obedient, tryin to make whatever trouble I am in go away.

"Anastasia Gilbert has made a complaint about you. She says you had an inappropriate conversation with her on the field trip to Hope Gardens last week. An inappropriate conversation of a sexual nature."

Not so sure about the *inappropriate* thing, but know what is sexual. "What she say, Miss? She say me ask her for sex? Is not true, Miss, I swear it not true. Me – I – wouldna do that!"

"She didn't exactly say you asked for her sex. She claims you were talking to her about pornographic – blue – films. Is that true?"

"*She* did ask me about it Miss! She ask me if me ever see a blue movie! I seen it one time and I tell her. What she complain for? Is *she* ask me, Miss. Not me bring it up. True-true. You call her in here and you ask her."

Mrs. Carpenter give big sigh. "I know being here is difficult for you, Raymond. There are all kinds of rules you don't know about. But one of them is absolutely no talking about sex with any of the girls – well, not with the boys either. No sex talk – do you understand? You have to try and fit in. I'm afraid I'm going to have to tell your sponsor about this and ask her to have a talk with you. I'm not going to give you any other punishment, because it's your word against Anastasia's and I hope things happened as you say they did. Perhaps Anastasia misunderstood you, or perhaps you were just too graphic." She stop talk, which is good, since I don't understand what she say.

"You are not to go anywhere near Anastasia Gilbert from now on, though. Just stay away from her. She's not in your grade so there's no reason for you to be together. Okay? Do I have your word on that?"

I understand this part. I don't want go near Anastasia Gilbert; I hate her. I woulda like turn Boston or Lasco on her, or even the boy in Racehorse Crew. Mess up her uptown prettiness, kill her with hood, give her *pure agony*. What am I here for? Tryin to get a education? For *what*?

"Raymond?" Mrs. Carpenter say. "Do I have your word?"

"Yes, Miss. Stay away from Anastasia Gilbert. No sex talk.

Fit in. But I *can't* fit in, will *never* fit in. Holborn Prep student call me *Big Foot*."

Mrs. Carpenter don't say anything to that and I know she a pretend she don't hear the last part. She start pick up paper and put them in file on desk. She just a try look busy.

"You're dismissed, Dexter. I think you're a good boy, I know you're trying hard. You just have to keep out of trouble, that's all."

"Yes Miss," I say. Can hardly breathe with all the things I want say. Keep outta trouble! I just sittin in the bus on field trip I have to go on – what them call it? *Compulsory* field trip, that right. Compulsory. Mean you have to go. I on compulsory bus and Anastasia Gilbert come up and talk to me and now she cryin for no reason at all and I am in trouble. And now Principal tellin me I must *fit in*.

I get up and leave the Principal office. Outside, Anastasia Gilbert still cryin, her mother still sittin there lookin vex. I want to cut my eye after Anastasia, wicked girl, but I don't do it. I look down at my shoe – humble, obedient – and go outside inna the heat.

Get call to the Principal office again. It about a week since I get call there last time and see Anastasia Gilbert and her mother. I never tell Mumma what happen, or Marlon. Mrs. Carpenter don't send note home with me, and I hope the lie Anastasia Gilbert tell on me is forgot. But when Miss Gordon tell me I must go Principal office, I know is not the end a trouble.

Walk up to office. It just after break and school yard quiet – all children inna class. Children not allow to run up and down outside when class keep, not like at Nightingale. I hope children keep them head down inna book and don't look up to see me.

It comin up for December and day is cooler now. I been at Holborn Prep almost one term. I don't make a single friend. I learn things, though, true-true. I learn about not takin off shoe to go on play field, how to eat at a table with knife and fork, how to make letter and spell better, how to write sum on paper. At Holborn Prep, I do things I woulda never imagine before I come here – like write a poem, shake a tambourine in a band, hold a turtle in my hand on environment day. I learn about many place in the world and sometime I wonder what kinda life I woulda have if I was born some other place, maybe Greenland or Australia – not inna small Caribbean island. But more than some different place, I wonder what my life woulda been like if I born a different colour.

Is true children at Holborn Prep come in every colour – white, brown, red, black, chiney, coolie. But not so many black children for sure. And black children is the ones that don't talk good and get into trouble most time. The whitest one can be the cruelest, laugh after you and call you Big Foot or Ghetto Boy, but sometime them just keep themself separate. White children have white friend and coolie children have coolie friend. It not true every time, like, Sarah Mountjoy is white-white and she is friend with Shawna Winston, who is black-black, but it true a lot a the time.

Standin at the office door. Don't want to go in. Look out at car park; wonder if I shoulda run. Then I see a yellow VW inna car park and know Miss Sahara must be here. I was 'fraid before, but is then my heart start beat fast and I feel dizzy. Trouble with Miss Sahara is worse kinda trouble. If she decide to leave us – no Holborn Prep. I hate 'nuff things about Holborn, but I know when I think it all going to be taken from me, I hate Nightingale All Age more.

I knock. "Come in," say the bursar and I go in. Instead of Anastasia Gilbert and her mother sittin in the room, there is Miss Sahara. She wear a jacket and a plain short skirt – I never see her wear that kind a clothes before this. Her hair more neat. She look confuse. She have a line go right down the middle a her forehead to between her eye and she shake her head at me. I know she already believe what Anastasia Gilbert say.

"Dex," she say. Her voice soft. "I can't believe you let this happen. Why can't you stay out of trouble?" I feel anger like hot coal inna my chest. She no different from Mr. Reckord at Nightingale.

"Is lie she tell on me, Miss Sahara," I say, but I know it hopeless.

140

"Why she pick you to tell lie on? Why you even talk to her?" Just then the door open and Mrs. Carpenter come out from her office. "Ah, Mrs. Lawrence," she say. "Thank you for coming so promptly. Good morning, Raymond. Please come in."

We go inside and Mrs. Carpenter tell us to sit down. She close the office door and walk behind the desk. She put her hands together on desk, like she prayin, and she look at Miss Sahara. She say, "Mrs. Lawrence, as Raymond's sponsor, I've asked you to come here because a complaint has been made against him and I thought you should know about it. I've discussed it with him and he has a different version of events, but still, what happened is worrying and the other party's parents are very concerned about their daughter's safety..."

"What happened?" Miss Sahara say, interruptin.

"Well, according to Anastasia Gilbert, a Grade 6 student, Dexter made inappropriate remarks of a sexual nature to her while they were on a field trip to Hope Gardens. Apparently, he described a pornographic film he had seen in quite some detail. The girl was very upset, felt threatened, and told her mother. Mrs. Gilbert then reported the matter to me.

"Dexter, however, says that's not exactly how it happened. His story is that Anastasia came to sit beside him in the bus and asked him if he'd seen a pornographic film. He said he had and when Anastasia expressed curiosity about the film, he told her what he had seen."

"Is that what happened, Dex?" say Miss Sahara to me. I so grateful she call me "Dex" in that gentle way she have, so happy she ask me what happen, I want to put my head in her lap and bawl like a five-year-old. "Yes, Miss Sahara. That is how it go. I think Anastasia and Travis have a fight and she want make him jealous and that is why she come and sit beside me. I don't know her, but Travis *hate* me and Marlon."

"Why does Travis – Travis, who, by the way? – hate you and Marlon?" Miss Sahara say.

"Travis Walters," I say. "In Grade 6. Him a footballer. He hate me and Marlon for being ghetto pickney. Him call us Big Foot and Baby Big Foot."

Miss Sahara flinch like something hurt her. "Really? That's what children call you here?"

"All the time, Miss. All the time. Them call us Big Foot and Ghetto Boy and Dunce Cap and Ignorant and Slow Learner and Buttu – coulda *never* remember all the name we get call."

Miss Sahara look at Mrs. Carpenter, who don't look too happy about what I say.

"When did the name-calling start, Raymond? Why didn't you report it to me?" Mrs. Carpenter say.

"Happen first day we come, on the football field. I take off my shoe, like Mumma always tell me, just to kick some ball. The children laugh after us and Travis call me 'Big Foot'. If I report it, Miss, I would be call *informer*. Everybody just hate us more."

Mrs. Carpenter sigh, like she tired and want go home. She say something like, "I suppose that was inevitable." Don't know why teacher must use so much big word, they really hard to understand sometime.

"I'm sure life is not easy for Raymond, or Marlon, for that matter, Mrs. Lawrence. But you've given these children a tremendous opportunity and if they can manage to capitalize on it, I'm sure it will be a worthwhile investment. We've got to come up with a strategy to help the boys fit in and keep out of trouble," Mrs. Carpenter say. I don't understand the middle part, sound like *Morning Talk* on the radio, but I hear the part about keepin out a trouble.

"Dex?" Miss Sahara say. "Do you have anything you want to say?"

"Dunno, Miss. I never trouble Anastasia Gilbert. She ask me about blue movie and I tell her. What I do wrong? Why she not in trouble too?"

Mrs. Carpenter and Miss Sahara look at each other. They don't say nothin for awhile. Then Mrs. Carpenter say, "Well, perhaps I'll have to ask my staff to keep a closer eye on the boys. Lord knows, we want to help. We think they're remarkable children and we'd like to see them succeed – and we understand the situation, the home situation. Hmm. How about this? Suppose Raymond apologizes to Anastasia for offending her, even if he didn't mean to. He'll have to avoid her in future, I'm sorry to say, but perhaps an apology will defuse the situation."

"She have to apologize too?" I say quick-quick. "Why I always have to say sorry? She get me into trouble – *she* wrong, not me!" My voice go up and I know I am shoutin.

"That's enough," say Mrs. Carpenter. "I know this is hard, Raymond, I know it's unfair, but I'm going to ask you to do it just the same."

"Dex," say Miss Sahara. "Please. Just tell the girl you're sorry for offending her and you didn't mean to. Then everything will be okay and you can go on with your education. Please. Do it for me."

This is what Miss Sahara mean: do it for food on Sunday night, for the shoe, because you lucky, you *ghetto* pickney, you *lucky* they even let you in the gate of this uptown prep school to sit inna classroom, even with the *slow* children – you lucky you is not here cuttin the play field, sweepin the classroom.

I think about Lasco all of a sudden. I know him woulda laugh out loud at these two woman, him woulda kiss him teeth and tell them two bad word. Mi? Him woulda say. *Mi*? Tell the white gal mi sorry? For *what*? Suck you madda, him woulda say, the worst curse him could think up.

"Dex?" Miss Sahara say. And I look at her, the line between her no-colour eye, her pale mouth, the way she dress up little bit to come to school for me. She look worry. She reach over and put her hand on my shoulder and she say quiet-quiet so only me can hear – "Please Dex?" I get up and she stand up too and she put both of her arm around me and hold me close-close. Is the first time she ever touch me like that – maybe the first time *anybody* ever touch me like that. I feel sad to dyin. This a good woman, even though she don't know, *can't* know about my life.

"Dex?" she say again. "What do you want? What do you want to *be*?"

I answer in a second. "*Carl*, Miss. Your son. That is what – that is *who* – I want to be."

Waitin outside for Marlon and Lissa. Don't go back to class

after Miss Sahara leave. I walk with her to her car. Don't know what to say. She put her hand on my shoulder and she shake her head a little and she get into the car. I shut the door and just stand there. "Sunday, Dex," she say. "Sunday night. Go inside now." I nod my head and she drive away.

I sit under the divi-divi tree outside. It cool and peaceful. Security sleepin in him chair over the other side a the car park. If him did see me, he woulda tell me to go back inside school yard. I can hear low sound a traffic on Holborn Road, grassquit cheepin inna the bush and the voice a the teacher-them behind me. Holborn is one quiet place.

I stay there, waitin for Marlon and Lissa. Don't know why, since Marlon just going want know why I get inna trouble again. But he my brother, my family, even though him younger and I suppose to be the strong one. And it hard for him to take Lissa home by himself. I want to walk down the street with my brother and sister to the bus stop, go back to Jacob's Pen, maybe stop in Papine and buy patty and soda. Maybe we talk about lesson in school today or the time Marlon did nearly wash 'way in the river or what Mumma mighta cook for supper tonight. I hope for the bus to be empty, for it to come quick, for Marlon not to vex with me.

The bell ring and I hear the sound a the children comin out a them classroom, collectin them lunch pan, makin plan to talk about homework later on them cell phone. Some a them talk about how Christmas soon come and Brandon Cook's birthday party is on the weekend. I hear say him live in a mansion up in Stony Hill with swimmin pool and tennis court.

The gate creak behind me and I look to see who is first out. Is Felix and Miss Gordon pushin him wheelchair. "Let's go over to Dexter," she say. "He'll keep you company until your mother arrives." She push the wheelchair careful over the ground which is kinda rough for a wheelchair. Felix head bobbin up and down.

"Hello, Raymond," Miss Gordon say. "Would you mind waiting with Felix until his mother comes?"

"No, Miss."

"Okay, boys. See you both tomorrow." Miss Gordon smile

at us and go back through the gate. I look at Felix and see him not sittin right. All this time in class with him, I get to know how him like to sit. Him don't like to complain, but if him don't sit right, it hurt him. I go over and settle him right. Him not a big boy but he heavy.

"You in trou-ble a-gain?" him say.

"Um-hmm."

"Travis?" Felix don't use plenty word; it hard for him to talk.

"Sorta. More Anastasia."

"She tell lie on you?"

"How you know?"

"Is not the first time," Felix say. Him can't move hardly at all, but him see everything.

"Why she tell lie on me?"

Felix raise him eyebrow. You have to look hard to see what him is feelin, but if you get to know him, you can read the small way-them he move him face.

"She get bad marks and she don't want her mo-ther to pun-ish her for it. So she tell a sto-ry about you and her marks don't mat-ter so much."

Waitin. Other children come out and car start to drive up. End a day at Holborn Prep. Some children stay to play sport or do club activity or have extra lesson. I don't ever do any a that. Marlon come out, holdin Lissa hand. Him face make up bad-bad.

"What you get inna trouble again for?" him say.

"Hush!" Felix say. "Take it ea-sy. Not his fault."

Marlon suck him teeth. "What you do?" he say to me.

"He don't do any-thing," Felix say. "Just Anas-tas-ia tell lie on him."

"We waitin with Felix," I say to Marlon. "We waitin until him Mumma come for him. That's it." The four a us sit under the divi-divi tree and watch the Holborn children leavin. Mrs. Munroe is late today.

Christmas presents

"Should we talk about Christmas opening hours?" Lydia said.

"I guess."

"Well, you're the accountant. Do we need to open?"

"Depends on what you mean by 'need'." I said.

"You know what I mean. How well did we do this year? Can we pay bonuses?" Lydia expects the production of accounts to be more or less instant, like baking a cake. Ingredients in; delicious concoction out. Tools: bowl, measuring implements, an oven, a modicum of creativity. Voilà.

"Well, I have figures up to the end of November. December isn't finished yet, obviously, and the final result will depend on how much we open over the holidays and how many customers we have."

"*Duh*. So tell me November's figures, Einstein." Lydia was supervising Londel in the making of our sorrel Christmas drink, which was famous. We sold it by the bottle and claimed it had all kinds of health and aphrodisiac properties.

I nodded in Londel's direction, meaning I didn't want to dish out hard figures. "We did better than last year, this time," I said. "About twenty percent better. We have less money on the road too. We can pay bonuses." Londel looked up from grating ginger, but said nothing.

It was early December. The evenings had already closed in and the sun was down by six. The white euphorbia was blooming and Christmas work had been given out by the politicians. Banks were being bushed, trees limbed and curbs painted white. Sound systems were being tuned up. Stores had already put up their decorations. Our house was the only one on our road without icicle lights, which were the rage this year.

I felt empty. I hated Christmas – the parties that went on until all hours of the morning, the snarled traffic, the hysterical count of each year's murders in the media that seemed to take on special significance in December. I hated the appeals for charity, the sad stories of fires and illness that required donations, the platitudinous speeches by politicians. I hated being alone. I knew why Lydia was asking when we should open – she'd met someone. She was just figuring out how to broach the subject.

When Carl was small, we'd had fun at Christmas. We used to drive up into the hills and collect pine cones in a basket. We'd take a picnic and he'd bring along a friend and while I sat on the soft needles under the pine trees, they'd chase up and down playing cowboys and Indians or trying to catch lizards with nooses made from coconut fibres. We'd take the pine cones home and spray-paint them. Each year I tried to decorate something different to stand in for a Christmas tree – a piece of driftwood, an old iron gate or the five-foot-tall blossom of the maypole tree that vendors dried and sold on Mountain View Avenue. I could measure Carl's ages by the way he reacted to these projects – first, glee and excitement, then resistance and the wish to have a regular tree like everyone else, and now, complete indifference. These last couple of years, he'd had Christmas dinner with Mark and I'd eaten with Lydia. Invitations to Lydia's house for Christmas dinner were sought after – the food was extraordinary and the company eclectic. No turkey and ham for Lyds. One year she'd cooked Moroccan food and we'd sat on the floor and eaten with our hands.

"Why don't you get it over with?" I said to Lydia.

"Get what over with?"

"You know. Tell me. You've met someone, right?"

She flashed me a smile over her shoulder. For all her bulk, for all her determined independence, men loved Lydia. She was rarely without a lover. Oh, she flirted with my "fucking men" ideology, but it didn't suit her. Whenever she met a new man, I worried she'd marry him. Lydia was my family and marriage changed everything.

"Could be, mah girl, could be. Stop – too much ginger, Londel! Scrape out some, quick! Here, give me the spoon." She began scraping the floating ginger particles from the surface of the sorrel.

"So, who?"

"Oh, just a guy I met at the National Gallery exhibition last weekend. The one you wouldn't come to because you had to go to *Jacob's Pen*. Ben Something. He grew up in New York but he's come back to fa-a-nd his roots." She said the last three words in a fake American accent.

"Ben Something my foot," I said, laughing. "You know everything about him already."

"Could be. Well, some anyway. He's an investment banker. We're going out for drinks later, so I'll fill you in on the vehicle and the attire tomorrow."

"I spoke to Lester," I said suddenly, wanting to avoid the fact of Ben Something.

"You *what*?"

"I called him. We met. He's balding, can you believe that? And he's got bad teeth and bad breath – still smokes."

"What you telling me? When was this?"

"Oh, couple of days ago. We had coffee at a dreadful place downtown. We talked about Carl. He says he's happy to help with college, he'll even give him a summer job next year, see if he likes law."

"Halleluja. How come you didn't tell me?"

"I'm telling you now."

"So are you happy about it?" Trust Lydia to go for the jugular.

"Yes. I guess. I dunno. I wanted to do it all on my own. But I can't afford college, so yes, I'm happy about it. I want Carl to go away to school."

"He won't be studying law, I can tell you. You have to work too hard at that."

"Lydia. Stop. Carl is a good boy... He asked me to Christmas lunch," I said, suddenly fighting tears, assailed by an image

148

of young Lester, long-limbed and shaggy-haired. Sexy. Promising a life I had not lived. Now had no chance of living.

"Who? Carl?"

"No, course not. Lester. And wife."

"Are you going?"

"No. I'm coming to you, as usual."

"Have a taste," Lydia said, offering me a spoon of the deep red sorrel.

We got our Christmas bonuses. They were generous. Carl announced he was going to Mark for Christmas dinner. Ben Something was coming to Lydia's. Two days before Christmas, I fought my way into the plazas and I spent every cent of my bonus on presents for the Jacob's Pen children – toys, clothes, shoes, food, even a new dress for Arleen. Summer Lion closed after lunch on Christmas Eve and I drove to Jacob's Pen with everything. I parked and got out, my hands full of packages wrapped in shiny Christmas paper. The light was fading and the sound systems were ascendant, but I heard Marlon's voice behind the half-open door, "She a come!" And I stood beside the car, my hands full, waiting for the children to help me carry their Christmas presents into the Habitat for Humanity house, now painted pale yellow with khaki trim.

PART TWO

DEXTER
Helpfulness and Most Improvement

This a one hot summer, but we lucky so far, only two tropical storm. No hurricane yet. Last Sunday I go church with Mumma. I don't hardly go church, but I go last Sunday. Pastor tell everyone that Jamaica is bless, look how many time storm draw bead on us and swerve away at last minute. He talk about Mitch, this one hurricane that start down by Mexico last year and come straight up the Caribbean Sea. When the storm see Jamaica, it draw brake and turn around and hit a place call Honduras. Plenty people dead over there, pure mudslide and floodin. Pastor say the Lord spare Jamaica, but I want know what sin people in Honduras do that Jamaica people don't do? Plenty sin right here. When I think about sin, I think about Lasco and Boston and all those people havin sex on TV.

The last storm, Tropical Storm Desmond, brush by the north coast two day ago. Coulda been a whole heap worse for Kingston. We get plenty rain and breeze and river swell up and wash away two car. Jamaican people can't understand not to drive into a river fordin in heavy rain. The two man in the two car get 'way – nobody drown this time. People go to the river bank to watch – yes, people come out a them house inna the rain to go watch car wash 'way. Them say the two man come out a water callin on God. One man, inna a blue Camry, him curse God, ask God why him bring down trouble on him when him don't done pay for the Camry yet and him only have it for two month, and if God don't know is a *serious* man him borrow the money from and the interest is fifty percent *per week*, and if God don't know what will happen if him don't pay it back, him *and* baby mother will be kill – prob'ly baby too – and now him have no car, and if God don't know him run taxi with the Camry, and is only that keep bread on the table. Accordin to Miss Betsy, this man use to live 'round Jacob's Pen, did grow up a ways up the road, near a squatter settlement call Bedrock, but him leave after him fail Grade 9 Achievement Test and him mother don't hear from him from that day to this. The day a the storm, when him Camry wash 'way, that was the first time him come back to Jacob's Pen and the community have it to say that him only did come back to show off. *That* is why him car wash 'way, Miss Betsy say, that is why God took it from him. Vanity and pride, Miss Betsy say, vanity and pride.

The other man, him was in one mash-up old pick-up, him come out a the river quiet-quiet. Him never call on God first thing. Him stand still in the river and look at him car hitch up on a rock with the water gettin high around it. Then the river tear it 'way, and it roll over and over, going down to the sea.

That man come out a the river soakin wet and stand on river bank in front a all the people. "Bwoy, man, you lucky," somebody say. "You coulda dead." The man fall on him knee and start praise the Lord. Miss Betsy say she *never* hear a man send praise to heaven in a rush like that. She say the man don't draw breath for fifteen minute. Nobody don't know that man; him not from round here, prob'ly takin short cut like people do when storm comin and they rushin to get home.

Summer takin long to pass. Sometime I want it over. Other time, I don't want September to come. September mean back to school. A new school. One high school. Because I pass for St. Stephen's.

We almost never go to graduation from Holborn Prep. Mumma never have a frock or shoe – well, to tell the truth, all a we almost never go to graduation because me and Marlon need white shirt and grey pants and school tie. If Miss Sahara never buy everything we need, none a us woulda go. Even with new clothes, I never did want go. Mumma too; I know she frighten to go. All a them uptown people in one place! You can say them is just people, same as we, some good, some bad, but when you see them, you know them a more different from us than goat is from butterfly.

But when Mumma say she not going to my graduation, Miss Sahara, she kick up one fuss! She stand up beside me and she put her arm around my shoulder and she say, "You're going, Miss Arleen! You *are* going. Dex has worked too hard for this. What is it – you don't have clothes? We'll buy clothes. You're going and so is Marlon and so is Lissa."

So all a we go. And it did hard for true – 'specially when we get out a Miss Sahara car and see all a the big car in the car park and all a the woman! Lookin so young and beautiful with them brownin self and them make-up and jewellery and high heel and fashion! Them call to each other and talk on cell phone and some a them walk in holdin hand with man; them *husband*, I suppose.

The Holborn children, too, look polish-up 'til them shine! Belinda Shoemaker walk past, very dignify, carryin her violin in a case. We did all hear her practisin 'til we sick a it. Holborn children dress in costume from different-different country. "Look Mumma," say Marlon, "see Sunana Roy, she from India." Sunana dress in a big orange cloth, wrap 'round her, over and over, and she stand up straight like a princess. "That her sari," Marlon say. The orange cloth look airy and you can see silver thread in it – this sari not like any cloth we ever seen. It look bright against her brown skin. Is hard to stop lookin at her, this Sunana Roy, she so beautiful with her black hair and black eye with the white so pure, her eyebrow shape like bird wing, her dark brown skin and her smilin mouth. "She not really from India," Marlon say, "she born right here, but her mumma come from a place call Bombay. Mumbai they call it now." I know from him voice that him like off this Sunana Roy.

Peter Lyn dress in a chiney costume and Keisha Smith a wear African dress. She have a long piece a cloth wrap 'round and 'round too, but is not like the silvery sari – no, this cloth made a cotton with a brown pattern, different type a brown, with thick black line, like the pattern you see when you close your eye after a bright light. She have a scarf tie 'round her head too, and she have tiny seashell around her wrist and ankle and big hoop earring. She don't wear any shoe. Why only the African girl is barefoot? Make it look like African people backward. Every other chile in foreign clothes a wear shoe.

The five a we stand together. Lissa did hold Miss Sahara hand when we did walk in, but then she turn to Mumma and raise her hand-them – she want Mumma to pick her up. Sometime I still surprise Lissa ever learn walk. "Shh," Mumma say. "Wi soon sit down."

Teacher call out to Miss Sahara – they all know her. Nobody talk to Mumma. She come to Holborn Prep one time – first day. After that, never.

Felix mother come over too. She not too dress up. She say, "Hi Sahara, hi boys. Is this your mother?"

"Yes, Miss," say Marlon. "This our mother."

"Nice to meet you, Mrs. Morrison," say Mrs. Monroe, givin Mumma name wrong. "I'm Tina Munroe. My son, Felix is in the same class with your boys. Raymond has been very good to Felix – you should be proud of him." Mumma don't say anything to Mrs. Monroe and I feel shame.

"Well, enjoy the ceremony," she say and walk away.

"A who Felix?" Mumma whisper.

"Him," I say. I point. I know Mumma is shock when she see a retard boy inna wheelchair.

Miss Gordon come up and say I must come with her. "Let's find some seats," Miss Sahara say, and she turn to find seat near the back. "We'll see you later, Dex." The crowd a people start settle down, the uptown people put away their cell phone and stop callin to one another. I go with Miss Gordon to the classroom. Children in costume gettin ready. A man on stage say, "Testing, testing, one, two, three," into the mike and it give out one awful screech. People laugh. We line up beside the blue shelf for lunch box and I think about the first day I come to Holborn Prep. Can hardly believe two year pass and I get good enough mark in G-SAT for St. Stephen's. I know nobody can believe it.

We line up and teacher tell us be quiet, and then we hear piano music and all the children who are to graduate today go marchin in line up to the seat at the front a the hall. Anastasia and Travis leave last year. Me, I glad I don't have to see them. Girl who are graduatin all dress in white, them have ribbon in them hair and them wear black shoe with little heel. A few a them have on make-up, them mouth too pink and them eye too bright. I know what Mumma have to say about that! Force ripe, she going say, inna young girl, bound to bring trouble.

The graduatin boy-them dress in white shirt and tie and grey pants. I am in line right in front a Felix, but he is being push by Charlton McKenzie. I wish Miss Gordon ask me to push Felix, but she say something about alphabetical order. We all stand in front a our chair. Piano playin stop and a man in a suit go up on stage. Him raise him hand over us like him preparin for blessin and everybody sit down together. This man tell us him is Chairman a the School Board and him is proud to be there and now we must pray.

Graduation take long – hour upon hour. I win two prize – one for Most Improvement and one for Helpfulness. I can tell the prize-them is book. Seem to me like every child win a prize – even Felix get one for Overcoming Obstacle. The Chairman a the School Board come down to where Felix a sit to give him the prize. Then the costume children come up on stage and do different kinda music – African drummin and singin and a few children play the violin. Graduation only end after night fall.

When it over, nobody seem to want to go home. Children come up to them family and they get hug and tell how good they is. I take Felix chair and push him over to Miss Sahara, Mumma, Marlon, Lissa. Miss Sahara say, "Congratulations, Dex. I'm so proud of you. Who's your friend?"

"This is Felix," I say. When I look at Miss Sahara, I shock to see she a cry, really cry. "I'm a fool," she say and look in her handbag for something to wipe her face.

"Supper?" Miss Sahara say, when she done dry her eye. "Let's go out and celebrate. Where shall we go?"

"Kentucky, Miss Sahara," say Marlon, quick-quick.

"Dex's choice," say Miss Sahara. "This is his night."

"Kentucky," I say.

"Really?" she say. "Don't you want to go somewhere more special?"

"No, Miss – Kentucky!" me and Marlon say.

"Can Felix come?" I say. Miss Sahara look confuse.

"Well, Dex, he's welcome, but I'm not sure we can fit his chair in the car."

"His mother will bring him. You want Kentucky, Felix?"

"Ken-tuck-y! Y-e-s, Kentucky," Felix say.

Mrs. Munroe come over then and Miss Sahara ask her very nice if she want come eat Kentucky with everybody. Mrs. Munroe smile and say thank you very much, but she have to get Felix home and is better if him eat food he accustom to. I squat down in front a Felix so his face and mine on a level. "I gone, Felix. See you." Both a we know that not true. Felix don't say anything but him look down at my prize in him lap where I rest them. "You keep mine for me," I say. Felix nod him head, but him don't look up.

"Don't you want your prizes, Dex?" say Miss Sahara.

"Felix will use them more than me." I can see Miss Sahara want say something about that, but she stop herself.

We all start walk away and I don't look back. End a Holborn Prep. Me hungry and me only eat Kentucky Fry Chicken one time in my life before this.

SAHARA
Going to college

"Have you got everything, Carl?"

"Yes, Mom, relax. You've asked me that a hundred times. I've got everything. Can I drive?"

"If you like." My son now driving – the L-plates had come off the car several weeks ago. He hated my car, of course, but it was wheels, and in the driver's seat he was a man. I knew it wouldn't be long before he braked suddenly at a traffic light and put out his hand to prevent me from hitting the windscreen – our roles turned upside down, my life on a downslope.

He loaded the luggage. Les had been generous in the end – not only paying Carl's tuition to Florida State, but sending two air tickets so I could fly up with him and get him settled. All summer long, we'd been engaged in preparations for college – a student visa, application forms, selection of classes, accommodation, clothes. I was calm. It was the right thing. I certainly didn't want a son who lived at home until he was thirty-five, comatose on the sofa or surfing the Internet. No, it was going as planned. Carl had graduated fifth form, Grade eleven, as it was called these days, did reasonably well in his CSEC exams and even better in his SATs. Another thing Les paid for – SAT classes.

Carl had never been much of a student; he did what was required but nothing more. He sent out six college applications – wouldn't even let me see them. Said it was between him and his father. "You've got to let go, Mom," he said, covering the prospectuses with his hand. I shrugged.

I was surprised when he selected Florida State – so close to

Jamaica. He'd always said he wanted to go as far away as possible, a statement that hurt me as it seemed to reflect on our relationship. I imagined him in Scotland, maybe, or Canada. But I knew he was averse to the cold. I don't know why, he's never seen winter, but he often said he was going to college somewhere warm, where he could still go to the beach and learn how to surf. I suspected his choice had something to do with a girl he'd just started seeing, Kimberly Foster. I'd asked him directly if she was going to Florida State and he'd said she hadn't decided yet. "Butt out, Mom," he'd said.

We drove to Lydia's house. She'd offered to drive my car back from the airport and get it serviced for me.

Lydia was waiting on her verandah; Ben was in her favourite rocker, reading the newspapers. I got out, tilted the front seat forward, waved to Ben and struggled into the back seat. "Hi Sar," Lydia said over her shoulder as she settled herself in the front passenger seat. "What's happening Carl? Going away to school, huh?"

We drove down Mountain View Avenue. I looked up the turn-off to Jacob's Pen, as I always did when I drove past it. I wondered where Dexter was right now. *Don't think about it.*

"Slow down, Carl, there are always police on this stretch. We don't want a ticket and a delay," I said. He made a little sound of exasperation and I had a moment of fear for him – the young are so *careless.*

I remembered Dexter telling me he wanted to *be* Carl – that was the time he'd got into trouble at school. I was surprised when he said it – he'd only met Carl twice. Eventually I realized it was the *idea* of Carl Dex longed for, not Carl the person. It was the idea of his life. The list of things Carl was and had was long – and Dex would never be or have those things. Dex would not be going away to college. Dex might not make it through high school. I prayed he'd see his eighteenth birthday.

Okay, enough. I'd done what I could, was still doing what I could. Isn't that what we all say? We do what we can. There's always someone in trouble; you can't help everybody.

We stopped at the Windward Road traffic light. A street boy

ran up to the car, knocking insistently on my window, making lewd faces, then switching tactics and calling me "Madda". How and when had I become "Madda", I wondered fleetingly, instead of "sweet gal" or even "browning". The boy plastered his mouth to the window in a parody of a kiss. Carl waved him away and he began swearing; we could only hear him dimly, but we could see his mouth contorting around every type of claat and hole. In a few years, he'd be more dangerous than a hungry crocodile.

We turned onto the Palisadoes Road and drove along the harbour. The wind was up and the water was choppy with whitecaps. Even though it was a weekday, a sailboat tacked its way east, its sails bright against the water. Kingston Harbour was polluted – only poor people ever swam in it now. I imagined the people in the sailboat flinching at the spray as it came over the deck – it would smell of sewage.

"So Carl," Lydia said, trying to be friendly. "Are you looking forward to college?"

"Yes," said Carl.

"What will you be studying?"

"Business."

"Ah. Maybe you can take over my accounts when you come back. Give your mother a rest."

Carl didn't answer. Everybody in the car knew I needed Lydia's job.

We drove into the airport. Horns blared, travellers shouted at their relatives, taxi drivers abandoned their vehicles in front of "No Waiting" signs. Carl pulled up on a pedestrian crossing and immediately a policeman came over and asked him to move the car. "We're leaving right now," he said.

"You no hear what mi say, yout'?" the policeman said. "Move di car."

Lydia opened her door and got out. "Officer," she said, "I'm just letting them off. We'll be gone directly." Lydia could speak like an old-time elementary school teacher when she was ready. The policeman sucked his teeth and moved off.

We struggled with the luggage, dragging it out from the back seat and the VW's tiny trunk. Carl waved away an enthusiastic

161

porter. Lydia was already back in the front seat of the car, so I couldn't hug her goodbye. I patted her shoulder through the window, surprised to find my eyes tearing up. It wasn't time for that, surely. "Thanks, Lyds, look after the old bug for me. I'll be back in a week – you've got our hotel. Don't forget to ask Londel about those receipts!"

"'Bye, Sar. See you soon. All the best, Carl." She put the car in gear and reversed into the chaotic traffic. She waved at the glowering policeman who was returning, no doubt to object to the length of time our departure was taking.

We fought our way into the terminal building. As soon as we were inside, I felt it was going to be a good journey – the air conditioning was working and the lines were short.

DEXTER
What to want

August: sun fryin Kingston. Independence Day is next week and I want go street dance with Lasco. I start see him in Jacob's Pen this summer – him never used to come up this way. One time I see him with Merciless and I 'fraid for him. Merciless a serious man, him run Racehorse Crew, even though him young. I see him and Lasco laugh and touch them fist. Lasco can take care a himself, all the same. Most day I sit on the wall and wait for him to come by. Last time I see him, he carryin cell phone. Maybe things gettin better for Lasco.

"What you doing up there, bwoy?" Miss Betsy call out on her way to church. Miss Betsy go church every day of life – if her church don't keep, she just go another one.

"Nutt'n, Miss Betsy. Just a wait for a frien'."

"You idle, bwoy. Idle hands come to no good. Why you don't look a work down a gas station in Papine? Or help Pastor up at the church? Big bwoy like you, a time you start bring home some money."

"Yes, Miss Betsy." I say. She pass by, shakin her head. No point tellin her is me still bringin home the money, no matter what Miss Sahara say about not beggin. True, it easier because she bring food every week. But we still need money and I still go Plaza to beg. Not Sovereign, though – could buck her up there like last time. I gettin too old to beg, comin on fourteen. People don't sorry for you when you start get big. Marlon soon have to take over.

I think about St. Stephen's, where I going next month. I 'fraid. Is a big high school, near downtown. I remember I used

163

to scared a Holborn. It was rough, but I glad I don't get expel. I still surprise I pass G-SAT. For one whole term at Holborn, teacher just give us G-SAT paper to do. Mumma tell everyone inna Jacob's Pen how I pass for St. Stephen's and even Ma'as Ken say, *Big up, bwoy. Never think you did have it in you.*

"Wha'ppen, star?" a voice say. I look inna the sun and can't see who hail me up at first.

"Is you Lasco?" I say, puttin my hand over my eye.

"A mi, Boston. But I lookin for Lasco? You seen him?"

"Not since mawnin. What you a do up this way?"

"Lasco and mi have a mission," Boston say, walkin over. I see him grow big, him one hand bulk up like him a lift weight or cut cane. Him put him one hand on the wall and jump up beside me. Him a wear 'nuff cargo.

"What kinda mission?" I say.

"Stay out a what don't concern you. See you now? You too young for di runnins."

"What runnins? After me is nearly fourteen. And me pass for St. Stephen's."

"Hear dis now! Jacob's Pen pickney a go high school! Dem going nyam you a dat school." Boston laugh and take some darkers from his pocket and put them on. Him look like a big man, cool, you know.

"What you know 'bout St. Stephen's?" I say.

"Plenty. Watch out for a yout' name Carlyle. Russian, dem call him. Him like to mek Molotov cocktail."

I don't know what is Molotov cocktail, but I don't want ask. We sit on the wall and wait for Lasco. We don't know if he will come today or tomorrow or never, but we don't have nothing better to do.

Lasco don't come that day or the next. Every day Boston come from Nevada and we sit on the wall, waitin. We don't talk. Old people in the community walk past, a shake them head. Marlon sit on front step a the house, watchin the two a we. I wonder how it feel to have one hand chop off, to see the man comin with the 'las, to not know if him going cut off you hand or you head.

"Dexter! Come here!" Mumma shout out. She going say she want me go a shop or to standpipe, but what she really want is for me come off the wall and get 'way from Boston. I don't answer.

"Time for madda soon done," Boston say. "I gone."

"Where you goin?"

"Dunno. Just gone. Hear say Merciless need lookout work over at construction site on Elletson Road."

"Pay work?"

Boston suck him teeth, meanin, a course, pay work.

"What you mean, lookout work?"

"You no watch TV, yout'? When someting bad going down, fryer look out for Babylon, give warnin if dem a come. Pay good."

"Me comin wit' you," I say.

"You sure, high school bwoy? You madda a call you." Boston laughin after me. I shame. This is what him mean: me still a pickney, me a mumma's boy, me *tryin* to be a uptowner, me want to be bigger than him, me think I can get 'way from Jacob's Pen with schoolin, and everybody inna ghetto know *that* a lie bigger than Dallas Mountain. Bigger than Blue Mountain Peak. My head go round and round and I close my eye-them. I see bright yellow spot and feel dizzy. Don't know what to want. To be like Felix, acceptin my life, lookin around, makin sense a it, still managin to smile. Or to be like Rayton and the big boy in Jacob's Pen, kickin over bucket, terrorizin small pickney. Them boy get respect. Or to be like Boston, whose hand chop off over nothing, and who still stand tall and look for work. Or Lasco, who nobody with any sense will ever mess with.

I jump off the wall and follow Boston. Lasco don't come today again, and I don't care what Mumma want.

SAHARA
Keeping vigil

Late August in Florida was hotter than Jamaica – the air was still and clogged with moisture. The drive from the Talahassee airport was short, along a road with strip malls. I drove too cautiously and Carl was irritated.

We drove into the university – a mix of fake old buildings, low-slung glass and steel edifices, lawns and landscaping. Carl found the instructions we'd been given to find his dorm. After an exchange of paperwork, a distracted woman with a head-tie gave us directions to his room. The hallways were full of students and parents, carrying TVs and laundry baskets full of modern-day essentials.

We found the room – a tiny basement room with very little storage, but he hadn't wanted to share. There was a desk under a high window and when you stood you could see the unnaturally green lawns, soggy with irrigation. At least being in a basement would be cool. I wanted to unpack and set Carl up, but resisted it. I'd never been particularly motherly, but just then I felt like mothering. He opened one of his bags and started taking out things. I could tell he wanted me to go.

"So," I said, sitting on the bed. "You're here." He didn't reply, just went on stuffing clothes into the only cupboard. "How do you feel?"

"Okay," he said. "Good. Could you pass that small bag?"

When all the bags were empty, there was still a pile of things on the floor. Carl picked up a poster and unrolled it – it was the Jamaican flag. He pinned it up on a large cork board that took up almost all of one wall. He put up no other pictures, no photos of school friends, no sporting moments, no picture of

Kimberly. No photos – I tried to dodge the thought – of me.

"Soon come," he said and opened the door. "Gone to check out the bathrooms."

I looked around the tiny room. I was jealous. I'd not been to college and I had a good brain – I could have done well in college. I could have studied literature, maybe could have had a life as an academic or a writer. Sitting in my son's college room, I was stung by the knowledge that I wasn't nineteen, with everything ahead of me.

There was a knock on the door and I said, "Come in." Two young girls peered around the door and one said, "Oh! Sorry. We're looking for Carl Lawrence. Are you his mother?" She checked a clipboard she was carrying. She was lanky; model material, with a blonde ponytail on the side of her head and a diamond in one nostril.

"Yes," I said, getting up and extending my hand. "Sahara Lawrence. Carl's just gone to the washrooms."

"Melissa Lang. Okay. We'll come back. We want to take him to a freshers' party."

"He'll only be a minute," I said. "Why don't you wait?"

"Well, like, we've got other freshmen to talk to. We'll come back."

"Nice to meet you both," I said, although the other girl hadn't spoken. Just then, Carl's head appeared behind them.

"There he is now," I said and my voice sounded bright and insincere, like a nurse talking to a terminally ill patient. "Carl, these girls are looking for you."

"Hi," said Melissa. "We've come to take you to a party."

"You're *Jamaican*?" said the other girl, speaking for the first time. She was Latino and chewed a large wad of red gum. "Like Bob Marley? You don't look like a Jamaican."

I smiled and said, "There're a few of us light-skinned ones around." Carl looked embarrassed.

"Go on, son. Go to the party. I'll finish up here and head back to the hotel. Why don't you call me later?"

"Sure. Whatever. 'Bye Mom. Later." He leaned down to give me a brief kiss on the cheek – I still wasn't used to him being taller than me. "Let's go," he said.

I'd better be cool, I thought. "Okay, son. Have fun."

"Your mother is okay," I heard Melissa say from down the hallway. "You should see what some others do." I imagined she was responding to Carl's apology for my existence.

I sat on the bed and waited for tears, but I wasn't particularly sad. Carl has left home. When you go back, you'll be in the house alone. You're officially middle-aged. You'll have an empty nest. None of these phrases had the desired effect – I wasn't sad. I was actually glad Carl had gone to a party and our farewell had been so low key. I congratulated myself on being sensible.

Yet that night I couldn't sleep. I lay on the scratchy bed-spread in my Holiday Inn room, the air conditioner at full blast, flicking through TV offerings. I'd ordered room service, ate a cream-laden soup that gave me indigestion. I'd bought Michael Crichton's new novel in the airport, but it failed to interest me. It was close to midnight and Carl hadn't called.

The party was probably still going on. Midnight was early for a teenager – like owls, emerging at night to hunt, spending days in the dark with their eyes closed to slits. Or Carl had lost the number of the Holiday Inn. Or he'd forgotten. Besides, once I went home, there'd be no one calling to say: I'm home.

And it was this thought that filled me with loss. If Carl didn't make it back to his room one night, who would know? This was college in the US – non-attendance at a few classes wouldn't be noticed. Perhaps he wouldn't make friends and there'd be no one knocking on his door – *Hey Carl? Dude? You in there?* No one to tell another set of friends – *Guys, I don't know where Carl is, any of you seen him recently?* No one to find the dorm manager and stand fidgeting at the door as it was opened to reveal – what? A bed neatly made with dust on the covers? Signs of a struggle, furniture overturned, books on the floor?

This was stupid. Carl was safer in Florida than in Jamaica and I'd never worked myself into such a state when he went out at home. But it was my vigil that had kept him safe all these years. I pleaded with the forces of the universe. Keep my son safe.

DEXTER
Lookout work

Summer over now and soon time for school. For three week now, I been doing lookout work on the construction site with Boston. I tell Mumma and Miss Sahara that I get a job sweepin up at a hardware store in Papine. Them don't ask too much question and Mumma love the money. I only give her some a it, all the same. Lasco come by the construction site sometime, but him don't do lookout work. Him say him never workin for any man, woman or chile. Him say if you work for somebody, you a slave.

Lookout work sound excitin, but it borin. I sit on a wall at one end a Border Lane; Boston sit at the other end. If we see Babylon, we take off our shirt. One other boy, Ted, him younger than me, him see we take off our shirt and him run, low to the ground like a mongoose, and tell man runnin the construction work that Babylon a come. Before you can look round two time, all ganja hide, all knife and gun put in sewer pipe.

I 'fraid a the man-them on the construction site, but I want to get to know them too. It hard work labourin inna hot sun all day, with the contractor bawlin after you for every slip you make, but the pay good. The man who work there is mostly young, from seventeen to maybe nineteen, very strong, fight over everything. Is a PNP construction site; no Labourite is allow. Jacob's Pen is a PNP area, so I can go there.

The construction man give us spliff to smoke and share them food with we. I learn to smoke and I like how it make the world go far away, but make it big and sharp at the same time, how colour get bright and how sweet sno-cone taste. I like how

169

the bitter tastin smoke make my head quiet down and my feelins turn mellow. I start learn how to cook, and almost when is time for school, I get cookin work, as well as lookout work. I start have money in my pocket.

"You a do awright, yout' man," Lasco say quiet-quiet. Him squat down beside me. I just finish make a huge Dutch pot a curry goat. Him hand me a spliff and I take a big drag. Spit come inna my mouth; can hardly wait eat the curry goat, but know alla the big man must eat first.

"You goin back to school?" Lasco say. "September 'round di corner."

"What you want know for?" I say. Lasco don't look so poor any more, him clothes look new, him not so thin. I think he going laugh after me for schoolin and I don't know how to explain that if I don't go school, Miss Sahara stop bring food and stop pay for Marlon and Lissa schoolin. We still a write letter to the foreign people who pay school fee. I learn how to do it after a while; make up story after story. Sometime me wonder if Miss Sahara believe the story I write down, I see her lookin at me funny, but she don't ask me anything. She like Marlon and Lissa more than me.

"Just want know. Schoolin a one ting, bein a man a different ting."

"What you mean?"

"Later you and mi go pon a mission."

After the construction site close down for the night, Lasco and me get inna taxi with five man. I don't know the man more than so; know their name, but not more than that. We squash up and I don't like being so close to the man-them. I think about the time when Boston and Lasco watch blue movie and how I did wonder if them was batty man. No, couldna be true. Boston not here tonight. All these man couldn' be batty man. The taximan is old and him hunch over the steerin wheel, like him a expect a lick from behind. The man-them is rowdy and make joke about the driver, tell him a bottle a white rum waitin for him after the night done.

The taxi start leave the city and climb up inna the mountain. There is no street light and all around is dark bush. I wonder if I will see the light a day tomorrow. I look over Carlton, the man who sit next to me, and I catch Lasco eye. Him shake him head and I know him tellin me not to worry. Him is with me and nobody – *nobody* – mess with Lasco.

We drive so long I start get sick. The moon come out and the mountain turn to silver. Road get narrow and bush scrape the car. The air rushin in the window is cool and I want shiver, but I hold myself. Not good to shiver in front a man. I don't know where we a go. I want to get there *and* I wish I never get inna this taxi. I want sleep; want to be inna my bed at Jacob's Pen, Marlon, Mumma and Lissa in the next room. Tomorrow is Sunday – I will stay home at night and wait for Miss Sahara. She been away – she take Carl to university in foreign. I don't want think 'bout that.

Must be near midnight before the taxi drive inna brokedown gateway. Can see the shape a buildins and hear man-them talkin. Car stop and we get out. Everybody stiff up in the taxi. Everybody stretch. Hear a wild shout a laughin.

We follow Lasco round the side a one a the building-them – look like one old farmin place – and see a whole heap a man sit around a fire. The flame leap up high, crackin and hissin. I can see the face a the man-them, them face shinin with the heat. One man stand up and say, "Lasco. Who you bring wit' you?"

"Just some a the man-them from Elletson Road."

"Hope you know what you a do."

The five a we sit near the fire. The man-them smoke and pass around a bottle a white rum. I take some and it burn my mouth. I want cough, but I don't. Nobody payin attention to me, not even Lasco. My head start to swim and I want sleep. White rum and ganja make the night one big confusion. I crawl away from the fire and lie under a bush. Maybe I will never get home. This a where I will end up, somewhere, I don't know where, with the moon hangin low in the sky, with man I don't know. Just before I fall asleep, I hear the sound a the patoo – *whaagh* – and I think a Marlon and how him 'fraid a patoo.

A terrible bawlin wake me up. I sit up and lick my head on the bush. Macca tangle up inna my hair. Need a haircut. I sleep so deep I don't remember for a minute how I come to be in this place. Day comin up and everywhere is grey. I feel sick and can't think straight. I crawl out from the bush, pullin the macca out a my hair. I stand up and look for who a bawl and for Lasco. I see him standin with some a the men, but the mornin foggy and I can't see what is happenin too good. The bawlin turn to a gurgle, like dirty water going down a drain. I am cold and wet – sleepin outside mean plenty dew. I want go home.

I walk over to the man, standin in a circle. I push through the circle and see them lookin at a calf, bend down on it knee, a wide red slash inna it throat, blood pourin on the ground. Lasco holdin the knife. Him see me. "Here yout' man," him say to me. "Come finish di job. You can cook and wi hungry." Him hold out the knife to me, drippin with blood, and the calf bawl one more time, and then it roll over on the ground. "If you want eat meat, you must learn kill it," Lasco say. "Tek di knife."

I walk over to him, slow, feelin the vomit in my throat, thick and sweet like molasses, knowin that gettin home depend on not showin weakness. I take the knife and look at Lasco and I don't know if him a friend or deadly enemy. "Here," him say. "Turn over di calf. Mi show you how to gut him." Him turn the calf over and it move it leg, like it a try run 'way. I can't do it, no I can't, not cut inna a livin thing, a young thing like this calf. The man-them laugh and shout and say, "Gut him, yout'. What you 'fraid for? You a pussy-claat!" I kneel down in the blood and put the knife to the soft white fur at the calf throat. I close my eye and press with the knife, and it easy in the end. I feel the skin a the calf part and warm blood wash over my hand, flowin, flowin. The man-them cheer and yell and clap me on the back and after that, cuttin up the calf turn easy. One a the man show me where the joint is and how to take out the gut. When I finish, the calf is nothing more than a slab a meat.

Sun is up now, but me still cold. "You have seasonin?" I say to the man who help me.

"What kind a seasonin?"

"Corn oil. Skellion and thyme. Scotchie."

"Come. Mek us look inna di kitchen," the man say. If I find the right seasonin, I cook food the man-them never forget.

SAHARA
The next thing

I asked for a window seat on the plane going home. Usually, I preferred the aisle, but I wanted to see out. Carl had telephoned the day after I left him at Florida State, apologizing for forgetting to call. I told him to work hard, take advantage of his opportunities, packed and left. I went to the airport early and waited, my mind empty.

I didn't read on the plane. I stared out the window at the skyscrapers of Miami and then the Gulf Stream, crisscrossed by the curving wakes of speedboats. We flew south, over Cuba, and then approached Jamaica's north coast. I saw the sugar cane fields of Caymanas and then the plane settled into its ponderous descent over the harbour.

Lydia was waiting outside. I wanted to fall into her arms and cry like a child. She embraced me and took my roll-on bag. "How'd it go?" she said. "You okay?"

"I'm fine. I think. It went well. He's there, Lyds. It's up to him now."

"Um-hm. That's a fact. Now you have to think about yourself, for a change."

"Everything okay at the restaurant?"

"Pretty much. It's been busy. I think we need another couple of tables."

"You don't think that's going to make it too crowded?"

"I think I've figured it out. I'll show you." We crossed the road to the car park and Lydia threw the car keys to me. "You drive," she said. "This car is way too small for me."

"What did Clive say?" Clive was the mechanic.

"Needs a new timing belt or something. You'll have to talk to him. But he says the bug still has some years in it."

"How's Ben?" I said. Ben had moved in with Lydia after they'd dated for less than three months. He'd been living with his parents. I was suspicious. An investment banker without his own, rather nice apartment? I suspected he just wanted Lydia's fine meals and enthusiasm for sex, but had to concede he was well educated and charming.

"He's fine. You want to go home or to the restaurant?"

"Restaurant," I said. I wasn't ready to face the Mona house.

Luckily there was a lot of work waiting for me. Lydia was always slapdash with paperwork. I restored some order to the restaurant office and went over the figures. Lydia was right; Summer Lion was doing well.

"Want to see where I think we can fit some more tables?" she said, standing at the door, licking a spoon.

"What you got there?" I said.

"Trying out a new kind of grater cake. Come and look at the table situation."

We walked outside. There was only one lingering couple in the restaurant. Was Summer Lion becoming a rendezvous for illicit lovers? Lydia walked around the side of the old building housing the office and the kitchen, where there was a narrow strip of land between the building and an exuberant privet hedge.

"Here?" I said. "Impossible. No one would see the customers, they'd never get any service. Plus they'd be bitten by wasps and the privet would scratch them."

"Where then?"

I saw she was determined. "Let me think about it," I said.

I stayed at the restaurant as long as I could, sketching new arrangements of tables. I managed to get two more in without putting customers in the hedge and without constructing any more huts. Lydia had left at five and I'd sent everyone else home. I began to lock up only when the light started to fade.

I drove home. There'd be no food in the house, but I wasn't

hungry. The evening stretched ahead of me. I felt untethered, like a loose balloon in an empty sky. It was Wednesday; I would clean. No doubt the house would be extremely dusty, having been locked up for almost a week.

I went inside and turned on all the lights. The house was spotless; there were daisies on the dining table and a "Welcome Home!" card leaned against the vase. "On to the next thing!" was written inside in Lydia's crooked handwriting. The house smelled of cookies. In the kitchen I found a note on the fridge: "Mac and cheese inside, and a nice Chardonnay and fruit salad. Bread in the microwave – you've got to do something about the ants! Lyds." There was a large jar on the counter, filled with the cookies I'd smelled.

Noise, I needed noise. I turned on the TV and went into the bedroom to unpack. There was no need to clean or to cook and it was only seven.

I went to bed at nine. I turned off the lights but I lit the candle on my dresser and lay in bed watching the flame. It was cool and I let down the mosquito net. *I'll meditate*, I thought. *Then I'll fall asleep*. The candle flame stood straight up and the room was filled with shadows. I wondered what Carl was doing. *He's doing what he's doing. He's in college. You raised a son and he's gone.*

I heard a noise outside and I sat up in bed, listening. I heard rustling. I wondered if Lydia had tidied up the garden too; it had been too dark to see. The rustling noises increased and then a dog barked, right by my window. I lay back down. Sadie's mongrel, Rusty, had escaped again. My heart was beating fast. *Calm down.*

I thought about Dexter. He'd start at St. Stephen's next week. I'd seen him less and less over the summer, and every time I'd seen him, it had been a shock. He was becoming a man and the boy with the bright smile was fading. *Don't think about it. It's up to him. To them.* I stared at the candle until the night breeze came up and the flame began to flicker. I got up and blew it out and stumbled back to bed. Kingston was never silent, but at that moment, I could hear nothing, not the faraway throb of a sound-system, not the squeal of truck brakes on Hope Road, not the grating yelping of the Mona dogs. My room was a tomb. I lay with my eyes open. Slowly, the familiar shapes of furniture grew visible and I saw the glow of street lights through the louvre windows. Then a dog barked, and another, and the irritating chorus started. I turned over. On to the next thing.

DEXTER
St. Stephen's

Ten day later, after the trip into the mountain, I go to St. Stephen's. Is much bigger than Nightingale All Age and Holborn Prep. Everything confusin. Instead a one teacher most a the time, we have different-different teacher for all kinda subject. Instead a being in one classroom most a the day, student have to walk around a big campus. Some a the classroom have name, like laboratory, or Spanish room.

I go to school alone on bus – Marlon and Lissa still at Holborn. None a the teacher at St. Stephen's say anything to me. Class them big, like Nightingale – maybe forty student – and I sit inna back and hope nobody see me to ask question. Most a the time, I don't know what the teacher talkin about. Them teach half the class – the half sittin in front. All I want is to stay outta trouble.

But it don't stay like that. Two week don't pass when I come outta school gate and find Lasco and Boston a wait for me. And my life start split in two – the daytime and the night-time. The schoolboy and the big man. Inna day, I get up like always, get water at standpipe, drink tea and eat hardo bread, dress, take bus, go a school, go to class, write test, pretend to study. Then last bell ring and I go from St. Stephen's onto Kingston street with Boston and Lasco. I put my khaki shirt with the epaulette inna my school bag, I drop my pants low. Lasco give me cargo to wear. We go all over and I learn all the bus route-them, and the name a the bus driver, and the higgler woman who will give you a brawta when you buy a stick a cane or a hand a banana. We go down to Kingston Harbour, out to Port Royal, even go as

178

far as Spanish Town. We steal from haberdashery shop on Princess Street, we smoke ganja in mash-up old buildin on Harbour Street, we throw stone after the homeless man-them. I start feel strong inna my arm and my leg-them and there is no fear inna my heart. We arm wrestle and Lasco always win, even though Boston one hand strong like a vice grip. I start sleep out a night-time. Sometime we crash with Boston, if him house empty, sometime we pretend we are homeless boy and sleep in shelter on Water Lane run by some missionary in long white robe. We make up story to tell the missionary and they believe whatever we tell them, and them say they will pray for we. If we need money, we try beggin, or if that don't work, we go back to Elleston Road and do this job or that job. I start get back test and assignment with bad mark and teacher call me up in front a the whole class and say me fool-fool and tell other boy not to be like me. I don't pay them no mind. I just wait for three o'clock and school to be over and then is me, Lasco, Boston and the streets a Kingston. Some night when I go home, Mumma make up plenty noise and say she going beat me and I going come to nothing, and if I don't know Miss Sahara waitin for me every Sunday night. Me, I just suck my teeth after her and go to sleep. She a woman, after all. When a man is a man, he must not listen to the voice of a woman. Marlon look at me like him hate me and this make me sad, but he will find out how it really go in him own time.

One day, Lasco alone wait for me after school. "Wh'appen to Boston?" I say.

"Him lyin low for a while," Lasco say.

"What him do?"

"Police catch him with some a Merciless crew and dem hold him until human rights people say dem must let go. But Babylon beat him first. Him awright, but him stayin a yard today."

We leave St. Stephen's and walk down to the Harbour. We go by Coronation Market and sit on the wall and look out over the water. I hungry. Lasco take a pack a cigarette from him pocket and light one. Him hand me the pack and I take one too and me and him, we sit on sea wall, smokin. Sea gull make screechin noise and dive for fish. Water look oily and plenty plastic bottle floatin. The smell a Kingston strong – sea, rottin fish, diesel, smoke, shit, people.

"You know your father?" I ask Lasco. As the word come out a mi mouth, me sorry. Lasco don't like talk about them thing. Most time him tell you to mind you own fuckin business. But today him seem calm and him answer.

"Not even mi madda know mi fadda."

"How you mean?"

Him look at me. "Mi madda was bare pickney when mi born, no more dan fourteen."

"She still musta know your father."

"Mi madda hate di sight a mi, from di day mi born."

"How you know dat?"

"How I know dat? You know what a battery, yout'?"

I 'fraid to say I don't know, in case Lasco laugh after me. I hear the word in Jacob's Pen, the old woman talk about keepin the girl-them away from man, so no chance a battery. I don't say anything. Lasco go on, "Battery a when a whole heap a man tek a woman and all a them fuck her, one after anodda, until di woman near split in two. That a how mi madda have mi. Some crew war where she did grow up, and one man want fight 'gainst her brudda, and them tek her one night and half kill her."

"Whoy. That rough. Where she is now?"

"Dunno. Don't want know. If mi see her, mi kill her."

"Why you want kill her? Is not her fault she get battery."

"Not my fault neither. You ask too much question, Dexy-bwoy. Some tings not good to talk."

I think about Lasco madda, a young girl, my age, I think a her with alla the man-them a rape her, hold her down, payin no mind to her screamin, to her beggin them to let her go. It seem like the time I butcher the calf – I know a person can get to a place where him don't feel anything, when him don't hear another person bawl out for murder, when another person come like nothing at all. I think about Lissa at home, still young,

180

but alla this could be in front a her. She will grow and she will turn woman and man will want to fuck her. That's it.

Two week don't pass, and I hear that word again. Battery. Battery inna the Sixth Form bathroom after last bell. The talk run through the school like a bush fire. St. Stephen's a boy school – who them going batter? I don't want see but I have to.

I walk inside the bathroom and it pack up with boy-them. I see Russian, who Boston did warn me about, and who the whole school 'fraid of. And I see him holdin a girl, maybe twelve, and I take one look at her and know she not so right inna she head. She a smile and when the boy ask her to pull up her skirt she do it and everybody laugh. She don't know what going on, what them want do to her. She a retard, like what I did think about Felix, until I get to know better.

"Take off her pants," Russian say. Him hold her arm-them, and she smilin, not fightin. A boy behind me say, *Yeah man, she really want it.*

"Bun dat," I say. "Let her go." And before I know what is what, I am standin in front a Russian with the knife I start carry from Elletson Road days in my hand.

"You raasclaat mad, yout'?" Russian say.

"You no hear mi, batty bwoy? Lef' di gal," I say. I take one step to him and the boy standin around take a step back.

"Who you callin batty bwoy?" say Russian, but him voice weak and I know the summer with Lasco and Boston teach me to face off a enemy.

"Leggo di gal, mi say. Find a big woman to fuck. Plenty whore down a Princess Street." I stare inna him eye-dem, black like ackee seed, and I see my own self lookin back. Nobody movin. Even the retard girl stand still.

"Master a come!" a boy whisper from behind me.

"Come," I say to the girl, holdin out my hand. She take it right away, trustin as Lissa. I put the knife away and pick up the girl – she solid like a bag a cement. She put her arm around my neck and we run around the buildin and do not stop until we reach the fence. I know a place where the chainlink cut.

"Go find you mumma," I say to her, holdin the fence open. "Go."

She wave like she and me are at a birthday party, usin her finger-them, and she walk off down the street, skippin and talkin to herself. Now I have to face St. Stephen's master and Russian. I feel rage like a burnin fire in my chest. Time for St. Stephen's over. I hide until the master and the boy-them leave and me go back inside the bathroom. Place like this need to destroy so not one concrete block left standin. Russian make Molotov cocktail and I know where him keep him things.

SAHARA
A boy with potential

I was in the kitchen making a grilled cheese sandwich when the phone rang. "Carl, can you get that?" I shouted, my hands full of grated cheese. There was no answer. Of course not. Stupid! I swore under my breath, brushed off my hands and ran to the phone. "Hello?" I said, breathless. There was no answer.

"Hello?" I said again, feeling annoyed. There was the sound of an open line. I wondered if this was going to be a threatening phone call.

"Hello! If you don't speak, I'm going to hang up," I said.

"Miss Sahara?" A voice came faintly and I knew it had to be Arleen.

"Yes? Miss Arleen, is that you?" This was the first phone call I had ever received from Arleen. Perhaps there had been an accident with one of the children. I wondered how she had found my unlisted telephone number. Then I remembered Marlon had asked for it once.

"Miss Sahara," Arleen said again.

"What is it, Arleen?" I said, impatient. I hadn't covered the cheese and flies were probably all over it.

"Dexter in trouble at school," she said.

"At St. Stephen's? *Already?* What did he do this time?" I was angry. There was the boy at a good high school, in itself a miracle, and he was going to squander the opportunity. Maybe Carl had been right about poor Jamaicans, you just can't help them. Dexter hadn't yet been at St. Stephen's six weeks.

"Well, Miss Sahara, the letter say him set fire to the Six Form bathroom."

183

"*Set fire to the bathroom? What?* Did he do it? Has he lost his mind? What did he say?"

"Him don't really say anyting, Miss Sahara, just give me di letter and go outside. Letter say mi have to see Guidance Counsellor." Arleen stopped.

"Hello?" I said, although I knew what the silence meant. Arleen wanted me to go with her to the school, to intervene on Dexter's behalf. *I won't do it*, I thought, *this has become impossible*. "Miss Arleen, I don't know how much longer I can go on doing this kind of thing for Dexter," I said. "He has to take some responsibility for himself. What am I going to tell his sponsors? It's quite likely they'll take away the funding when they hear about this."

The silence went on. I knew Arleen would be thinking – why tell the sponsors? They don't have to know. It's the Jamaican way – if you pretend something isn't happening, then it isn't.

"Read me the whole letter," I said.

I'd taken Dex to school on the first day of term, as I had at Holborn, except that Arleen had not come with us. I dropped Marlon and Lissa off at Holborn first, and watched them run with confidence across the car park. I thought: *One down. Two to go*. I felt the two younger ones would make it, however that could be defined, but despite his high marks at Holborn, I was afraid for Dexter. And supervising the children at two different schools was bound to be more difficult, especially as St. Stephen's had no Gail Carpenter to smoothe the way for Dexter.

That first day, Dexter and I stood by the VW and took in his new high school. A high school, not a comprehensive high or a technical high or a vocational school – places he would have been bound for, had it not been for Holborn Prep. He'd really come a long way in two years of good schooling. I touched his shoulder, but he moved away.

St. Stephen's had graceful old buildings and lawns. Curbs and tree trunks had been whitewashed. Modest cars were parked in a shady car park. A bell rang and boys surged to their

184

classrooms, noisy and exuberant. We were late. I watched the boys for a moment. The very oddness of boys together struck me. They clustered in groups and punched and shoved each other. They ran off and came back to their friends, they played imaginary sports – bounced a basketball, dribbled a football, made cricket strokes in the air. They danced to imaginary music, their hips imitating the sexual act. I saw two boys aim their fingers at each other. *Pai, pai*, they shouted. Their shirts were untucked. They laughed and swore, taking no notice of a group of teachers walking nearby. I'd been to an all-girls school fifteen years ago – this was alien. When we'd been out of our classrooms, we'd fallen into groups too, but we'd walked slowly, whispering and comparing classroom notes. We'd got into trouble for eating sweets in class. In comparison, the boys were a force – uncontrollable, destructive, murky – like a gully in spate. I imagined Dexter in the middle of the swirling mass of male energy – would he be included in their games? Or would he always walk on the edges, excluded? And which would be worse?

I'd hurried him to the office. A brusque woman said she'd show him to his classroom, pointing out our lateness. I remembered Miss Gordon's warmth on the first day at Holborn Prep.

Six weeks had passed since that first day and I'd not seen much of Dex. True, I'd been over a week in Florida, taking Carl to college. But even when I visited Jacob's Pen on Sunday nights, he was rarely there. Arleen shrugged her shoulders when I asked where he was. All she'd been able to offer was, "Him don't come home yet, Miss Sahara." I was angry with her. Why couldn't she be a mother to her children? I turned my attention to Marlon, still safe at Holborn and doing really well. And Lissa – she'd go into Kindergarten next year. Every Sunday, I said, "Tell Dexter I want to see him when I come next week." But in the six weeks since he'd been at St. Stephen's, I'd only seen him once. He'd had a bruise on his cheek, which I asked him about. "Fall down," he said.

"What, playing football?" I said, trying to touch his cheek.

He shook his head, avoiding my hand. "Football? No, Miss Sahara. Not football. Just fall down." He was wearing his clothes differently; his pants low on his hips, his shirt open to the chest. He looked like he belonged to a gang. I didn't know how to ask about gangs. I remembered the picture he drew in red and black of men and guns.

But there was nothing I could get out of him that night. He sat on the front step, his back to us. Everything was fine. He wasn't hungry. He didn't want to talk. And then he got up and walked out into the darkness.

Two days after Arleen's phone call, I collected her to go to the school. I'd made an appointment with a Mrs. Darby, who'd sounded tired when she heard why I was calling. "Yes, Mrs. Lawrence, I'm glad you've called. We're having a real problem with Dexter. When can you come?" Arleen was uncomfortable beside me in the car, dressed in her graduation frock, sweating in the heat. The dress was tight; she'd gained weight. I wasn't sure she deserved to be better nourished. She really was an ugly woman, her splayed teeth visible between her lips, her hair badly creamed and styled. She smelled slightly too. It was hard to be sorry for her. I did feel sorry for the boys – they had no advantages. But Arleen – no. Why had she had not one, but three children, all for men who were worthless? Why couldn't she get a proper job?

We drove in silence to St. Stephen's. I wanted to be doing something else. Dexter had set fire to the bathroom – why? I doubted we'd find out. It was hard to remember the boy he'd been that night on the steps of Sovereign Plaza, a small boy with a hopeful smile and deferential manner.

We reached St. Stephen's. I saw Arleen was still sweating, despite the admittedly inefficient air conditioner in my old car. She struggled with the door handle, as she always did. I was impatient with her ineptness, her unsuitability as a parent. Often I thought about getting the children away from her. Perhaps my first solution had been the right one – a boarding school. Perhaps there was no point in paying for schooling for the children if they remained in Jacob's Pen.

We walked up to the office, Arleen two paces behind me. She acted like a slave, head bowed, afraid of authority, child-like. Stand up straight, I wanted to say. You're a big woman with children.

We were told to wait by a sullen woman behind a door cut in half. We found a row of plastic chairs in a corridor. There was a short flight of back stairs in front of us with a water cooler at the top. As we sat there, boys came up to drink. They looked at me with predatory sexual interest and no respect.

After half an hour, I went back to the office window. "What's happening?" I said to the sullen woman. "We've been waiting over half an hour."

The woman didn't answer, but picked up a telephone and spoke inaudibly into it. I knew she had only then called the Guidance Counsellor; she intended us to wait. "Mrs. Darby is on her way," she said. If it were up to her, no one would be allowed to come to her window to bother her. Arleen *would* have fared worse if I hadn't been there – for a start, she wouldn't have come back to the window. She would have just continued sitting there until school closed for the day. Perhaps a janitor would have found her; perhaps he would have insulted her and thrown her out.

"Mrs. Lawrence? Mrs. Jones?" An enormously fat woman stood at the bottom of the back stairs. "I'm Elaine Darby. Would you come with me, please?" No apology for keeping us waiting, but then, she probably didn't know we had been there for a while.

We followed her across the parking lot and then into a two-storey building. Classes were in session and there were no boys in the corridors. I was glad of this – the frank stares of the boys who had visited the water cooler had been unnerving. Arleen still walked two paces behind us and Mrs. Darby didn't speak.

She led us into a small, neat office on the ground floor. She squeezed her bulk around the side of the desk and sat on a sturdy wooden chair. I doubted she could have made it in a regular swivel chair. There was a file on the desk in front of her and she opened it and reviewed the top page.

"Well, Mrs. Lawrence, Mrs. Jones, thank you for coming. As our letter said, Raymond has been suspended indefinitely for attempting to set fire to the Sixth Form bathroom. I thought I should have a discussion with you both – Mrs. Lawrence, I understand you are Raymond's sponsor – before we consider allowing him back in school. He's obviously having great difficulty settling down here."

"Shouldn't Dexter – Raymond, I mean, be here?" I asked.

"We can have another meeting with him present, if you like," Mrs. Darby said. "But right now I wanted to gain some understanding of his home environment and talk to you both without him being here." She was obviously an educated woman, but not a warm one. I felt anxious, as if *I* were in trouble. I glanced at Arleen. She was looking at her hands, which were folded in her lap. There were patches of sweat visible in the fabric of her dress wherever it touched her skin.

"Could you tell us what happened?" I said, keeping my voice calm. It was important to gain this woman's cooperation.

"Certainly. Last week, Friday, I think it was," she referred to her file, "yes, last Friday, the 18th, one of the groundsmen reported smoke coming from the Sixth Form bathroom. The Sixth Form has its own block of classrooms with sanitary facilities. The groundsman tried to open the door, but it was locked from the inside. He called out, but no one answered. He was afraid a boy was still in there. Anyway, he called for help and the door was broken down. The bathroom was empty, except for a pile of materials, which were burning. I understand there was a strong smell of kerosene. A window had been broken at the back of the building and there was a piece of khaki cloth caught on the broken glass, obviously from the uniform of the boy who had set the fire, as he made his escape from the building. The men put out the fire – luckily it hadn't spread and there was a fire extinguisher nearby – and reported the matter to the Principal."

"How did you decide it was Dex – Raymond who set the fire?" I asked.

"We called an immediate school assembly and checked everyone's uniforms. Raymond's pants were torn."

"No other boy had torn pants?" I asked.

"Mrs. Lawrence, as soon as Raymond realized we had the piece of cloth from the window, he confessed. He said he'd set the fire. There's no doubt about it."

I didn't correct her use of "Mrs". "Did he say why he'd done it?'

"No. He didn't seem sorry either. He said the place deserved to be burned down. He wouldn't answer any other questions. We asked him if he'd taken the rags and paper into the bathroom and where he had obtained kerosene, but he wouldn't answer. He told the Principal … Let me read for you what he said. 'Better you expel me. I've had enough of this place. Nothing here can help me.'" Mrs. Darby closed the file and looked at me.

"You said in your letter that Raymond was obviously having difficulty settling in here. Have there been other incidents?" I asked.

"Several." Mrs. Darby flicked through papers in her file. "Let's see. He's late most mornings for school. He's been absent eight times. He has failed to hand in four… no, five assignments. He has missed three class tests. His mid-term exam results are extremely poor – he failed to sit some mid-terms and earned zeros. His other marks are quite unsatisfactory – often in the teens and twenties. In addition, he appears to be friends with a very questionable group of street boys."

"Teens and twenties out of a hundred?" I said, for something to say.

"Yes, out of a hundred."

There was another silence. Arleen continued to look at her lap. I wanted to shake her.

"Mrs. Jones?" Mrs. Darby said. "Are there any particular difficulties at home? A new stepfather? Crime problems? Possible abuse?"

Arleen lifted her head. "Dexter just bad mind, Ma'am. Mi try and try and try wit' him. Miss Sahara here try wit' him. Nutt'n new at home to cause him trouble. I pray all night for him, ask Pastor to pray for him too, but nutt'n work. He don't

189

want change. Is true him have bad frien'. Better you just expel him and done."

I was shocked at how easily Arleen condemned Dex.

"Mrs. Lawrence, how did you get involved with Raymond? I assume Dexter is his pet name?" For a minute, I didn't answer. How *did* I come to be sitting in a boy's school with a woman I don't know, intervening on behalf of a doomed boy?

"Why does it matter?" I said. "I met him, I decided to help. Why do you need to know any more than that? And yes, Dexter is his pet name." *Which you should know.*

Mrs. Darby looked down at her papers. "We wondered if you were related to the boy," she mumbled. Oh, so that was it. The sniffing out of scandal.

"We're not *related*. I met Dexter begging at Sovereign and decided to see if I could help. I got him into Holborn Prep and he passed for St. Stephen's. That's it. That's why he's here. That's why I'm here."

"Well, that's very commendable. Raymond should be grateful for your interest." Mrs. Darby looked down at her papers again. She didn't seem to know what to say next. I wished someone would knock on the door and bring this interview to an end. It was hot in the small office and I was sweating. I could smell the two women – Arleen, metallic and poor, Mrs. Darby powdered and perfumed, but the black smell was there underneath. I could smell the school – chalk dust, bathrooms, gasoline, too many children. I reminded myself I'd read that slaves had been horrified by the smell of white people.

"I'd like Raymond to stay in school," I said. "What would we have to do to achieve that?" My choice of words was bad – it sounded like I was offering a bribe. "I mean, can he apologize, do detentions? If you throw him out, he'll be on the street. He's a bright boy. He deserves a chance."

"*I* won't be throwing him out, Mrs. Lawrence," said Mrs. Darby. She inflated herself like a puffer fish. Her features were small in the middle of her fat face; her lips were pressed together. I'd lost her cooperation. I needed to be humble.

"No, of course not, Mrs. Darby. I didn't mean you personally. I meant the institution. And I quite understand the school's position – what Raymond did is inexcusable. I'm just asking if he can be given a second chance."

Mrs. Darby raised her eyebrows. "The school board is still deliberating. There's a disciplinary procedure and we've set that in motion. This meeting is part of that process. We need to establish if there are home factors that are causing the boy to act out. Now that I've met with you, I'll send a report to the Principal and he'll make a recommendation to the board."

This sounded like a long process. "What will happen to Dex in the meantime? If he stays out of school too long, we'll never get him to come back." Mrs. Darby shrugged. I saw her indifference – Dex was just another troublesome ghetto boy. I felt angry that he could be so easily discarded. If I had not been in the picture, would this meeting have taken place at all? Arleen would just have got a letter saying Dex had been expelled and that would have been that.

"I'd like to request a meeting with the Principal," I said, abandoning efforts to gain Mrs. Darby's sympathy.

"That's your right, of course," she said, puffing up more. She looked over my shoulder and shouted through the door, "Devon! Come here!"

A teenage boy came over. "Yes, Miss?" he said.

"Take these two ladies back over to the office. They want to set up a meeting with Mr. Bancroft." She looked at me. "Devon will escort you to the office and you can request a meeting with the Principal. Good day." Her manner said: *It won't do any good. The boy is a criminal. You've wasted your money. These people can't be helped.*

"Thank you, Mrs. Darby," I said. "You've been very kind. I'll be in touch." I knew my voice sounded sarcastic. Mrs. Darby didn't get up as we left the room.

It took a week to get a meeting with the Principal, Mr. Bancroft. I went to see him alone. This time I remained standing in front of the sullen woman in the office until she told his secretary I was there. I refused to sit on the plastic chairs around the corner; I paced up and down the lobby area. I'd taken trouble with my clothes – I knew I had to look important.

I was wearing my only suit, black, with a plain white blouse. I wore Aunt Gladys's gold earrings. I'd even put on make-up. It felt like it was melting in the heat.

"Mrs. Lawrence?" said a voice behind me.

I turned to see the sullen woman standing nearby. "Yes?"

"The Principal is ready for you now."

Mr. Bancroft looked harassed. He was younger than I had expected; maybe in his late thirties. There was chalk on his fingers – he still taught, then. I thought this was hopeful.

"Mrs. Lawrence?" He extended a hand. "Please sit down. I understand you wanted to see me about Raymond Morrison. I've asked Mrs. Darby, our Guidance Counsellor, to join us – I believe you met her? She's more familiar with Raymond's situation."

Shit, I thought. I don't want the puffer fish here. "Thank you for seeing me, Mr. Bancroft. I was hoping we could talk privately, but if that's not the school's policy, then that's fine…"

"It's not a matter of policy, Mrs. Lawrence, but convenience. Of course, if you want to speak to me alone, I'll call Mrs. Darby and…" His voice trailed off. He sounded defensive and I wondered why.

"No, that's okay. Please. Whatever works for you. It's just Mrs. Darby gave me the impression she'd already made up her mind about Raymond."

"I'm sure that's not the case. We try very hard with all our boys. Raymond seems to be having an unusually difficult time settling in here – I've been eight years at this school and have never had a fire set by a student. Some members of our school board wanted him expelled right away, but you might remember the Lindsay case at Garvey College a few months ago and after discussion, the board asked me to do some investigation before a decision was made."

I remembered the Lindsay case. Three boys had been found smoking ganja on the school grounds of Garvey College and the boys had been expelled. One of the boys had been a member of a prominent political family – the Lindsays – and they'd sued. The government stepped in and told the school board to reinstate the boys. Half of the board resigned in protest.

"Well, Mr. Bancroft..." I began. What could I say on Dexter's behalf? That late at night on the steps of Sovereign Centre, he'd beguiled me with his smile? That he loved his sister Lissa and was gentle with her? That he was bright – a boy with potential, a boy who might do things? Or should I tell the part of the truth I knew: that he confused me, he'd gone silent, neither his mother or I knew what influenced him, but there must have been a reason he tried to burn down the Sixth Form bathrooms.

"I came to see you because I wanted to see if there was any way Dex – I mean, Raymond – could stay in school. I know what he did was indefensible and I know he's not been doing his homework and all that, but if you throw him out, he'll just end up on the streets. If he apologized, would that make a difference? Could he be given duties, like, I don't know, picking up litter on the school grounds? Working in the library? Cleaning the blackboards?" These were all sanctions from my school days when we got into trouble for eating sweets in class.

"It's not just the fire incident, Mrs. Lawrence. Raymond's teachers think he's a disruptive influence." Mr. Bancroft fiddled with his pen. "He doesn't do his work, he causes trouble. I know of your involvement with his family and I congratulate you on your charity, but really, having talked again to Mrs. Darby and Raymond himself, I'm afraid I'm going to recommend expulsion to the board."

"You spoke to Dex?" I said. "What did he say? Did he tell you why he did it?"

"He said the rags were in the bathroom and he had matches in his pocket and he just did it without thinking. But, Mrs. Lawrence, we don't believe that. The rags were soaked in kerosene and there was no reason for those rags to be there. Litter, yes, but not kerosene-soaked rags. Raymond went into the bathroom with the intention of burning it down."

"So what happens now?"

"I have a letter for you; well, for Mrs. Jones." Mr. Bancroft reached into a drawer and took out an envelope addressed to Arleen.

"So all this pretence at meeting me was just a formality?" I said, my voice rising.

"You have no reason to say that." Mr. Bancroft stood. "You requested this meeting. We tried with the boy. He didn't take advantage of the opportunity to be at St. Stephen's. I know you mean well, Mrs. Lawrence, but it's hard to help these people. In all my years of teaching, I've seen only a handful of boys like Raymond Morrison take school seriously and do well. It comes down to character and not many of them have it." His face was set and I saw he was angry.

I left Mr. Bancroft without seeing Mrs. Darby. I drove to Jacob's Pen and gave Arleen the letter. I watched her open it and read it slowly, her brow crinkling over the long words. She looked at me when she'd finished and I shrugged. "Where is he?" I said.

"Him leave out from last night, Miss Sahara, and him don't come home. Him go wit' dat bad boy, Lasco – the one you did meet dat time – and another one name Boston."

"Well, I guess Dex didn't want to be in school. I – we – couldn't force knowledge into his head." I turned to leave.

"Miss Sahara?"

"Yes?"

"You comin on Sunday evenin?" she asked. And I saw fear in her eyes.

DEXTER
Mining sand in Rocky River

More than six month pass since I been home to Jacob's Pen. Since I expel from St. Stephen's, I leave out and don't go back. Time for madda is over. If I think about it, I miss Marlon and Lissa and I miss seein Miss Sahara on Sunday night. I even miss Holborn; I miss the time when I did sit in class and feel like things comin clear to me. I try don't think about it, but it hard, especially when I put down my head to sleep. Then the board house at Jacob's Pen come inna my mind and it seem far away, gettin smaller every night, like it at the end a one long, dark, dirty, dry water pipe. Marlon must be bringin home the money now.

Lasco and Boston and me move around pretty much every night. Lasco say is trainin; say Babylon can't find you if you is on the move. We talk about joinin Racehorse Crew. Boston prefer Rustler; him say Merciless too dog-heart. We talk about it, but we don't do anything.

Work on the construction site on Elletson Road closing down. Work hard to find. We go down to Half Way Tree, see if the street boy will let us clean windshield, but them ready to fight we. We talk 'bout leavin Kingston, going to May Pen, or even Mandeville, where Lasco say it cool and fresh and people not so 'fraid a gunman like Kingston people. But we still stay in Kingston, a move around, smokin, drinkin when we can get it, sometime buy Cash Pot, or play drop pan. Lasco know plenty a the night girl outside New Kingston hotel, one special one name Cherry-Oh, and she ready to fuck anytime, for hardly any money. Cherry-Oh like me, say I am a good boy, and I hold onto her sweaty woman flesh like it going save me. Nearly every night we try find Cherry-Oh.

One night we find a half bottle a white rum in a garbage drum turn over by goat or dog. We drink it dry and drop asleep in the buildin on Harbour Street. We wake up when sun high in the sky and ground hot like coal pot to find one a the homeless man standin over us, naked, backin him fist. Him hood big like a donkey own and him eye roll up inna him head when him discharge on the ground at him feet. Him put him foot inna it and rub it around. I want go home.

"Mi hear about a job," Lasco say. We all dirty, hungry, desperate.

"What kinda job?" I say, saliva comin into my mouth, thinkin a the curry goat and rice and dumplin big like a plate at the Elletson Road construction site.

"Sand minin. It illegal, but it safe. Not like breakin house or t'iefin car."

"What wi have to do?" Boston say.

"Wi shovel river sand inna di truck. It hard work, but pay good. It near where you live, Dexy-bwoy. Rocky River, near you mumma."

My head fulla picture a the river, dry most a the year, but sometime runnin fast, hidin janga. I remember the day Marlon and I go there, and him almost drown and Rayton take away the janga. Rayton not going mess with me now.

I get up. "When?" I say.

"Tonight," Lasco say.

That is how the three a we end up on a open-back truck with man holdin long gun. That is how we drive past Miss Betsy house and Ma'as Ken shop and Mumma house, dark and quiet. The truck fight down the road, fallin into pothole, tearin out the macca bush. We stop at the river bank, see the pool a water-them, even though the night dark with no moon. We get out and I start shovel sand, even Boston with him one hand shovel. We shovel until I think my back going break and my hand-them blister and bloody. Lasco stand with the man-them. Look like

196

the truck will never fill and this is what I will do until I die, stand inna wet sand, mosquito around my head, shovelin shovelin shovelin, with men carryin long gun, men who do not talk except to make a grunt or a shout, men who do not say a kind word or hear one either, shovelin until the end a the world.

But the world don't end like that. The world slow down with the sound a police siren and the headlight of a car through the night and then a searchlight like day fall on the truck by the side a the river bed. A voice call out: *Police! If you move, you dead!*

We scatter, every which way inna the night. We fling the shovel down and run. "Follow mi!" I say to Lasco and Boston. I know every track a the Rocky River. We must can get 'way.

We climb up the hill behind our house, macca tearin at our skin. "Hush!" I say. "You a mek too much noise." From the top a the hill, we try see down to the river, but it too dark.

"Mek wi hide inna you madda house, Dexy," Lasco say. He hardly out a breath and him eye shine inna the night.

"No," I say. "It too dangerous."

"Too dangerous for who? Police can't search every house inna Jacob's Pen. We hide dere until dem gawn."

"No," I say, but Lasco and Boston already start down the hill.

"You knock first," Lasco say. I too tired to argue and I go up to the door. I knock and call out, "Mumma! Is mi. Dexter." The door don't open at first. My back a open to the night. But then, just as I raise my fist to knock again, the door open and Marlon standin there. I push him one side and the three a we get inside the house and slam the door.

Nobody don't say anything. Mumma face like a stone. Lissa asleep on the bed. "Go inna di back room," I tell Boston and Lasco. "Hide." Them don't give me no argument.

"Get inna bed, woman," I say to Mumma. I take off my pants and shirt. I climb into bed like me been there all night. Mumma eye get wide, that I call her "woman", but she don't answer. "You too, Marlon. We all go sleep now. Turn off di light."

The four a we lie inna bed. I think where there is place to hide inna back room – not much in there. Maybe them can fit inna barrel, or maybe inna roof behind cardboard. I close my eye and try breathe slow. I try brush the sand off my hand-them, but sand and blood all mix up. I think about how I used to sleep with my family.

It happen, just like you hear 'bout, but is a different thing when you live it. *Bam!* the door kick in and two police stand there, long gun point at we. Soldier is behind them; yard full up a police and soldier. "*Raid!*" the first police through the door shout. Lissa start to bawl and Marlon try shush her.

"We lookin for bad man; shotta, man from Racehorse crew. Tek you pickney dem outside, madda, we searchin dis house," Babylon say.

The first police grab Mumma and shove her outside. She nearly fall down on the step. "Come Marlon, Lissa, come outside, run, come nuh!" she bawl. The three a we don't move. If me get outta bed, police will see my hand-them. Lissa bawlin out her heart. "Get out pickney," the police say, "you want dead?"

"Come Lissa," Marlon say, and him try pick her up. I still in bed.

"You no hear mi, yout'?" the policeman say to me. "Come outta di bed." The gun point straight at me. I get up and the police spin me around against the wall, and something hit the back a my head. I fall. Everything is bare noise and confusion. I hear a crash and someone say, "Bumbuh-claat!" and I hear a sound like water. Them must turn over the bucket. I try to wipe the blood outta my eye. "Don't move! You want dead?" the police shout. I want tell Marlon and Lissa to run. I lift up my head and there is a explosion inside my head, behind mi eye-them.

"Lissa, Marlon!" I hear Mumma screamin. She don't call my name. "Mi pickney inside! Get dem out! Lord God, get mi pickney out!"

Police haul me up and pull me outside inna the yard. Then I hear them call out, "Dey in here! See dem here!" And I hear gunshot upon gunshot, until the world is full a the sound a war and agony. Over the road, I hear a woman screamin and pickney bawlin out and I know them cryin for Mumma and her children.

The police force me to my knee inna the yard and handcuff my hand behind my back. I shame to be naked, except for my brief. I feel the gun muzzle cold against my neck back. "So where you get sand 'pon you hand, shotta?" the police say. All I can see is the ground in front a me. I turn my head to answer the police and out a the corner a my eye, I see him reverse the long gun inna him hand and swing it at me, like a cricket bat. Then the world end in a sledgehammer a light.

SAHARA
After the raid

The phone woke me out of a deep sleep. *Carl*, I thought and grabbed for it. "Hello?" I said, wondering if my life was going to change for ever in the next few seconds.

"Miss Sahara?" said a voice I didn't recognize. *Not Carl*.

"Yes?" I said, sitting up and turning on the bedside light. "Who is this?"

"Is Miss Betsy. From Jacob's Pen. Miss Arleen frien'." I remembered an older woman who lived across the road from Arleen. Something terrible must have happened.

"What happen, Miss Betsy? Why you calling me so late?"

"Is Marlon, Miss Sahara."

"What happen to Marlon?"

"Him stone dead, Miss Sahara."

"*What*? How?"

"Him dead. Police kill him in a raid tonight."

"Oh my God. What about the others? Arleen and Lissa?"

"Dem okay. The police arrest Dexter."

"Oh my God," I said again. Marlon dead. Killed by police. I didn't know what to say. My stomach clenched. I looked at the clock – quarter to five. It wasn't late; it was early. It would soon be light. "I'll come in an hour or so," I said. "Tell Miss Arleen I'll soon be there."

"They at my house," Miss Betsy said.

"That's the concrete one across the road?"

"Um-hm. Come quick."

I made coffee and drank it. I couldn't face food. I dressed in jeans

200

and put my restaurant clothes in a bag. I would go straight to Summer Lion after visiting Jacob's Pen and change there. It was too early to call Lydia. I wished there was someone who could come with me – I had no idea how to cope with violent death. I knew nothing of funeral homes or coroner's inquests. And what could I say to a mother who'd lost her son, a mother I thought was partly responsible for her children's difficult lives? I didn't want to go to Jacob's Pen. I stared out of the front windows until the deep shadows disappeared and then I got into the car.

Miss Betsy was waiting in her doorway. She beckoned and I walked up to her. I offered her my hand and she shook it awkwardly. "Where are they?" I said.

"Inside. Come in. You want some bush tea? I just mek it. Calm you down."

"No, thanks, Miss Betsy. Not right now." I walked inside. The room was clean but overfull of furniture. Arleen was sitting on a red velvet couch, her hair unkempt, wearing her night clothes. "Miss Arleen," I said, "I am so, so sorry. What happened? Can you tell me?"

"Nutt'n more than so happen," Arleen mumbled, not looking up. "Happen inna ghetto all a di time. Police raid; fire plenty shot and chile get kill. Read it in di *Gleaner* tomorrow or di next day."

I sat beside her on the couch. She held a bloody plaid handkerchief and her feet were bare. I thought I should embrace her, but I couldn't. We were not on those terms. "Is Lissa okay?" I asked.

"She not hurt, but she don't talk since it happen."

"Where is she?"

"Back room."

"Call her for me?"

"Lissa!" Arleen called. "Lissa! Miss Sahara here. Come and mind your manners." I started to protest and Miss Betsy intervened.

"Mi will get her." She went through a door and came out carrying the little girl.

"Miss Sahara here, Lissa. Say hello to her now," Miss Betsy said. Lissa turned her head into Miss Betsy's neck.

"Lissa?" I said. "Won't you talk to me?" I got up and went over to Miss Betsy, who tried to give Lissa to me. Lissa clung harder. I tried to take one of the child's hands from where it held tight. She grunted.

"What happened?" I said to Miss Betsy, giving up. "Why did the police shoot Marlon?"

"Wi dunno. Look like dem was a look for some man from Racehorse Crew, doing sand minin. Look like Dexter and him frien' was hidin inna di house and shot start bust. Marlon tryin to get Lissa to come out a di house and di shot catch him inna him head. Police lick Dexter wit' a gun and kick him while him on di ground. Den dem throw him inna police car and tek him 'way."

"Dexter bad frien was a hide inna di house. Dat is why di police come," Miss Arleen said. "But dem get 'wey." She covered her face with the kerchief.

"Where is Marlon's…" I couldn't say the word. "Where is Marlon now?" I asked Miss Betsy.

"In di other room. You want see him?" I didn't, but I knew it was expected.

"Show her, Miss Arleen," said Miss Betsy. "Let mi tek Lissa back to bed."

Marlon lay in a tiny room, more storeroom than bedroom. There was an army cot in one corner and he lay flat on his back, covered to his neck in a flowered sheet. His eyes were closed and his skin was already looking waxy. Blood seeped from the back of his head and stained the cot. The questions about his future had been answered. I went back to the living room.

"What's going to happen to Marlon's body?" I asked Miss Betsy.

"Madden's comin for him. Dem have to keep him until police autopsy."

"Will they come today?"

"Um-hmm." Miss Betsy paused. "Lissa don't speak since it happen."

"When is the funeral likely to be?" I said.

202

"Is dat mi want talk to you about," Miss Betsy say. "Miss Arleen don't have any money. She don't want ask if you can help with di funeral, but I tell her she must ask. I tell her you can only say no. Marlon must bury right. He a innocent boy, don't deserve to die so young. Funeral have to do right, or him not going rest in peace."

"How much money?" I said.

"Roundabout twenty thousand," Miss Betsy said.

"I think I can find that," I said, wondering how. "But Miss Betsy, maybe we don't need a really expensive coffin and flowers and all that."

Miss Betsy looked at me. Her mouth was grim. "If it was your son, though, him would bury right."

"That's not fair. I said I'd help. I know a big funeral is important to…" I stopped. "When do you need the money?"

"Soon as you can bring it." She sat heavily in one of the chairs and picked up an old-fashioned paper fan. She fanned herself. It wasn't yet seven, but the house was hot.

I sat on the couch again. "Miss Arleen, I'm truly sorry about Marlon. I'll bring the money tomorrow and if there is anything else I can do, please let me know. Where's Dexter? Does he know?"

Arleen shook her head. "Dunno. Police tek him. Wi dunno where him is. Maybe dem kill him too."

"What they take him for?"

"Dem just tek him. Him was inna di house, him bring some frien' home last night. Police kick down di door and shoot up di place and take Dexter away. Marlon get kill. That's it."

"What happened to Dexter's friends?"

"Dem run."

"You going to the police station to try and get Dex out?" I said.

"No. Yes. Maybe tomorrow. But if dem even give bail, is not even forty dollar in my purse."

"Can't be today," Miss Betsy said. "Wi have to wait until Madden's come."

I got up. "Okay," I said. "I'll be back tomorrow. I'll bring food. And the money. I'll try and find Dex. Call me if there's anything else." I turned to Miss Betsy. "I don't mean any offence, but can you read?"

"Surely."

"Then read Lissa a story. A happy story. She likes 'Green Eggs and Ham'. The book is over at the house. But if you can't find that one, anything will do."

Miss Betsy nodded her head. "You a good woman, Miss Sahara. The Lord will bless you."

I didn't feel blessed or even sad about Marlon. I was angry. And I needed help to sort out this situation. I couldn't afford twenty thousand dollars. I didn't know anything about the court system. Damn the night I had spent a few minutes engaging a young street boy in conversation! I walked out into the hard sunlight and left Jacob's Pen.

DEXTER
Bad man into mad man

Something stickin me inna chest. I try take a deep breath, but it hurt too much. I breathe with my mouth open, like a dog chain to a fence inna the burnin sun.

I hear plenty noise; man shoutin, clangin, metal on metal. Concrete floor under my cheek. Try open my eye-them. One open; the other one stick shut. I don't know what happen or where this place is. Maybe somebody will soon come and take the knife outta my chest. I want Mumma.

I try reach the knife. Maybe I can pull it out. My hand-them tie behind my back. I try loose them, but I can't. I move one leg and then the other. Leg are okay. I move my head slow and look at my chest. No knife. Something must break inside. I am wearin only brief.

Smell vomit. I am lyin in it. Who vomit on me, star? I kill him when I find him.

"Di bwoy no wake up yet?"

"Him don't move since you finish wit' him. You beat him 'til him dead."

"Shut you mout' or you next. Him nah dead. See him a breathe."

I dream I am pissin on a bush down at Rocky River. The floor wet up. I must a been standin in the river.

205

How this place stink so bad? I smell man and shit and vomit and piss. Some cook food too. My stomach roll and I try to vomit. Knife that is not there turn inna my chest and I bawl out. Must be me vomit before, but nothing come out this time.

Open my one eye and look around. I try lift my head, but my brain come loose inside and everything spin around like a gig. I try vomit again; bawl out bawl out at the pain inna my chest.

Lay still. Open one eye slow-slow. Dark. I am lyin on a bare concrete floor. It cold. Other man here; them sleepin in corner, lookin like pile a old clothes. Prison. I think a Pastor in Jacob's Pen. Him say, prison turn bad man into mad man, and mad man into bad man. Lasco say I am a man now, but what kind?

"Di bwoy still a sleep?"
    "Him nah sleep, him beat up bad-bad. Him bawl out di whole night. Wait 'til human rights people hear 'bout dis."
    "You a chat bare foolishness."
    "Him a juvenile. Him not supposed to be in cell with plenty man. Him suppose to be in place a safety or him own cell. Him suppose to get medical attention."
    "Where mi to get empty cell?"
    "Clear a space where di woman is. Hardly anybody down dere."
    One man suck him teeth. The other man say, "You have to tek him to clinic. The one on Maxfield Avenue. But try wait a week so him don't look so bad. And mek sure you clean him up first."
    The cell door open and three man come in. Them pick me up and I scream out. Them carry me down some steps and put me in another cell. Them drop me hard and I scream out again. The cell door bang shut. Must not move. Movin hurt too much. I pretend I am a tree trunk cut down.

"Water," I say. "Please." Nobody hear me and no water come.
    "What you name?"

"Me?"

"You see anybody else here, shotta?"

"Dexter."

"Dexter what?"

"Raymond Dexter Morrison."

I don't know what day it is. I try remember what happen. I remember shovelin sand in Rocky River. I remember runnin to Mumma house to hide. I remember police comin and shot firin. Mumma bawlin out to save her pickney-them. Then I see the police swing his gun at me and after that, black. Then I am locked somewhere small and movin and smellin of gasoline and oil. A car trunk. Then nothing.

"Where is dis place?" I say. There is another boy in the cell with me.

"Half Way Tree lock up."

"Mi need water. Please."

"You see dis line?" The boy point to a line I can barely make out on the concrete floor.

"I see it."

"Mek sure you don't cross it."

Don't know long I been in jail. Day and night is the same. Them take off my handcuff. Them give me tear-up shirt and pants. The other boy in the cell don't even say his name. The cell have two concrete slab for bed. No mattress or sheet or blanket. We piss and shit in a plastic bucket. We get food two time every day. Wonder what happen to Boston and Lasco? Know I must not tell Babylon anything. Them give me basin with water and cloth and I wash off some a the blood and vomit. I still smell stink. I have big coco on my head, my face beat up, but nothing hurt worse than my chest.

"Morrison?" Police stand at the cell, holdin key and handcuff.

"Yes sir?" I say. Don't hurt to be mannersable. Even if I am a man now.

"Get up. We a go clinic."

I stand up and walk over. Him open the door a the cell. "Turn around," him say.

I turn around. Him put on the handcuff, take me outta the cell and slam me against a wall. "Hear mi now, yout'," him say quiet-quiet. "You see what happen to you? *You fall down inna cell*, you hear mi? Nobody don't lay a hand on you. If you say anyting different, you don't see tomorrow and you madda don't see tomorrow. You understan' mi, shotta?"

"Yes sir," I say.

SAHARA
Carl comes home

"Mom? Hello, Mom? Can you hear me? It's me…"

"Carl? What time is it? Are you okay?" I heard a burst of laughter and crashing noises.

"Shut up, guys, I'm on the phone here! It's not late, Mom, it's only eleven. Yes, I'm okay."

I'd been sleeping deeply. It was the night after Marlon's death and the lack of sleep had caught up with me. Why was Carl calling? He was due home in a week after his first year at college. Was there some problem with his air ticket – but why at eleven o'clock at night?

"I'm awake. What is it, Carl? Is there a problem with your ticket? Have you finished your exams?"

"Exams're over." There was something in his voice. "More than a week ago." He sounded accusing, as if I should have remembered his exam timetable. He didn't seem to have many exams. His course work seemed to be mostly papers and projects. He'd been vague about college for the whole year and I'd tried not to pry. When he came home last Christmas, I saw one of his textbooks was on folk art and I wondered what that had to do with a business degree.

"So why're you calling?"

"What? Can't phone to say hi? There has to be some special reason?" I knew he'd pick me up like that. But there was a tremor in his voice, an uncertainty.

"Spit it out, son. What's the problem?"

"I got a letter from the Dean. I've been thrown out."

"*What?* Why? What did you do?" I turned on the light and got

209

up. I saw my face in the mirror and looked away. I imagined my son dealing drugs, pimping – it had to be something very bad for him to have been expelled. I thought of Dexter. Setting fire to the bathrooms. Now in prison.

"I don't have sufficient grades to continue." Carl's voice cracked.

"How is that possible? They don't expel you for poor grades without a warning, surely?"

"I've had warnings, Mom. Basically you have to have a certain GPA or they put you on academic probation. I've been on academic probation since my first semester and my GPA is only 1.8. So they've thrown me out. You need a 2 to go into second year."

I was stunned. I'd worried about dozens of things where Carl was concerned over the past ten months, but his grades hadn't made the list. He'd always been a decent student, not brilliant, but never failing.

"Say something," he said.

"I don't know what to say." I wanted to shout at him, call him an idiot. Ask him whether he thought his father would keep paying his tuition now. "Why didn't you tell me you were having trouble before?"

"I thought I could fix it. None of my friends took grades seriously. I dunno, Mom, I thought it would be okay." He sounded close to tears.

"Well, Bugs, what to do." I pretended a calmness I didn't feel. "You're coming home in a week. We'll talk then. I suggest you go and see the Dean and find out what your options are."

"Okay," he said, sounding like a ten-year-old.

"We'll sort it out, Bugs." I didn't tell him about Marlon.

Carl phoned many times that week. He seemed to have lost his ability to make a decision. Should he put his stuff in storage or bring it all home? He'd planned to move out of the dorm next year into a house with some friends. He'd given them a down payment towards the rent, should he ask for it back? Should he make an appointment with the Dean or speak to his academic advisor first? Would I meet his plane in Kingston? Could I send a little money? He didn't want to ask his father, didn't want to explain what had happened.

"He'll have to know sometime, Carl," I said.

"Could you tell him for me?"

"I think you should tell him, son. Look, I can't say I know exactly how your father will react, but we've all made mistakes. Don't assume the worst."

"You don't understand," Carl said, sounding like more his old self.

Towards the end of the week, he told me not to meet him at the airport.

"Why ever not?"

"I can get home by myself, I'll take a taxi."

I knew he was afraid of confronting me as well as his father. "I'll be at the airport, son. I told you, we'll work this out."

I got to the airport early and stood on the waving gallery. I remembered being taken there as a child, before my father left and my mother died, standing close to the railing and staring into the sunset, trying to see the planes. It was entertainment – in those days people went to watch the planes. There was even a place you could have a drink and watch the planes landing and taking off through huge glass windows. I always had a lime squash just for the red cherry at the bottom.

Now the waving gallery was a squalid place. A concrete counter ran along the back wall and a listless woman presided over the selling of cheese crunchies and banana chips. Litter blew unchecked into corners. A ragged man held out his hand without appearance of hope to anyone reasonably well dressed. He encountered averted eyes and shaken heads.

I walked to the railing and stared into the setting sun for my son's plane. I was angry with him – how could he have squandered an opportunity I would have loved? I wondered if it would do him any good to try and rescue him – perhaps it would be best to let the expulsion – if that was what it was called – take effect. Then what? He'd have to get a low-paying job, struggle to work on public transportation or beg lifts from people. It might do him good.

Perhaps the situation at Florida State wasn't rectifiable – I was falling into the Jamaican trap that assumed anything could be fixed with entreaties and connections. I had no connections at Florida State – well, no connections anywhere. Perhaps there would be no going back.

I watched a pregnant woman walk to the end of the waving gallery. She was young and wore a too-tight red dress. Her hair was done in cornrows. She put her hands in the small of her back and stretched her back, looking up to the sky. I remembered that backache. The woman turned around and I saw she was hardly more than a girl, the remnants of acne still peppering her face. I had been a girl like her, not yet eighteen and pregnant. I remembered the fear I felt at confronting Aunt Gladys. I remembered the hot tears at night while I tried to decide what to do and no course of action seemed possible. I'd thought my life was over.

Carl had made a mistake. So had I. And yet I was waiting now to meet the result of that mistake. Perhaps there are no such things as mistakes, because we never know what's going to happen. Perhaps if Carl had stayed at school some other, some worse fate would have greeted him.

I told myself to stop agonizing. It wasn't the end of the world. If Florida State wouldn't take Carl back, he could work for a year and try again. People get scholarships all the time and work their way through college. "It'll work out," I said out loud. The ragged man approached me and I gave him the small change I always kept in my pocket for such moments. Always better not to have to dig in your handbag.

A man pointed towards the sun and I saw the plane, its wings glinting as it sank towards the earth. I thought of my empty evenings and was glad my son was coming home.

DEXTER
Fall down inna cell

The police drive me to a clinic. This time they put me in the back seat of a car. Outside a the lock up, the sun so bright I think it must have come down to earth. I close my eye-them. I glad to smell outside, glad to hear car horn and music and people. Nobody pay me any mind in the back a the police car. The clinic is not far and I sorry when the journey over. I wonder if I can escape, but two police hold me.

We go inna the clinic. It crowd up with woman and bawlin pickney. Nobody look at me. The police go to a woman behind a desk. Them don't say anything. She jerk her head to show the way to go and we go into another room. A young Indian man wearin a white jacket sit behind a desk. Must be the doctor.

"Could one of you wait outside?" him say to Babylon. One a the police leave. Wonder if I can escape now.

"Hello, youngster," the doctor say. "What happened to you? What's your name?" Him talk funny, like Mr. Malik, the sports master at Holborn.

"Him name Raymond Morrison. Him a shotta from Jacob's Pen," the police say.

"Officer, please let me do my job. I need *him* to tell me his name." The police suck him teeth and stand behind me.

"Well, son?" the Indian man say to me. "I'm Dr. Saipu. What's your name?"

"Dexter, sir. My real name is Raymond Morrison."

"How old are you, Dexter?"

"Fourteen."

The doctor shake him head. "Let's have a look at you then.

Can you get up here?" He point to a high bed on one side a the room.

I show him my handcuff. "Officer, please take off his handcuffs," the doctor say.

The police suck him teeth again, but he do what the doctor say. I get up on the table, my chest still stabbin me. Lucky there is a stool to climb on.

"Where hurts?" the doctor say.

"Chest. Someting stickin mi."

"You've probably broken some ribs." The doctor start pressin my chest and I scream out. I shame. Big man not supposed to bawl.

"Um-hmm," he say. "Definitely broken or cracked ribs. What happened to you?"

I see the police lookin at me. "Fall down inna di cell," I say.

"Of course," the doctor say. "Let me see your head." The doctor feel my head. "You have a big lump here, young man. But I don't think there's any fracture. It's healing – it should have been stitched, but it's too late for that now. Fell down in your cell, you say?" I don't answer.

"I would like to take this boy for an X-ray," the doctor say to the police.

"No vehicle today," the police say.

The doctor shake him head again. "What about the vehicle you came in?"

"It due to go on patrol," the police say.

The doctor make me take off the stinkin clothes. Him clean me up as best he can. Him put tape on my ribs and dressin on my cuts. "Not much I can do about this eye," him say. "You're quite a sight, young man." I want bawl livin eye water. Better not to have this doctor being nice to me. Better no one nice to me again. The doctor give me back the same clothes and I put them on.

"You finish?" the police say.

"Yes. For now. Call me when you can arrange the X-ray," the doctor say.

"Yes doc. We going *definitely* call you."

Babylon put back on the cuffs and take me outside. The other police come. "Him say anyting?"

"No. Look like him know what is good for him."

Them push me back in police car. I wish the prison was far – I wish the drive was long-long. But not even ten minute gone and we back at the Half Way Tree lock up. When they take me in and I go a my side a the cell, I know this is where I going be until I am an old man with bend back and no teeth. I want Mumma. I want know what happen at Jacob's Pen the night the police come on the raid. No one here to tell me.

SAHARA
Finding Dexter

Three days after Carl came home, he and I went to the Half Way Tree lockup to find Dexter. I'd told him as much of the story I knew; Dexter had gone bad, Marlon was dead and Lissa struck mute. Carl seemed shocked.

"What will happen to Dexter?" he asked.

"I don't know, son." I waited for his "I told you so". It did not come.

It had taken many phone calls and educated insistence to find out where Dexter was being held. The Half Way Tree lockup was infamous for overcrowded, inhumane conditions and I was afraid to go. I wished I had a lawyer friend who would come with me. Carl suggested asking his father, but I couldn't face his unspoken judgement. Lydia was out too – I knew her views on what she called the "Jacob's Pen project".

"I'll go with you, Mom," Carl said. "How bad can it be?"

We waited until the worst of the traffic had eased and drove to Half Way Tree; Carl was silent beside me. He'd been awake when I got up, as he had been each morning since his return. He'd shaved expertly, not inaccurately (and infrequently) as he used to. His room was neat. He seemed to have stopped eating breakfast, drinking only a single cup of black coffee. One day he wore shorts and I saw his toenails needed attention. I began to feel like he was a house guest I didn't know very well.

At every traffic light we passed, street boys gathered at the car windows. Some of them were children, skinny and dusty, others were men. Some were probably crackheads, their eyes showing the whites, their manner vague. Some boys looked like they were at play, like the boys at St. Stephen's, pushing each other, aiming karate kicks in the air. We didn't roll down our windows. I always left space between my car and the one in front, in case it was necessary to get out of the lane of traffic in a hurry. Often, there were cars on all sides so it was only possible in theory.

There was a red Prado in the lane beside me, driven by a woman who was talking on a cell phone. One of the men approached her car, and without waiting for permission squirted slimy water from a plastic bottle on her windscreen, eased the wipers off the windscreen and began cleaning. The woman gestured angrily at the man and eased the Prado forward. The man threw the contents of the plastic bottle at her car, splattering the windscreen and the paintwork, and sauntered off, leaving the wipers sticking out like an insect's antennae. The light changed and cars started moving. The woman's mouth was working furiously; she was obviously cursing the street man. No doubt she was considering whether she would have to get out of the Prado and put the wipers back down. Cars started to blow their horns and our lane moved. In my rear-view mirror, I saw a street boy put the Prado's wipers down, his manner obsequious.

I couldn't see any parking at the Half Way Tree Police Station – wrecked cars occupied many spaces. Vendors plied their trade at the gate. I asked a uniformed policeman where we could park. "Try 'round the back," he said, uninterested.

We inched around the building and luckily a taxi pulled out of a parking space right in front of us. I turned into it; it was tight.

There was no indication about where to go. People milled around at every entrance to the building. They were mostly women. Some were carrying baskets with the contents covered with cloths, as if they were visiting the sick. Many people stared at us, our light skins setting us apart. They parted to let us through. "Brownin'," a man whispered as we passed.

We guessed a doorway to enter. It was dark inside. A rusty ceiling fan stirred fetid air. People sat on wooden chairs around the sides of the room, some leaning their heads against the wall as if they'd been there for a long time. No doubt they had. A policeman sat behind a desk with an enormous ledger open in front of him. I wished I knew more about the ranks of the security forces – whether he was a constable or a sergeant or what. I was sure if I addressed him by his correct title it would win me points.

He looked up at us, but didn't speak. "Good morning, officer," I said. "I'm here to inquire about a prisoner."

"No prisoner here."

"I was told he was here. Maybe we're in the wrong place? Is this the Half Way Tree lockup?"

"Is di lockup. We have detainee here, not prisoner."

"I'm sorry," I said, holding in my irritation. "Detainee, then. We're here to inquire about a detainee."

"Name?" he said.

"Sahara Lawrence, and this is my son Carl Lawrence."

"Not your name. Di detainee name."

"Dexter – no, Raymond Morrison."

The policeman reached behind him for another book. The phone on his desk rang and he answered it. "Yow. Yeah, bred'ren. Get off 'bout five. Wha' you a sey?" He listened and laughed. The conversation went back and forth, while he thumbed through the book. He paid no attention to us.

Eventually he finished his call. "When di detainee bring in?"

"Two weeks ago." I said. "The second. He was arrested after a police raid in Jacob's Pen."

"So is a shotta you come look for. You one a dem human rights people?"

"No, officer, I'm not. We're friends of the family." As I said this, I realized how ridiculous it sounded. *Friends of the family*. The phrase belonged in a drawing room in another century.

"Don't see any such name," said the officer, not looking at the book.

"Could you look again? I called earlier and they said he was here."

"Who you speak to?"

"Corporal Hylton."

"Him off duty now," he said, as if that settled everything.

"I don't need to see Corporal Hylton. He just told me that Dexter – Raymond was here. I know he's allowed a visitor and Corporal Hylton told me I could come this morning."

"Hylton not here," he repeated, looking over my shoulder, seeking to end the interview. "Check back tomorrow."

I summoned some backbone. "Officer, I know Dexter is here. I would like to see him. If you won't ..." – what would be the right term for a prison? – "...admit me, I'd like to talk to your supervisor."

The man sucked his teeth, but he said nothing. He went back to the book, his finger tracing the lines of names, some, I saw, with only first names. "See him here, Dexter Morrison. Never see it di first time, dat man Hylton, him handwritin bad. I get somebody to bring di detainee."

We sat on rickety chairs. They were placed very close together and we had to squeeze between two large women, one who appeared to be sleeping. I stole a look at Carl. Before he went away to college he would have hated all this. His face was impassive, but I didn't sense impatience. The policeman behind the desk continued to pore over his ledger.

We waited. Every now and then, a policeman came in and called out a name, and someone would leave with the policeman. Someone else from outside the room would immediately take the chair. I could see no system. I hadn't seen the policeman behind the desk give Dexter's name to anyone else. I wondered how long we'd have to wait. I realized I'd made the mistake of not asking the policeman his name.

Another policeman walked in and the man behind the desk said, "Hylton. Dese people here to see Morrison."

"But..." I started to say. So it was a lie, but decided against completing my sentence. There was nothing to be gained by antagonizing these men.

"You family?" Hylton said, with an air of disbelief.

"In a way. My name is Sahara Lawrence; this is my son Carl. We've known Dexter and his family for a couple of years. Dexter was arrested after a raid in Jacob's Pen and his brother,

– his eleven-year-old brother – was killed. His mother is grief stricken and asked me to enquire about Dex."

"Di boy you call Dexter, we know him as Matrix. Him a bad bwoy; a shotta. Him kill a man over at Portmore. We find illegal firearm on him. Better you look out for a different bwoy."

"Were you on the raid, Corporal Hylton?" I asked.

"Not you business. You a lawyer?" There was a hint of anxiety as well as truculence in his voice.

"No, I'm not a lawyer. I told you why I'm here."

Corporal Hylton looked over at the policeman behind the desk. "Gone to get Morrison. Tek her to room four. You..." he said to Carl, "...you wait here."

Room four was a dirty cubicle with a small table and two chairs. I hoped Carl would be okay waiting. He hadn't objected or raised his eyes to heaven or sighed audibly. I felt anxious about my son and resentful that I had to be dealing with this situation. Why couldn't Dexter have kept his nose clean? Was he really a shotta, one of those cruel men who slaughtered in multiples?

The door opened and Corporal Hylton pushed Dexter into the room. He staggered and almost fell. His hands were handcuffed behind his back. His head was lowered and he did not look up. His pants were ripped and soiled. His shirt was many sizes too big for him. His head was bandaged. He stank.

"Five minute," Corporal Hylton said and left. Dexter sat heavily in the other chair, still looking down, leaning forward to allow his hands space behind his back.

"Dex?" I said and the gentleness in my voice surprised me. I'd been angry seconds before. Dexter looked up and I saw the damage to his face, his mouth swollen and split, one eye closed and bruised. He breathed shallowly. He looked at me with his one open eye.

"What you doin here, Miss Sahara?" he mumbled.

I leaned forward and held his chin in my hand, and remembered when I had touched him the first time we met in Sovereign. He had flinched. I had asked him not to send any children he might have in the future to the plaza to beg. What

220

a ridiculous thing to have said! I remembered his graduation night, his eyes luminous with hope. He winced, tried to turn his head away, but I held his chin firmly.

"What happened, Dex? Did they beat you?"

"Wha'ppen to everybody, Miss Sahara? Mumma and Marlon and Lissa?" he said.

"Aah, Dex, I'm so sorry, but Marlon is dead."

"Marlon *dead*?"

"I'm sorry. Yes. He died in the gunfire. He died immediately though, he didn't suffer."

Dexter sat in silence for a moment. I still held his chin. Then he met my eyes. "Him suffer, Miss Sahara," he said. "Him suffer him whole life. Prob'ly is better him dead. Him woulda just end up a sit where mi a sit now."

"Your mother and Lissa are okay," I said. Dexter didn't answer.

"Did they beat you?"

He twisted his head free from my hand. "No, mi fall down inna cell." The sarcasm bit.

I felt helpless. I had no idea what to do. I didn't even know what I felt about him – was he a victim, deserving my sympathy and assistance, or was he a violent, antisocial male who was right where he needed to be – in jail? Both?

"I'm going to try and get bail for you," I said. "Get you out of here until your trial. Have you been charged with anything?"

"No. Dem not going give bail – or it going be too high. Miss Sahara, you can't do nutt'n for me. Better you try help Mumma and Lissa. It over for me." Dexter looked over my shoulder and I turned, expecting Corporal Hylton. Carl stood there.

"Dexter," Carl said. I was sure that was the first time Carl had uttered his name.

"Carl? You come home, huh? What you mumma bring you here for?"

"I'm sorry about Marlon. Who beat you up? Mom, can we get him out of here? Look at him, he's hurt."

"I can try, Carl." My spirit lightened at my son's words. Had his own failure brought him empathy?

"Them say you is a shotta," Carl said, lapsing into patois.

221

"Them say you name Matrix. Them say you kill a man over in Portmore and them take a illegal gun from you. Is true?"

"Mi never kill nobaddy. Mi never have no gun. Mi never been to Portmore. Mi was down at Rocky River with some badman and dem did have gun."

"Why, Dex?" I said.

"*Why?* 'Cause what else there is for mi to do, Miss Sahara? 'Cause mi tired a bein Big Foot, tired a borin schoolroom and bwoy and teacher disrespectin me. 'Cause what all the schoolin you t'ink so important going bring me? Nutt'n, Miss Sahara, *nutt'n*, you hear? Schoolin going bring me labourer job at construction site. Maybe mi could wash big man car, maybe if mi lucky-lucky, get a job as a security, and is *mi* gunman shoot after at night. You know what badman and gun give mi? *Respect*, Miss Sahara. Respect mi couldna get no other way."

"But now you're in jail and your brother is dead!"

"Mom!" Carl said. "Take it easy!"

"No other way," Dexter said, and I saw his cheeks were wet. He was a boy without a future and he was the cause of his brother's death. I was no use to him; to any of them. Yes, I could bring a basket of food, buy shoes, even get them into a good school. Dexter passed for St. Stephen's, but here he was sitting forgotten in a jail cell, beaten by the police, another statistic, another criminal. I stood up. "I'll try and get you bail, Dex. Even so you can go to Marlon's funeral."

"Don't want go to Marlon funeral. Don't want *you* here. Lef' mi, Miss Sahara. Go 'bout you business. You want do someting for me? Take food for Mumma and Lissa – mi in here and Marlon dead. Nobody at home to get food for Mumma. You tek food for her like always. That is what mi want."

"Five minute up," said Corporal Hylton behind us. "What you doin in here, bwoy? Don't mi tell you to wait?"

I thought of Lydia. She would not be silent. "You told us," I said, and I was ashamed of the tremor in my voice. "And now I see why. The police beat the crap out of this boy. He's just a kid, a boy. He…"

"Shut you mout', woman. What you know 'bout it? Nobody beat di yout'. So wi find him. And we find him wit' a gun – you

222

better say you prayer he don't get outta jail; you coulda wake up inna night and dat gun be point at you. Then you want call 119 and you want police to answer. You and you son get outta here. Go back to whichever *gated community* you come from."

"We're going," I said. "But we'll be back, Dex, we'll be back with a lawyer and clean clothes and food. And, you...," I said to Corporal Hylton, "I'm going to report you for your unprofessional conduct. We have laws. I have *never*..."

"Mom. Stop." Carl put his hand on my shoulder. "Let's go."

We heard Corporal Hylton laugh as we left the cubicle. "So you have uptown frien', bwoy," he said. "Good fah you."

DEXTER
Dead is just dead

In prison, it hard to tell day from night. No window inna cell, but there is a window in the passage outside. It high and small and the glass dirty. When I first come here, I think when light come through that window, must be day. Hour upon hour go by; night never come. I ask the boy inna my cell if that is daylight. Him laugh. "You a eedyat, star. Is a street light dat." Is the only word him ever say to me. After that, me learn to tell day from night by the food we get. Police take me back to cell after Miss Sahara and Carl visit. Lie on concrete slab and feel my chest. It seem better. Run my hand over my head top, under the bandage. It don't feel too bad. I want sleep. I don't want think.

But I can't keep my brother outta my head. Him come to me like a duppy – Marlon livin inside my brain. I see him strugglin to carry him water bucket, holdin on tight to me inna bus, I see him bringin in food from Ma'as Ken, I see him sittin at him desk, quiet-quiet at Holborn Prep. Marlon dead. The police-dem murder me brother. Them kill him because I bring them to Mumma house. I make Marlon into a duppy.

What dead feel like? Pastor say if you good, you go heaven and angel will be there. No more being hungry, no more gunshot, no more hurricane to wash you 'way. No more bad thing at all. Will Marlon feel okay with a whole pile a angel? Maybe him will be alone, like at Holborn Prep. Maybe the angel-them call him "Big Foot". No. Bad thing not suppose to happen in heaven.

But maybe dead is just dead, like the calf me kill. Maybe

dead mean you is just meat. And me, I am not good; if Marlon is with some angel-them, I will never see him. I will never see my brother again; never see Lissa or Mumma. Them forget me in jail. Me, Raymond Dexter Morrison, forgot. Now I'm a prisoner, a shotta, a dog-heart yout'. I am not the boy who pass for St. Stephen's. Not no more.

Wonder what happen to Boston and Lasco. Better to think about them. I don't think them get catch by Babylon, but I not sure. Them could be take to another lock up. Them bigger – them could be upstairs in the cell with the bad man. Them could dead after the police leave Jacob's Pen.

Miss Sahara say she will get bail for me. She too ignorant 'bout how things go. One thing I know – if I come out, I never comin back. Them never find me. Go find a place up inna Dallas Mountain to hide.

Fool-fool, Marlon say in my head. What you going eat inna the mountain?

I going come down inna early mornin and catch fish inna the river. Fish and janga.

What kinda foolishness you a chat? You mean the one-one fish inna Rocky River?

Shut you mout'. Is better than jail. Must can find tamarind and mango and banana and ackee inna the mountain.

Best thing you do if you get out is find Merciless. Find Boston and Lasco. Them not dead – you woulda hear if them was dead. Get inna Racehorse crew. Big man protect you then.

And how long before I am back in prison?

Be smart. Lay low. Merciless man-them show you how to survive. Bwoy like you and me never going live long anyway. Me know that now. You join Racehorse Crew and you get bling and 'nuff gal. You shine for a time. Better than going to jail until you a grown man.

Shut you mout'. You not Marlon. Leave me in peace.

I turn over and hide my face. Look like a man can never escape the voice he carry with him, inside him head. A man can never escape what him is, what him is born to be. What a man is born to be is waitin for him, no matter what. It wait for him, hidin in the mud bottom in a shallow pool in the dry season, waitin for the day when rain start fall and the river swell and overflow and carry everything before it to the sea. And this is what I know. Everything drown in the sea, sinkin to the bottom, to rotten in the dark, lost for ever and ever.

SAHARA
The summer of storms

It was Monday, two days after Marlon's funeral and I was still raw. Carl had been out all day and I'd had no idea where he was.

I'd been sleeping badly since the funeral – it played over and over in my mind, the crowds of sweaty people, the women dressed in frills and hats, the men in shiny suits, Arleen's embarrassing keening, the too-loud, out-of-tune organ, the incoherent speeches and sermons, the flies on the open coffin, the smells of excited, sponge-bathed, over-perfumed people. It all felt so unseemly, so unrestrained – the chapel was like a bathroom with glass walls, where immodest people did their private business in full view of the world. The people seemed to relish the rituals of death and it all had little to do with the boy Marlon had been.

Then, I hadn't felt sad. It was too noisy and uncomfortable and I was too out of place, especially standing beside Miss Arleen in the front row, where I'd been ushered by Miss Betsy, and given Lissa to hold. I didn't know how to act, didn't know when to stand and sit, didn't want to join in the "hallelujahs" and "praise Hims!" and "Amens!" At first I longed to put Lissa down; soon I was glad of her dead weight – holding her gave me something to do, something that wouldn't be judged by anyone. I was being useful. It was not until I got into bed that night, after I'd showered and washed away the grime of the long afternoon, that I thought of Marlon, and that I'd never know how he would have turned out, and that thought shamed me. He'd never been real to me.

It was inevitably Carl who felt the blast of my tension.

"Where've you been, Carl? Your phone's off; I've been worried sick. I know you've been away at college and you've come and gone as you pleased, but now you're back home and if I don't know where you are, I worry. You have to start thinking about someone other than yourself!"

"I got Dexter out of jail," he said. In truth, I'd been more upset by the lack of a phone call than truly worried – I imagined he'd found a friend and was off at the beach or Lime Cay.

"You did what?"

"I got Dexter out of jail. And I finally told Dad about being thrown out of school."

"What? How? When?"

"Just now. I called Dad, asked to see him, told him about school, told him about Dexter and he bailed him."

"Your father bailed Dexter?"

"Yes."

"How is that possible? The police say he was found with an illegal gun!"

"I don't really know – something about improper process for a juvenile and the beating he got. Plus Dad knew the judge. Anyway, the point is, he's out. We dropped him home."

"Your father dropped him home?"

"Well, to the corner. We didn't go right up to the house."

"So you didn't see Arleen?"

"No. We didn't see anybody."

"Why'd you do that? Arleen and Lissa are probably still at Miss Betsy's and Dexter won't find them."

"Mom, you're a control freak! Let go, nuh. You don't have to organize everything. That's what Dexter wanted. He asked us to drop him on the corner. He said he'd find his way."

"Did you give him money?"

"Yes, a few thousand dollars. Dex has to go back to court, though. Next month, on the 25th. Dad's handling his case."

I heard pride in my son's voice. He had done something good and his father was helping him. I didn't know how to feel about it. I didn't like the way the word "Dad" was falling so easily off Carl's tongue. "Dad" had achieved something I hadn't imagined could be done.

"So what'd he say about your being thrown out of school?"

"He was upset. We talked about that first. He says I have to figure it out. He says if it costs more, I'll have to pay him back. He thinks you should get in touch with the school and go and see them. Maybe I could switch programmes or something. He thinks we can work it out, Mom."

I heard excitement in Carl's voice. I'd told him things could be worked out, but it hadn't had the same effect. What did Lester know? Had he been around for measles or bullying – for thousands of sleepless nights?

Afterwards, I remembered that summer as the summer of storms. They came in waves off the coast of Africa, much earlier than usual, strengthening into storms as they approached the Lesser Antilles, building up into hurricanes over the warm Caribbean Sea. Carl battened down the house and I shopped wearily for provisions – canned soup, candles, crackers, kerosene oil, batteries. Rivers burst their banks and swept the dwellings of poor people to the sea. Many drowned and some were never found. Huge slabs of hillsides fell away, carrying boulders as large as houses on a relentless tide of mud.

Between storms, Kingston baked – the bougainvillea exploded in blooms and the hills around the city caught fire. Then the storms came again and sheets of water ran off the cracked earth, turning the streets into muddy rivers. Flowers fell from the uncontrollable shrubbery and lawns became pastures. Every seed germinated, weeds erupted from the earth and the limbs of trees bowed under the weight of their leaves. Then the rain stopped and the island dried out until it was no more than a tired, dusty rock in the sea.

We were spared the wreckage of a direct hit, but we were exhausted by the constant state of worry – the hurricane watches, the evacuation instructions that no one heeded, the lines in gas stations and supermarkets. Then we struggled though the aftermath of these near-misses – days and nights without electricity, people lost in shelters, wild young men in the streets – and the savage, sodden heat.

Lester gave Carl a summer job at his law practice and Carl started to talk about taking L-SATs and trying for law school. We made an appointment at Florida State with Carl's advisor in mid-August. Carl seemed happy – his father collected him for work most mornings and he seemed interested in his job. He was still dating Kimberley. A nice girl, I thought. It was time to breathe easier about my son.

I'd not been to Jacob's Pen since Dexter had been bailed. I'd thought of the family often during the storms and hoped they were safe in Miss Betsy's house. I hoped the money Lester had given Dexter was keeping them fed. I didn't like to think about where he was and what he might be doing, but I was sure I couldn't help. Mostly, I was angry with him. I wrote Josephine Blanchard in the US and told her of Dexter's arrest and Marlon's death. I asked if she would continue her sponsorship of Lissa's education, adding that girls were so much easier. I waited for her reply.

Dexter's court date was June 25th. Carl dressed in his only suit that day; he intended to go with his father to court. "Wanna come, Mom?" he said. "I think Dex would like to see you."

"I don't think so, Carl. I think I've had enough."

"So you're going to abandon them, then?"

"Abandon? I think I've done more than could reasonably be expected. Dex's not going to get back into school. He's got to figure things out for himself now. Maybe Lissa will make it. I don't know. I've asked Mrs. Blanchard if she'll keep Lissa on; I guess I'll hear back from her soon. Anyway, I thought you were sure *those people* couldn't be helped."

Carl shrugged. "I guess. But I got angry when I saw how the cops beat Dex. He made a mistake, Mom. He's a boy. It shouldn't be the end of his life. Come with us."

"No, Bugs. I have things to do. You'll tell me about it later. It's just a formality anyway; nothing's actually going to happen today."

Two hours later, Carl was back. He looked sad.

"What happened?" I said.

"He didn't show up. They've issued a warrant for his arrest."

The three boys waited in the dark behind the Chinese restaurant in Sovereign Plaza. The Sunny was parked nearby with the trunk half-open. The boys had lined it with used cattle feed bags and enlarged a small rust hole for air. Dexter had suggested including a bottle of water, but Boston and Lasco said there was no point, the white woman's hands would be tied. "Nah tek any time drive from Sovereign to downtown. She can't dead in dat short time," Boston said.

"So what if she dead?" Lasco said.

"She not suppose to dead," Dexter said. "You no hear we suppose to let her go?"

"How wi going get it inna di Gleaner?" Boston said.

"We just call her fambly and ask for money. Preten' like it a kidnapping. Dem will phone di police and it wi' get inna di paper." Lasco smiled. "Wi going be famous after dis."

"How we going find out who she people is?" Boston asked.

"She going tell wi, eedyat. You no tink she 'fraid for her life? She tell wi anyting wi want know!" Lasco hit Boston lightly on his shoulder.

"Who you callin eedyat?"

"Awright, awright," Dexter said. "Mek us just find a old woman who not going gi' trouble."

Sahara, Carl and Carl's girlfriend, Kimberly, joined the group of people leaving the movie. "It's hot," Sahara said as they came out of the air-conditioned cinema. "I think it gets hotter every year."

"You always say that," Carl said.

Sahara could no longer go to Sovereign without thinking of Dexter, but she said nothing.

From the shadows, Dexter saw Sahara and Carl and a young girl he didn't know. A tide of fear flooded his body. They should not have come to Sovereign; the chances of an encounter with Sahara were too great. Now Lasco might see Sahara; he might pick her, might decide she was the one who would take the ride in the trunk of the Sunny. Not any woman; *this* woman. This woman who had touched him, fed him, listened to him, visited him in prison. This woman, whose son had bailed him. He imagined her held by Lasco, bound, gagged and thrown into the car trunk. She'd be in complete darkness with only a chink of light coming through the rust hole. He turned his mind away from what she might feel. It was best to make sure Lasco didn't see her and picked some other woman.

Dexter watched Sahara walk through the car park, chatting easily to her son. He stepped in front of Lasco and Boston, blocking their view. He pretended to look for something on the ground. Hurry up, hurry up. Go before they see you.

After a while, he looked over his shoulder. He saw the yellow VW parked in the dark at the end of a row. Perfect for a kidnapping, but there were three of them walking together. It was too risky. And anyway, Lasco knew Miss Sahara and surely he'd realize the danger of being identified. And she wasn't white-white; she was more a browning. Dexter breathed easier. It wasn't going to happen. They'd just wait some more, although he doubted there'd be any old women out this late. They needed a better plan.

Then Lasco said, "Sweet brownin dat." He nodded towards the young woman with Carl and Sahara. "Wi could tek her…"

"Tink she white enough?" Boston said.

"Yeah, man. She white enough."

"How wi going get her away from di other two?" Dexter said.

"But wait – don't dat a you uptown woman, Dexy-bwoy?" interrupted Lasco. "What she name again? Say-rah, some name like dat. A she for sure. You no want wi trouble her, nuh true? You soft for she. "

232

"Not soft for nobody," Dexter said. "Tek di young gal if you want. Just tell mi what wi going do with di bwoy and di madda."

"Shot dem is what. Tek di girl, she nah recognize wi. Two uptown people dead inna Sovereign, one kidnap – mus' mek di *Gleaner* tomorrow an' den wi in wit' Merciless."

"You crazy, star," Dexter said. "If wi shoot up di place, every security come runnin. Mek us just do what wi come to do. Find wi a old woman by herself who can't fight. That what wi here for."

As the three boys watched, Sahara, Carl and Kimberly walked past the yellow VW. They went over to a Toyota, parked near the gate. Sahara kissed Carl and hugged Kimberly and the three said their goodbyes. The car park was emptying and the security guard at the red and white barrier settled down in his seat.

The Toyota drove out onto Liguanea Avenue. Sahara watched until they were out of sight and then turned to go back to her car, parked near the back of the Chinese restaurant. She was suddenly afraid – her car was in darkness and there was no one around. It's Sovereign car park, she told herself. No one would try anything here.

She took out her cell phone and turned it on. The low battery signal beeped and the phone turned itself off. Blasted cell phones. Never work when you need them. She began walking the short distance to her car, keys in hand. She heard scuffling noises and a stifled curse behind her. She turned and saw the shapes of men too close to her – way too close. Then hands clamped, trapped her, spun her around. She smelt bodies long unwashed. A hand closed over her mouth and she tried to bite it, but her teeth could find no purchase. Her bag was pulled from her shoulder and the cell phone pried from her fingers. She felt herself lifted and carried for a few feet; she saw the Sunny and the slightly open trunk.

"Tie her hand-dem," a voice whispered and she heard the rasp of some kind of tape. Her hands were bound behind her. "Gag her," the same voice said. Another piece of tape was slapped across her mouth. And then her captor swung her completely off her feet as if she weighed no more than an empty cardboard box, and slung her into the trunk. She hit her head and the world fell out of focus. She felt her feet pushed inside the car, one of her shoes fell off and she let herself hope that the one shoe found in the car park would lead rescuers to her. Foolishness.

The trunk lid slammed and she was in a smothering darkness. She smelled oil and something musty and fermenting. She sneezed helplessly and snot ran from her nose. Her fear was oceanic. The car started to move and she knew she must not vomit or she would suffocate. Why was she thinking of living? Why not suffocate? Surely that might be better than what lay ahead. As the car picked up speed, there was more air in the trunk. The darkness lightened and saw there were a few holes in the trunk, one larger than the others, either rust or deliberately made, she couldn't tell. She wriggled to become more comfortable, but there was no space. She flexed her fingers, trying to keep the circulation going. She could dimly hear the voices of the men who had kidnapped her. She supposed when the car stopped, she would fight. She saw herself struggling and kicking and then on the ground, limp and bloody, her legs spread. She saw Carl's ruined face at a muddy grave. She thought of Lydia and the warm light of day and the sight of green hills and the comfort of her bed, soft, with clean sheets. She bargained with the God she did not believe in to deliver her unharmed from the hands of the men who held her.

Dexter thought of his own time in the trunk of the police car, the nausea, the fear, the pain of his broken ribs and beaten face. He hardened his heart. Why should anyone escape such journeys? Where was the justice in a world that issued him a life of struggle and failure, while others never went to bed hungry a day in their lives? But this was Miss Sahara, who had talked to him, and had listened to his answers, and for a few years at least, had let him glimpse a future he had never allowed himself to imagine.

Sahara heard the men speak, but she would only make out some words – their patois was thick and hard to understand. She had no idea how much time had passed, but she thought they must have left Kingston. She wanted the car to drive forever. I can do this, she told herself, I can be in this car trunk. People can adapt to anything. I'll use my brain. I'll talk to them. I'll find a way to escape. And how bad can nothingness be?

The car stopped and the flow of air ceased and Sahara struggled to breathe. She called out to the men, "Please, I'm suffocating, please let me out." They did not respond, but they began to shout, and she realized they were arguing about her.

"What you want kill her for? Just bring down more police. Mek us stick to di plan, kidnap her, keep her, let her go."

"If wi kill her, Merciless have respect."

"Mek us just batter her."

"Let her go, big man. What do you?"

"Is mi you a talk to?"

Please. Let me out. I have money. Take what you want. Sahara screamed in her mind, desperate for breath, for light, for the touch of night air on her skin. She heard scuffling noises, a slammed car door and shouting. The car shook. Then the explosion of a gunshot cracked right over her head, and she heard a dull, final falling sound. The men were fighting. Maybe they would kill each other and leave her in the car trunk, undiscovered for days. But if they let her out, they would probably rape and murder her. This was where it would end, her small life, precious to no one but herself and those few who loved her. Everything would go on without her. She imagined the skin of the earth closing over her coffin, as dark and airless as the car trunk. Dust to dust. She closed her eyes and waited, each gasping breath loud in her ears.

Then the trunk opened and air flooded in, cold and rejuvenating, and she inhaled it like a drug, in love with every breath. All she wanted was to breathe. She opened her eyes and saw a figure standing over her, extending a hand. She could not see his face; the only source of light was faint and behind him. She wanted to reach for him, but her hands were tied. "Get her out," a voice said. The man standing in shadow pushed one hand under her and pulled her roughly out of the car. She fell over the edge of the trunk to the ground. She turned her face to a filthy concrete floor, breathing as deeply as the gag would allow, not having understood until that moment the gift of unfettered breath. She waited uncaring for a bullet to the back of her skull. Just let me breathe until the end, she prayed.

"Get up, Miss Sahara." Her name. It was Dexter's voice.

She struggled to her feet, falling once, because she couldn't use her hands. She stood and faced the men who held her. They were not men. One boy lay off to the side on the ground, blood spreading around him. The one who had helped her out of the car faced her, a solid, terrifying youth with one arm. And then Sahara saw Dexter, behind the one-armed boy, holding a gun to the back of his head.

"Cut she hand-dem," Dexter said to the one-armed boy.

"You dead, yout'. You dead before one week pass."

"Shut you mout'. Do what mi say or *you* nah see tomorrow." Sahara felt the edge of a knife and her hands fell apart, the tape remaining stuck to her wrists. Dexter stepped forward, still keeping the gun trained on the other youth, and ripped the tape from her mouth. "Run, Miss Sahara, run," he said. "Run and don't look back."

She fled towards a faint glow of street lights, away from the hulking building, limping with only one shoe, ignoring the pain of returning circulation in her hands, the rough ground under her one bare foot. She realized she was still in the city, but she had no idea where she was. She ran blindly down darkened streets until she saw light coming from an open door. A homeless shelter. She ran through the front door and collapsed into the arms of a young priest. Dexter saved me, she thought. Now he's probably dead. Then another voice: Yes, but he kidnapped you too. The police were right – he's a shotta.

Sahara would never remember exactly how the entire sequence of events unfolded. She would feel the emotions for years, crashing one after the other in her mind and body, each one like a massive hillside rock set in motion by an earthquake. Fear of dying without breath. The relief of half-running through the squalid streets of downtown Kingston, the men left behind. Hope. Realizing there were no sounds of pursuit. Then the anger, the righteous, energizing anger that her commitment to the Jacob's Pen children had not bought her exemption from violent crime. I tried, she thought, over and over. I tried. It should have worked. Why didn't it work? And then: it's finished. No one can help him now.

That night's images would keep coming back to her in fuzzy, unconnected scenes, like the flickering black and white movies her father used to show at her childhood birthday parties. She tried to describe where she had been and the police went to find the building. Somehow Lydia was there with Carl; she didn't remember using a telephone. She was at the police station giving a statement to a young officer who laboriously transcribed it onto a long piece of paper with a wide margin. He kept going over the same ground. How did you escape? They let me go, she said. Why? he said. I don't know. Other policemen came back and then she was asked to identify a dead man in an abandoned building.

The police took her to a derelict building on the waterfront. She was surprised to see the gutters full and water dripping from roofs. She had not heard the rain. The building was close to the homeless shelter – a matter of two blocks. She was sure she had been running for hours. The sky was lightening – it would soon be dawn. The rain had stopped, though lightning still flared, more powerful than the coming daylight.

She stood staring down at the boy's face, his eyes half open. The dead boy was the one she'd met at Jacob's Pen. The boy named for powdered milk. Lasco, she thought. Or Carnation. No, Lasco.

"Do you know this man?" the policeman said. "Do you know any of them?"

Sahara said, "No. I don't know him. I told you already. I never saw any of them before. Can I go now?" She turned and walked into Lydia's embrace. It's over, she thought. That's all I have left to give you. We're even.

When Sahara was out of sight, Dexter lowered the gun. "You too," he said to Boston. "You run too." He watched Boston run. When he was out of gunshot range, Boston stopped and pointed at him. "You dead, yout'," he shouted. Then he disappeared. Dexter walked over to a broken window and threw the gun into the dark waters of Kingston Harbour. He watched it fall into the sea.

He ran alone from the building where he, Boston and Lasco had lived, off and on, for so many weeks. He jumped into a gully, a long drop, over eight feet, and despite the pain in his ribs, he did not pause in his flight. Lasco had shown them how to use gullies as escape routes. He ran through the gully, hugging the walls where the shadows were deep, avoiding towering piles of garbage and rusting appliances and dead dogs and black plastic bags he knew held human shit. He smelled sewage from houses along the gully banks and he heard the scurrying of rats. The ground was slippery with waste, but he ran without stopping, high on adrenaline, until he was no longer afraid. He ran accompanied by the noises of a Kingston night – dogs barking, trucks changing gear, hammering dancehall music. He began to laugh, as if the events of the night had been no more than a boyish prank gone wrong. As if Lasco was still with him. As if the full weight of the Racehorse Crew would fail to hunt him down.

It began to rain and he climbed out of the gully at Papine. The adrenaline ebbed and he felt sick. The pain in his chest from his healing ribs was beyond bearing and it was raining harder. He'd go to his mother's house and sleep. He'd decide what to do in the morning.

He lay on his old bed. The rain beat on the zinc roof and he could hear nothing else. The house had been damaged in the storms and it leaked badly. The door had been nailed shut, but it hadn't been hard to break in and the rain drowned the noise. He figured his mother and sister were still at Miss Betsy's. They were lost to him anyway.

He wanted to mourn Lasco. He'd wanted to know all his secrets and now he never would. Dog-hearted Lasco; dead in a condemned building, populated by rats, feral dogs and lost people. Dead at *his* hands. He had made another duppy. He looked at the hands that had held the gun and pulled the trigger. He'd made a choice between the brethren of his boyhood and a stranger, a woman, who had held out hope of a different way. Could a man escape what he was born to be? How to tell?

He wondered which was easier – death, jail or a life hiding from Merciless. He imagined the years ahead – filthy prison cells and the company of brutal men. Or when the police came, he could choose a single flash of light, a gunshot, the end of pain. And Marlon might be waiting with the angels. Marlon would beg for him, he was sure. Or he could leave Kingston, maybe hide in the mountains, as he had imagined while in prison. Maybe he could work on a farm. He remembered being asked to write about a day on a farm while at Holborn Prep. He had never seen a farm and the words had eluded him then, but lying in his own bed, he saw a peaceful place with fields and animals and food that came from the earth, a place less wild, less bleak than Dallas Mountain.

He thought of Miss Sahara. She'd be safe at home now, in the house he'd never seen. Perhaps she'd be crying and Carl would comfort her. He remembered how she'd bought him a set of draughts, food, clothes, and how she'd cried at his graduation. He knew she'd have told the police where to find him – perhaps they'd be at the door this very night. He turned his battered face into the mildewed mattress and wept.

Arleen got out of bed. She was tired of trying to sleep. It was impossible in the torrential rain. She went into the back room and looked for her daughter, who had still not spoken since the night of Marlon's death. The sheets were crumpled, but Lissa was not in the bed. Arleen knelt down and peered underneath. Lissa lay on her side, her knees drawn up, eyes open. "Come, baby," said Arleen. "Come stay wit' mi in my bed. I frighten too." Lissa stared at Arleen for a moment and then she closed her eyes. Arleen sighed and sat back on her heels. She waited without hope. Then she saw Lissa's dim form move and she leaned down again. Lissa uncurled her small body, crawled out from under the bed and, finally, raised her arms to her mother. Arleen stood. Through the window in Miss Betsy's spare room, she looked across at her own house and saw a pale glow in the window. Dexter. She turned her back and climbed into bed with her daughter.

Dexter woke after a few hours. The rain still drummed on the roof and the room was dark. He was surprised the police had not yet arrived. Maybe the rain had kept them away. He wondered if there was still electricity in the house. He put the lamp on the ground and threw an old T-shirt over the bulb, and then he turned it on. A weak light lit the room, leaving shadows in the corners. He sat up and looked around the house. It was damaged and dirty, but everywhere there were artifacts of his childhood. He saw Marlon's school bag hanging high on a nail, a nail he himself had driven, proud of the three blows that had sent it straight and strong into the wood. He looked for food, but found nothing except a few tins – bully beef and condensed milk. He weighed them in his hands. And then he reached for Marlon's school bag and started to pack it with everything that could be useful, even clothes he had long outgrown.

When he was ready, he looked around for the last time. He saw an old calendar on one of the small desks Miss Sahara had given them and one of his Holborn exercise books. He saw the name on the front: Raymond Dexter Morrison. Raymond. He found a crayon and sat on the floor, studying the plain, white reverse side of the calendar. Who should he write to and what could he say? In the end, all he could summon were a few sentences for his mother. He wrote that he was alive, but the police were looking for him, and he had to go away. He could not think what he could write about his brother.

He turned off the single lightbulb and hefted the bursting school bag. He went out into the rain. He had money in his pocket, the proceeds of Miss Sahara's handbag, shared in the car, and the remnants of the money Carl had given him. He thought again of Dallas Mountain, but the prospect of living like an animal frightened him. And it was true – the river was

240

almost lifeless. There was nothing to eat in its murky pools. The storms had taken it all.

He remembered Lasco talking about Mandeville. Lasco, too, lived with him, inside his head. They were all with him, the dead and the living – Sahara, Marlon, Lissa, his mother. Even Felix. If Lasco's gift was manhood, Felix's was endurance. Dexter thought he could probably find his way to Mandeville. He liked the idea of a town in the hills. He would find a place where he could set his back against a mountain and gaze over green plains to the sea. And perhaps, he thought, when his ribs healed and his bruises faded, he might find someone there who needed a cook named Raymond – no questions asked.

ABOUT THE AUTHOR

Diana McCaulay is a Jamaican writer, newspaper columnist and environmental activist. She has lived her entire life in Jamaica and engaged in a range of occupations – secretary, insurance executive, racetrack steward, mid-life student, social commentator, environmental advocate. She is the Chief Executive of the Jamaican Environment Trust and the recipient of the 2005 Euan P. McFarlane Award for Outstanding Environmental Leadership in recognition of her 15 years of leadership within the environmental conservation movement of Jamaica. She was awarded a Musgrave Medal for Merit from the Institute of Jamaica in 2009. Her film, made with Esther Figueroa, *Jamaica for Sale*, on the dangers of large scale tourism to the environment of the north coast of Jamaica, was released in 2009.

Dog-Heart won first prize in the 2008 Jamaican National Literature awards.

Opal Palmer Adisa
Until Judgement Comes: Stories About Jamaican Men
ISBN: 9781845230425, 2007, £8.99

The stories in this collection move the heart and the head. They concern the mystery that is men: men of beauty who are as cane stalks swaying in the breeze, men who are afraid of and despise women, men who prey on women, men who have lost themselves, men trapped in sexual and religious guilt, men who love women and men who are searching for their humanity...

Jacqueline Bishop
The River's Song
ISBN: 9781845230425, 2007, £8.99

Gloria, living with her mother in a Kingston tenement yard, wins a scholarship to one of Jamaica's best girls' schools. She is the engaging narrator of the at first alienating and then transforming experiences of an education that in time takes her away from her mother, friends and the island; of her consciousness of bodily change and sexual awakening; of her growth of adult awareness of a Jamaica of class division, endemic violence and the new spectre of HIV-AIDS.

Kwame Dawes
Bivouac
ISBN: 9781845231057, Feb 2010, £9.99

When his father dies in suspicious circumstances, Ferron Morgan's trauma is increased by the conflict within his family and his father's friends over whether the death is the result of medical negligence or a political assassination. Ferron has lived in awe of his father's radical commitments but is forced to admit that, with the 1980s' resurgence of the political Right in the Caribbean, his father had lost faith, and was 'already dead to everything that had meaning for him'.

Ferron's response to the death is further complicated by guilt, particularly over his recent failure to protect his fiancée, Dolores, from a brutal rape. He begins, though, to investigate the direction of his life with great intensity, in particular to confront his instinct to keep running from trouble.

This is a sharply focused portrayal of Jamaica at a tipping point in its recent past, in which the private grief and trauma condenses a whole society's scarcely understood sense of temporariness and dislocation.

Curdella Forbes
A Permanent Freedom
ISBN: 9781845230616, 2008, £8.99

Crossing the space between novel and short fiction, *A Permanent Freedom* weaves nine individual stories about love, sex, death and migration into a single compelling narrative exploring the profound courage, integrity and folly of which the human spirit is capable. Each story surrounds migrant or migrating characters seeking to negotiate life on the margins, and taken by love, rape, AIDS, murder and family pain out of the safe places of conventional behaviour and belief, to the farthest reaches of themselves. Characters cross over into each other's stories in uncanny networks of meeting orchestrated by a dark angel who also bears witness to these tales and the nature of stories as a form of haunting.